Nat Burns is a talented author who lives in New Mexico, the Land of Enchantment, after spending much of her early life in the state of Virginia. Her unique and rather bohemian upbringing has gifted her with a unique perspective on life and love. She is truly one of life's originals, and her free spirit clearly comes through in her writing. Her stories are original, unique, and sometimes spiritual, but always based on love and respect for living beings…human and otherwise. As a fellow author, I appreciate, and envy her talent. Nat's books run the gamut of many genres, including poetry, romance, speculative, sci-fi, horror and general fiction, among others. Her roots are in journalism, reporting, editing, and medical publishing, and she has fully used the skills she learned in these fields to enhance her writing abilities. To top it all off, Nat is a genuinely wonderful person…a trait that many of her characters share. I highly recommend Nat's books to anyone who wants a thoroughly enjoyable, entertaining, and easy read!

Karen D. Badger
Author and Co-Owner of Badger Bliss Books

As a fan of Nat Burns's writing, I especially like her thrillers, such as *The Rustle of Leaves* and *The Quality of Blue*. Now, I can add science fiction to my favorites with The Desert Willow Series. Book one, *The Liaison*, introduces the reader to characters who are put into dangerous situations, including the threat of sinister aliens from another planet. Book two, *Rosemary*, continues the story of the main characters yet introduces us to a whole new set of engaging personalities. A great deal of research went into the science of this series, and *Rosemary* is a fast-paced, dramatic work with a satisfying ending that I wasn't expecting. Well done!

Nina Knapp, Owner
Crone Productions LLC

# Rosemary

*Book Two in The Desert Willow Series*

## About the Author

Nat Burns is a retired editorial systems coordinator—once managing computer systems and editing medical journals—who now writes novels and short stories full time. She is also a columnist and music editor for *Lesbian News* magazine. *Rosemary* is her sixteenth novel. She lives in New Mexico with her partner, Chris, and an aging cat named Boo.

# Rosemary

*Book Two in The Desert Willow Series*

## Nat Burns

BELLA
B O O K S
2023

Bella Books, Inc.
P.O. Box 10543
Tallahassee, FL 32302

Printed in the United States of America on acid-free paper.

First Edition - 2023

Editor: Medora MacDougall
Cover Designer: Heather Honeywell

ISBN: 978-1-64247-448-0

*PUBLISHER'S NOTE*

## Acknowledgement

Quantum physics is the study of matter and energy at the molecular, atomic, nuclear, and even infinitesimal levels. It aims to uncover the properties and behaviors of the very building blocks of nature. Even space and time, which appear to be continuous, have the smallest possible components.

Quantum physics came to the forefront in Max Planck's 1900 paper on blackbody radiation. Albert Einstein, Niels Bohr, Richard Feynman, Paul Dirac, Werner Heisenberg, Erwin Schrödinger and others contributed to this field of study.

## Dedication

I'd like to dedicate this book to creating reality. And to Schrödinger's cat.

A popular thought experiment by physicist Erwin Schrödinger in 1935 stated that if a cat is placed in a chamber with a radioactive atom, which may or may not decay and emit radiation, that cat will remain both alive *and* dead until the chamber is opened. Whereupon the superpositional nature of reality collapses, and a result is observed. One theory, a personal favorite, states that before this observation, the cat exists in two dimensions.

This experiment implies that a quantum system, atom or proton, remains in superposition, one thing above another, traveling side by side, until shifting when observed by the external world.

Schrödinger posed the question, *when* does a quantum system stop existing as a superposition and become something else? This was asked in a sarcastic manner, as he—and Albert Einstein—originally wrote that quantum science was absurd and reality constant.

This is just one of many interpretations of quantum theory, but suffice it to say, science has since progressed in leaps of observational proof, so that today, the reality of quantum existence has become a true branch of science. In quantum mechanics we discover that the entire universe is actually a series of probabilities.

# PROLOGUE

*Aili's Journal*

## On My Birth

After my human birth on this planet, I quickly realized that I had the knowledge and power of the universe in my hands. Literally. I looked at those small, pudgy baby hands and knew instinctively, even then, that everything I would ever need and want could be made manifest by those hands.

But I was just an infant then, a newborn. I could do nothing on my own. I spent many hours pondering this, wondering at it. What good is having the universe in one's hands when one's physical form is so limiting? And then there were the voices that spoke to me constantly, trying to answer all my questions, and the dazzling, smiling facial features that appeared and faded back into bright energy almost instantly. My other family. They were the source of my knowledge and power and they, the Collective, made me giddy as their shared energy shook my tiny body to the core.

My beautiful mother, so young and so jaundiced by past events, had to meet all my physical needs in the beginning. Plus, she had to tolerate the surges of energy that ran through me. I could tell they alarmed her each time they occurred, so I tried to radiate soothing thoughts when I was close to her. I think there was the full knowledge somewhere within her about how special I was. How I was but one small cog in the vast Collective, but that my very existence was unique and important. It was as though she waited, watching me. I could see it in her eyes. I waited as well, creating toys of light alone in my crib, understanding my destiny, knowing that one day I might have to give my all to protect this new round of humanity. The human line that one day might evolve into their own energy collective. If I could help them survive.

# CHAPTER ONE

## *The Desert Willow*

There was only one more left. Lily looked down, judging the distance to the hard-packed desert dirt below. A good eight feet, at least. She lifted her eyes to the unsightly branch high to her right, wondering if her obsessive-compulsive need to remove the final dead limb was worth the risk. She sighed and the pungent scents of desert willow greenery and bark filled her nostrils anew. The potent scent was making her head hurt.

Small, drab birds watched her cautiously, hopping from branch to branch but staying always out of reach as she worked. They didn't complain so she knew there wasn't a mama bird with a nest nearby, but they certainly avoided her. She looked up again. The harsh sun was dappled here in the leafy shelter of the willow, and she leaned her head back to rest and reflect.

The accident or, actually, the *rescue*, had changed her life in so many ways. Once a capable, energetic waitress, filled with determination and a bit of intolerance, she was now disabled, or challenged, as they say, missing a finger and with one leg crippled by limb-saving surgery. And yet here she was, up a tree.

A tree that was as majestic as it was ancient and one that certainly deserved a perfect pruning. She ran a hand along the gnarled bark. Like her, the willow was a survivor, sending roots down unbelievably deep and wide to glean any moisture lingering below the competing dry scrub that littered the nearby landscape. Lily admired these trees in general, and this one, old and stately, had been in the front yard of Good Neighbor Ranch long before Lily and her family had moved there more than two decades ago.

She took another deep breath and, using her strong arms, hoisted herself a little higher, securing her denim-clad bottom against a protruding scar that was all that remained from a fallen branch. Clumsily repositioning the loppers, she leaned to one side and tried to lock the cutting blades onto the thick dead branch. After much maneuvering, she managed it. She'd need both hands and some sort of leverage to pull the handles together, though. Unfortunately, this wasn't a skinny feeder branch. It was substantial. Easily handled by the loppers she was sure, if she wasn't twisted into an absurdly awkward position.

She glanced around, seeking a solution to her dilemma.

"Just do it," she muttered, seeing no ready way to reposition herself.

Gingerly, she shifted and placed her hands on the lopper handles. Tongue clasped between her teeth, she leaned away from the trunk and toward the dead growth.

Fixed in concentration, she was startled by the sound of gravel crunching loudly under the tires of an approaching vehicle. Looking toward the long driveway, she spied Hunter's SUV, the dark blue vehicle surrounded by a billow of sandy dust, as her weaker leg, braced against the trunk, failed her. In seconds, she was grasping at air as her world turned upside down. The loppers spiraled away from her, the heavy handles coming dangerously close to clocking her on the forehead. Her good leg folded instinctively and curved around a branch below her as her upper body swung into free fall. Tree litter swirled around her like a green snowfall as she perilously swayed to and fro, trying to calm her racing heart.

"Shit," she whispered, pressing one hand to her chest. The other hand swung out, trying in vain to connect with anything of substance. She peered toward the trunk of the tree, realizing that the hold her leg had on the branch was tenuous, at best. She gauged the distance to the ground again, calculating it now to be only six or seven feet. Far enough to still do some damage, especially if she landed headfirst.

"Shit," she said again, much louder.

"You are definitely between a rock and a hard place," Hunter said in her quiet, level voice.

Twisting her neck, Lily saw Hunter standing on the porch steps, regarding her with unbelievable calm. She held a paper grocery bag with both arms, and her long, dark braid was laying crossways on her shoulder. If not dressed in jeans and a T-shirt, she might have been a stereotypical Indian maiden from the eighteen hundreds. As Lily pondered this new upside-down view, their daughter, Aili, who they called Birdie, approached the tree, her huge neon blue eyes stretched even wider than usual.

"Mummy?" she queried. "Why are you hanging in the tree?"

Lily groaned. "Will you two please help me get down from here?"

Hunter sighed a beleaguered sigh and placed the bag of groceries onto the porch floor. "You know, Lil, we live on a ranch and have a handful of people who would have been glad to do this—whatever it is—for you."

She walked to Lily and raised her strong, gym-toned arms, but her hands barely reached Lily's short blond hair. Birdie moved under Lily and extended her arms to either side.

"You're gonna have to drop, Lil," Hunter said. "We'll catch you."

"You can get the ladder. It's behind the tree."

"Oh, okay," Hunter said, backing away. "Hold on, don't fall."

Lily studied her daughter as Hunter stepped away. "Was school okay today, hon?"

Birdie shrugged, squinting into the sunlight behind her mother. "I can't go anymore, and I'll miss him. He was a lot of fun. He says he's taken me as far as he can."

She was standing beneath Lily, arms extended still, as though she would catch her mom if she fell. The platinum-haired preteen had never looked cuter or more Nordic. Aili, a Finnish name given by the Collective seemed apt, physically. It also meant blessed and the girl surely was.

Hunter came around the tree, stepladder in hand. "You used this?" she accused. "Seriously?"

"It was high enough," Lily said defensively. "I've always climbed trees. Just get it over here."

Hunter opened the ladder and placed it securely beneath her wife, muttering in a low tone. Lily was glad she couldn't hear the details of her exasperated rant. Mounting the ladder, Hunter grasped Lily's shoulders and pushed upward, enabling Lily to grasp the branch being held crooked in her now numb leg. She swung both legs down, levering the stiff, damaged one out and away from the trunk. Hunter wrapped her arms about Lily, supporting her on the stepladder, and Lily let go of the branch and fell against the solid heft of her. She kissed Hunter on the nose. "Welcome home."

Hunter shook her head, a bewildered but tolerant smile on her lips as she helped Lily down the ladder. Birdie fetched her mother's cane from where it leaned against the trunk of the tree and handed it to her.

"Thank you, sweetie," Lily said as she patted her good leg, trying to get the blood flowing again.

Hunter put the handle of the stepladder over her shoulder. "Aren't you supposed to be inside entering data into the computer?" she asked as she and Lily moved haltingly toward the house.

"I finished it. What's this about Birdie and school? Did he finally give up?"

Hunter nodded as she lifted the grocery bag from the porch. "Yep. He says that this is as far as he can go. Our Birdie has surpassed his Mensa-level IQ. He says every time we pay him, he feels guilty, that he's merely helping her find stuff on the Internet at this point."

"Shoot." Lily slowed her lurching walk up the porch steps to take a deep breath. "We knew it was coming." She glanced at the girl mounting the steps silently next to them. "Now what do we do?"

"Birdie, whatcha want to do, kiddo?" Hunter asked.

Birdie glanced up. "Don't know, Hunny. I'm only a kid. Not much I *can* do."

Hunter frowned at the porch steps. "True. Kinda sucks, huh?"

Birdie sighed. "Yeah, kinda sucks."

As soon as they entered the house, Birdie dropped her purple backpack by the door and raced into the family room. Moments later, the sound of television static engulfed them.

"About time you got home," Sage said as she approached them along the long central hallway. She peered into the noisy family room as she passed. "That girl," she muttered, shaking her graying head. Her merry eyes belied her annoyance. She took the grocery bag from Hunter and silently carried it into the kitchen at the back of the house.

Hunter leaned the ladder against the hallway wainscoting, turned to Lily, and then pulled her into her arms. "Stay out of trees, okay?" she whispered. "You scare me."

Lily smiled at her and ran her palms along the sleek sides of Hunter's dark, center-parted hair. "I'm sorry. I'll try."

They kissed briefly and moved to the family room doorway, arms wrapped around one another's waists. Birdie was kneeling before the large-screen TV, both palms lifted high and pressed against the screen. Her head was down, her chin on her chest, as she listened.

"I guess we continue to homeschool on our own. Thank goodness she's an honorary member of Sage's pueblo so it's all legit."

"Yeah, and it's easier to hide the hyper-age thing, of course. But seriously, we can't be of much help to her," Hunter murmured in a worried tone. "What can we teach her that she hasn't already learned?"

"More life skills, maybe? And I think we should sign her up for every advanced course we can find on the web."

"You're assuming she hasn't been there already? We don't monitor specifics, Lil. She's on the computer a lot."

Lily lifted her gaze to her daughter. "I know. She is so much more, knows so much more than we ever will."

Hunter cleared her throat. "Does it ever, like, scare you a little? I mean, look at her. She's communicating through a TV, for Pete's sake!"

A chuckle bubbled up in Lily. She tried to squelch it, but it escaped her lips in a short spasmic snicker. Hunter arched one eyebrow but caught the merriment fever, giggling helplessly into her own palm. They touched foreheads, and both shook their heads as the laughter abated.

Lily sighed, then raised her voice to address her daughter. "Everything okay?" she asked. "Is Flynn talking to you?"

Birdie nodded briefly, eyes fixed on the TV. "And the others."

Lily shrugged at Hunter, and they turned away, holding hands as they strolled toward the kitchen to help with supper. A call from Birdie arrested them, and they hurried back to the family room archway. She was staring at them with wide blue eyes, the freckles on her nose a bas-relief against the translucent paleness of her face. Her hands were clasped in her lap as she knelt on the worn rug.

"Mummy? Hunny? Something very weird is happening to me."

## Aili's Journal

### Rosemary's Call

She kept calling to me, sporadically at first, then somewhat regularly. In the beginning, it was faint, hovering at the edges of the Collective. But I could tell the call was directed toward me, even though it was confusing to be singled out that way in the midst of the vast Collective energy field.

Then Flynn told me about her, that she was like me, a hybrid child, part Collective and part human. And that there were others. Only a few, true, but I was pleased. Am pleased. It will be amazing to talk to someone going through the same things I am.

Not that my life is bad or even difficult. Mummy and Hunny are amazing parents, and they should be called saints, the way they have patiently dealt with raising a child like me. I'm mostly normal and fit well into this human realm, I'm simply too smart, with the limitless knowledge of the Collective buzzing in my head every minute of every day.

I study photos of myself as a baby, then as a toddler. I don't look too different from others that age, though my hair and eyes are lighter than most. Luckily, Mummy is a blonde—so it's expected. What wasn't expected is that I would age normally until about age two and then jump ahead approximately ten years overnight.

I immediately realized it wasn't a progeria thing, as Hunny first surmised, the Hutchinson-Gilford Syndrome that leads to premature aging but within the same body size. It's more like my younger, smaller body couldn't contain the powerful, substantial energy of my Collective half. I remember my two-year-old self and how limited I was in speech and in strength. I could barely communicate with the Collective by glass back then, but when I became twelve-ish, that shifted. I understood better. Communicated better, even through the pixels of flat-screen televisions. I could also suss out the facts and language of our history, as well as the powerful means of our universal order.

Oh, the confusion it caused in those who knew me. Pure humans couldn't understand how my molecules could shift in such a way. To age me ten years as though it were a normal occurrence. It terrified them and it took every bit of influence I could manifest to calm their fears and charm them back into liking me.

# CHAPTER TWO

## *Trust*

A shock of terror raced through Lily's body. Her hand tightened around Hunter's as her heartbeat escalated. How could anything be stranger than a child who ages a decade overnight? "What do you mean, sweetheart? What's happening to you?"

Birdie furrowed her brow as she seemed to be lost in deep thought. Lily knew from experience that she would want to make sure her thoughts were in order before she spoke. This placid thoughtfulness was one of the reasons Hunter had given her the nickname Birdie several months after she'd been born. When thinking or, especially when listening to the Collective, she often cocked her head to one side in a very birdlike movement.

Hunter's hand loosened as she crouched down next to Birdie. She laid one hand on Birdie's forearm, causing her to open her eyes. "You've got to talk to us, baby. We need to know what's going on."

Birdie lifted gemlike blue eyes and studied Hunter's face. "I know, Hunny. I know."

Lily moved close, both hands clutching the handle of her cane tightly. "Did Flynn and the Collective speak to you?"

She nodded and looked surprised. "Always, of course. This… this is different. I'm being pulled to someone. Someone here in this dimension, on Earth, in this flesh."

Hunter rubbed her nose thoughtfully. "Pulled?" She peered up at Lily questioningly.

Lily shrugged. "This is new," she said, lacking an explanation.

Birdie continued, "It's like something I need to do. A mission."

Lily took Birdie's hands and lifted her to her feet. Hunter rose as well, and the three stood silently in the family room, the static of the television an angry buzz in the background. Hunter lifted the remote and turned off the TV. The resulting silence seemed to have substance, seemed to have actual weight.

"So, the Collective has given you a mission? What is it and when do we start?" Lily said into that sudden silence.

Birdie hung her head, silky, silver-blond hair sliding forward to cover her face and shoulders. She took in a deep breath, and Lily felt her heart lurch with compassion. And worry.

"No, it's not us. Them. Well, it's her. She's calling me."

"Someone is calling you?" Hunter frowned in confusion. "Who? Who is calling you? And why?"

Birdie hesitated before speaking. "I'm not sure. I just keep hearing the word Rosemary."

"Rosemary." Hunter turned her frown of confusion on Lily. "Rosemary? Like the herb?"

"Aili, what is it, honey? What do we need to do?" Lily watched Birdie with intense concern.

"I don't think it's a what, Hunny, I think it's a who. Not an herb, a person. I dunno exactly, Mummy, but I will soon."

"Someone named Rosemary? That's a name?" Hunter said, her tone one of disbelief.

"Sure, like Rosemary Clooney, the singer," Lily explained impatiently.

Hunter nodded as Birdie shrugged.

"I think so," Birdie said. "I can see her, sort of, and hear her."

Lily had been through a lot since Flynn, the interdimensional being, or IDB, had appeared in her bedroom more than four years ago. She'd been kidnapped by aliens, weathered an alien viral plague as those she loved died or were maimed, gotten pregnant with a hybrid child by passing through an energy field, and accepted a position as Government Liaison between the United States Government and the IDBs. She'd also lost most of a pinky finger and a lot of the muscle in her left leg from passing through that radioactive energy. But this—this was all new. As Liaison, she worried about another attack on the people of Earth, but as a mother, she worried that her exceptional hybrid daughter was losing her mind.

*No, I won't go there*, she thought firmly. Who knew what special gifts and abilities Birdie would develop as time passed? Being called by someone in the grand ether of time and space was not so weird, comparatively speaking. After all, Birdie had once gone to bed a two-year-old, then awakened the next morning a preteen. Now, *that* was weird.

Lily sighed, trying to grasp some meaning from Birdie's words. "What does she say when she calls to you?"

"Nothing, really. It's hard to explain. It's through energy, like my people, the Collective, but it's not them and not words exactly."

"Not words? Not words." Hunter threw her hands up in frustration and changed the subject. "Hey, I'm hungry. Can we eat?"

Lily and Birdie exchanged knowing, fond gazes, then grinned at one another. Hunter was comfortably predictable. "Well, we'll talk about it more later, when we can glean a little more information, okay?"

Birdie, rebounding from her earlier distress, nodded, then took Hunter's hand and pulled her toward the hallway that led to the kitchen.

"Let's have a big salad tonight," Birdie suggested as they made their way along the hallway. "With some of the tomatoes SaySay grew in the back garden. I'm really glad you like them as much as I do. You still do, right? They're originally American, you know. The Aztecs loved their tomatoes and used them in almost everything."

Lily followed along behind, her thoughts rioting above Birdie's chatter. She knew that, as soon as possible, she needed to check in with Flynn. Needed to find out what was going on with her daughter.

"Gonna pop in here," she said as they passed the door to her office. "Be right behind you."

Once inside, she pushed the door mostly closed, then stood next to the crystalline two-foot-tall sculpture on her desk. It was spectacularly beautiful, not like an obelisk, but more feminine-curved and beguiling. And it always drew her in, mesmerizing her. She loved resting her palm in one of the smooth, abstract concavities as she used the device to communicate with Flynn. She did this now, mentally asking the IDB to come to her. Usually, if the coast were clear, it would appear to her in one of its many guises. Today, though she stood there for many moments, Flynn did not appear.

"Flynn!" she muttered angrily. "This is my daughter we're talking about." Her voice fell into an angry hiss. Colors swirled suddenly in the statue, creating a pearlescent beauty that was awe-inspiring. Lily almost let her hand fall away but held on with steadfast determination.

"Flynn..."

Then the message came, traveling along her arm and settling comfortably in her brain. It was one word only and Lily knew that there would be no more information today. Obviously, Flynn and the Collective were busy at that moment, but she hoped, believed, that all would be okay. The word that settled in her mind, like the cozy nestling of a duck mother onto her fragile eggs, was *Trust*.

## *Aili's Journal*

*Missing Leon*

I already miss my tutor. He isn't the friendliest of people, not an Auntie Tess or Margie by any means, but even though he's a loner, a mostly solitary desert rat, he loves the bandying of ideas and theories. Some days we'd talk philosophy the entire class time, as we tried to understand fundamental truths about ourselves and the world in which we lived. We discussed and examined the many philosophical theories posited by the great thinkers from the past. Of course, my particular experiences were, by far, very different from his, so I always tried to drag more opinions and even random thoughts from him. I need to know about regular humans and their relationships to the world and to one another.

Leon Schoolboy Robbins's mother, Glory, is an Arizona Navajo, so this obliquely colored all our talks. He told me, early on, that she was the one who made sure he continued his education. She pushed and pushed, using every government option or New Mexico offering possible to raise her son's educational opportunities high above those of his peers. Luckily, he was interested in everything, *all* things, which stood him well as degree after degree was easily earned, hence his nickname, Schoolboy.

Schoolboy is lucky because his father was a well-funded banker in Mexico City and he was never forced to find work in the casinos. He simply wanted to be a lifelong learner, tutoring to round out his simple life and to further that goal. He's become a good friend to me, beyond being my tutor, accepting my subtle oddness without question, just as Lanny and Saysay do. I have promised myself that I will keep in touch with him.

Rosemary. What is it about her that draws me so incessantly? I think it's our common genesis. And the fact that I think she needs me somehow. But then it occurred to me that our meeting had been engineered by the Collective. I know if I asked any of the Collective consciousnesses directly, they would not lie, but I couldn't bring myself to do it. There is something too appealing about thinking that this girl, on her own, wants to meet me as much as I want to meet her. I have decided to chew on this fantasy as long as the taste is sweet, and I eagerly look forward to meeting her.

I wonder how my earthly family will welcome her into our lives. I sense that what she and I have between us is beyond romance. That emotion is there, certainly, an undercurrent that is inescapable, but at this point in my life, what did that mean?

I believe a wait and see approach is best. I hope my mothers will accept how much she means to me. Oh, there will be the usual arguments—too young, date more people of both genders to broaden your horizons.

It's laughable. Rosemary is my horizon. We are meant to be.

# CHAPTER THREE

## *Just Alabama*

The evening meal was subdued and all five diners seemed lost in thought. Sage's eyes rested on the dining room window as though she were keenly interested in the dusk encroaching outside. Her dark eyes were serene, and Lily wondered if she sensed any foreboding about the impending changes. Lily had no idea of what these changes would be but knew that their peaceful ranching world was in for another shakeup. It had been more than four years since the Greys had inexplicably poisoned Earth's water with a killer virus. They'd been lucky then, but the time was ripe for another attack.

She sighed and made mountains and mesas out of her mashed potatoes. And now this someone, neither human nor interdimensional being, but maybe both, was beckoning her baby daughter to them. What did that even mean? Were the Greys back and trying to lure Birdie away? Rampant destructive scenarios toward the aliens filled Lily's thoughts, interlaced with concern for her child.

"Cletus Borrows wants to buy thirty head," Lanny said, drawing Lily away from her worried reverie.

Lily nodded and finally ate a forkful of potato. "Sounds like a plan. Can we cull the western pasture? It's overfed."

Lanny slathered a biscuit with fresh churned butter from Sky Village. "Yes. I noticed."

Lily smiled and shook her head. "Of course, I'm sure you did."

"So, what does she tell you? Do you know where she is?" Hunter whispered to Birdie.

Sage glanced at Hunter as Lily gave Hunter a loaded gaze. Hunter fell silent and sat back, her fork picking at a lentil patty. Lily hated the secrecy that shrouded their lives but knew that the less Sage and Lanny knew about the IDBs, the safer their lives would be. In fact, Lily's work as the IDB Liaison of the federal government carried the burden of need-to-know security.

"Do you like them, Lanny?" Birdie asked, wisely ignoring Hunter's question. She leaned across the table so she could more closely study Lanny's face as he responded.

"Well, it's not beef, sure," he answered slowly, looking down at his plate then up at her.

"But it's growing on you?" she added hopefully.

Lanny smiled fondly at the precocious child who had been gradually turning them all into vegetarians. "It's growing on me. At one time, we had no meat, only squash and beans, and corn, so this seems like going back to our old ways."

"It sure is healthier," Birdie said, plopping back into her chair and spearing a hefty bite of carrot. "Have I told you about Dan Buettner's book *The Blue Zones*?" She eyed Hunter archly.

Hunter, who enjoyed a good burger better than most, nodded her head slowly. "Yes, Birdie, many, many times."

Sage laughed and turned her attention back to her own food. The use of her left hand, damaged years ago by the alien virus, had almost completely returned, and she was able to use it to lift a glass of iced tea to her lips.

"How has it been for you, SaySay, learning how to cook like this?" Lily asked. "Do you like it?"

Sage nodded and carefully placed her tea on the table. "I do. Seems lighter somehow, not killing things. Animals."

Birdie moved to Sage and placed a hand on her forearm. "It's the right way for us," she said in a low, solemn voice. She crawled into Sage's lap, her thumb finding its way into her mouth. Sage cuddled her close, moving her chair back to better accommodate the lanky child.

Lily often wondered what Sage thought about Birdie's sudden age leap a couple years ago from two to about twelve. Sage would never ask, though, as was her way. Upon espying the larger child, she had merely blinked repeatedly and prepared Birdie's breakfast as though it were any old morning. Sage knew a lot more than she let on and was damned good at keeping her own counsel. Always had been.

For the past two years, they'd had a preteen instead of a toddler and every day had been a new challenge, from finding a way to educate her to hiding her as much as possible. Plus dealing with the changes her physical body was going through. The hardest thing had been trying not to explain those changes to the ranch workers who had adored the toddler from two years ago. There had been some tense moments and Lily was sure the change was common gossip fodder, but twelve-year-old Birdie had brought the hands as much joy as Birdie the toddler had, wrapping all of them around her little finger, readily helping them to forget her strangeness.

Lanny had been terrified by Birdie's unexplainable shift two years ago. He'd crossed himself repeatedly, looking to Sage for answers and studying the platinum-haired child as though she were a complete aberration. These days she had come to be his angel, though, and Lily knew he truly believed that she was one. An angel come to Earth to bless Good Neighbor Ranch. It was why she could get him to eat lentil patties instead of a beef steak.

Lily smiled at her wandering thoughts and, having emptied her plate, rose and started clearing her place. She really needed to talk to Flynn, her recently elusive IDB contact, and find out what was going on with Birdie. She needed some answers before approaching the government with this new development.

Sage and Lanny rose as well and carried their plates and silverware to the kitchen and the dishwasher. Lanny was hopeless in a kitchen, so Lily and Sage silently loaded the dishes while he made his way back outside for evening rounds.

Birdie had returned to her own chair and she and Hunter were giggling and whispering, foreheads almost touching. Lily watched them, smiling helplessly. How she loved those two.

"Okay, guys, are you finished?" she called out, enjoying the identical way their heads swiveled to face her.

Hunter met her gaze and grinned sheepishly. "She's helping me with a patient."

Birdie appeared at Lily's side in a bright flash as she handed her plate to Sage. She wrapped one thin arm about Sage's waist, and the older woman smoothed Birdie's shiny hair with one hand. "Hunny said Colonel Geneva Dendridge's heart is too friable for her upcoming transplant surgery and she's afraid they are gonna lose her and the heart."

Hunter approached. "So, Little Miss Smarty Pants here tells me that the surgeon can use stem cell injections to revasculate the area below the heart to strengthen…"

Lily held up a staying palm. She glanced at Sage, whose face was inscrutable. "Yeah, I get it. Go make your call."

She studied Birdie as Hunter hurried away. The girl appeared to think she'd done something wrong, so Lily smiled at her and, pulling her from Sage's caress, wrapped both arms around her daughter. "Good job, my brilliant bird."

"Out of here, you two," Sage said. "I got work to do."

"So, are you going to look up rosemary on your tablet?" Lily asked as they walked toward the family room.

Birdie sighed as she lifted her supercharged, IDB-enhanced tablet from the coffee table. "I will, just for fun but it's not that way, Mummy."

Lily sat on the sofa and pulled her daughter closer. "Okay. It's just us. Tell me what's going on. Did Flynn say something private?"

Birdie shook her head in the negative. "Mummy, you know there's so many more of us than Flynn, right? Sometimes many millions speak to me, all at once it seems like. I've gotten good at sorting who's who, but I find it surprising the others in the Collective don't contact you."

"Flynn is the only one I'm allowed to talk to, hon. It's their liaison with me and I'm theirs from our government. Besides, when I'm speaking with Flynn, quite often the entire Collective knows what we are talking about anyway and it tells me what they all think. Your situation is very different. I'm only human while you are half human and half IDB. Your communication is more direct."

"I know," Birdie said with another loud sigh. "I think Rosemary is, too, but there's trouble there. I'm not sure why she is calling me, but the Collective says we must go."

"Go?" Lily blinked her eyes in new worry. "Go where?"

Birdie had become engrossed in an encyclopedia page on her tablet. "Just Alabama."

Lily's mouth fell open. "Just Alabama," she repeated quietly.

## Aili's Journal

### Humanity

Alabama. I don't know much about the state. I know it's a conservative Republican state, according to Schoolboy and what I had read online. But it's where Rosemary lives. I find myself wondering about her political leanings but only briefly. I sense that she, like me, knows how vacuous and postering those in politics were. Well, most of them. Blanket statements are usually foolish. Some people go into politics for true altruistic reasons. Unfortunately, their hands, due to the political machine, are often tied. Schoolboy told me about his uncle on his mother's side. He, as a Native, sought out and won a seat on the New Mexico House of Representatives, thinking it would be good for his people to have ears and eyes in the local political caucus. He soon discovered that he was in a helpless minority when it came to having certain new legislation read and passed. Disheartening but an unavoidable reality.

It isn't what matters, the mores and social structures humans have made for themselves. What matters is humanity and how people relate to one another. The Collective has worked tirelessly behind the scenes for millennia to try to make humans more aware of their humanity. Oddly enough, specially selected human leaders across the world had agreed to this aspect of the Collective rules and even its inclusion in the human-IDB written agreements.

Humanity. The word says it all.

Now that I am almost on my way to Rosemary, I feel something that I could only class as trepidation. I don't usually have the same emotions as other humans, though compassion ranks high as it is an important part of Collective energy, so this nervousness surprised me. It wasn't an act, something I am often guilty of to get by with the adults and children around me, but it was a true worry about what to expect. Chief of all, again odd, was will she like me? We were two albino whales swimming in a sea of seals. We had to connect.

Things are changing. My energy is changing, and I feel revelatory each day, as though much new knowledge is coming my way. My body feels strange, as though I didn't fit it anymore and though it's exhilarating, maybe frightening, I welcome it. My energy half knows well that the only constant is change.

# CHAPTER FOUR

## *Our Baby*

Lily crept back to her office through the darkened house after Hunter had fallen into her characteristic heavy slumber. Foregoing her noisy cane, she braced herself on the hallway wall, steadying herself as she walked. She quietly closed the office door before blindly finding and switching on the desk lamp and seating herself at the desk. These late-night office visits had begun when she and Hunter started sharing the same bed. Flynn had routinely visited Lily's bedroom in the wee morning hours, but Lily wanted to make sure that Hunter wasn't disturbed. As a busy doctor, an internist based in the emergency room of the veteran's hospital, sixty miles away and yet the hospital closest to Morris, Hunter needed all the sleep she could get.

Besides, according to the agreement between the Collective and all the world leaders of Earth, only specific liaisons could see and communicate with representatives from the Collective. If the Collective, the energy field that encompassed the planet and had created mankind, was made common knowledge... Well, the entire social fabric that humans had created for themselves, millennia after millennia, would be deconstructed, no longer a practical security blanket.

This night found Lily waiting with sharp impatience. This new issue was of alarming importance, if not to the world and maybe the universal order, then certainly to the Dawson-Moon family. When it came to her daughter or Hunter, Lily was fiercely protective. Not unwarranted, given what she knew about how crowded the universe actually was, peopled with some truly evil creatures as well as the good IDBs. No, she was taking no chances. She was seriously worried about the sudden changes that were occurring.

She rose, limped to the window, and opened the blinds slightly so she could look out at the desert darkness. The only light was from a fingernail-like waxing moon and maybe a bit of starlight. The plaintive cries of a band of coyotes carried to her across the vast expanse of land surrounding her home. For some reason, she found the sound comforting.

She turned away and took her seat again, sighing in frustration. Her hand shot out to the glass sculpture, and, grasping it, she whispered angrily to the powerful beings of light, Flynn, in particular.

And then Flynn was there, a woman again, in its glowing pajamas and bright silver hair, standing on the other side of the desk.

"Oh, thank God," Lily muttered. "I am getting pretty frantic here, Flynn. What the hell is going on with my daughter?"

Flynn smiled and its glowing eyes softened somewhat. "Our daughter, you mean?" it asked.

Lily felt chastened, but she continued angrily, "Yes, our daughter. Why is this Rosemary person calling her? Now Birdie is saying we have to go to her. To Alabama!"

Flynn manifested a chair from bright atoms generating light and sat in it, its silky tunic and trousers flowing about its body like a waterfall. "There is much to say," it said with a very human sigh.

Lily sat back and tried to relax. "So, say it," she urged.

Flynn tilted its head, as though conferring with the beings of energy it was connected to. It looked like Birdie in that moment. "There is a problem."

Lily leaned forward and pulled a notepad close. She often took notes in waitress shorthand and later entered them into a protected tablet given her by Wendell Ames, her secure contact with President David Anderson. "What do we need to do?"

Flynn lifted its hands and waved them back and forth, light trails—maybe photons—making them blur together as they moved. "There is…nothing."

"Wait. What do you mean?" Lily frowned in confusion.

"This…problem…is not some…thing that can be fixed by humans. You may deal with the…fallout…but it is a battle for the Collective."

Lily felt her heart leap into her throat. "Battle?" she gasped. "What battle?"

Flynn fell silent again, chrome-colored eyes watching Lily closely. When it spoke next, Lily could hear the sorrow in its usually inexpressive tone. "Much will be asked of you… emotionally. And I…apologize."

"No." Lily's head automatically swayed from side to side, reinforcing her negation. "No, Flynn. She is my…our daughter. She is half human and your kind cannot cause harm to humans. It's in the agreement, I read it, Flynn. I fucking read it." Her voice had risen, ringing too loud in the quiet house. She fervently hoped neither Hunter nor Birdie would awaken and come to investigate.

Flynn seemed taken aback. "We mean no harm to Aili. She is one of us as well, and we would never…"

Flynn's attention suddenly veered from Lily and fastened on the window next to her.

Lily glanced in that direction. "What are you…"

"We are not alone," Flynn hissed as it, and its chair, disappeared instantly.

Lily stumbled to her feet and separated two of the blind slats so she could see outside. She turned her head, checking in both directions but saw no one, nothing but the expanse of moonlit desert beyond the ghostly posts of the ranch fencing. She watched for some time, her heart beating fast. Was it one of the ranch hands? She'd never known them to wander the ranch this soon before dawn. Yes, they were early risers but not before four or five in the morning.

After some time, she sighed and pulled the cord, closing the blinds. She pondered what the intruder might have seen, and new alarm grew in her chest. She could only hope that Flynn's quick disappearance had given the intruder pause, allowing them to disbelieve what their eyes had seen.

Lily sat at her desk and one hand reached to caress the statue. "Flynn, I didn't see anyone," she whispered.

Flynn appeared in the statue's interior. It didn't take the time to form so was only a swirling mass of bright liveliness within the statue's depths. Its voice rang clearly in Lily's head, though. "Aili is one with us, dear Lily. Do as she instructs, for she knows the way."

"But, Flynn, she's just a baby," Lily responded, hating the pleading tone in her voice.

"Our baby," Flynn said before the light faded away, taking Lily's sense of comfort and assurance with it.

## Aili's Journal

### Dark Matter

Thought for the day, via Rosemary. Does the Collective energy use dark matter as stepping stones to travel the ether of the universe? The Collective is split on this issue, most saying that this is a valid fact of the quantum cosmos. It has been argued among us since the beginning of time in this newer cosmos and yet a determination has never been settled upon.

Others say that the Collective is all powerful and needs only their photons of light to use for momentum. After all, dark energy is only the absence of the packets of the energy that sustain us.

I posit that light doesn't exist without darkness. I am definitely leaning toward the usefulness of dark matter. After all, dark energy is the biggest entity in the entire universe. Look around. Well, in empty spaces.

I also believe it may be that the Collective brought the dark matter with them when their energy was thrust into this new, empty plane of our universe. It may be the remainder of the large black hole that twisted time and space around us. It may have dissipated with the impact of transference and become the dark matter that buoys all things. Such lovely food for thought and debate.

# CHAPTER FIVE

## *The Cork Accepts*

Breakfast was oatmeal with a ton of fruit on top. Birdie, using her spoon, idly divided the blueberries from the strawberries and made hills of them atop the grain. She stacked the banana slices into a near perfect tower. Lily ignored her own breakfast as she watched this process with jaundiced, puffy eyes. Hunter, her long black hair already smoothed into a ponytail and pinned on the back of her head, periodically studied Lily while loading her mouth with oatmeal and fruit and chewing thoughtfully.

Lily flashed back to the day they'd met. Hunter had been so handsome in her Air Force uniform and she'd made Lily feel safe, even in the midst of the deadly Polar Purge, the illness brought to Earth by the Grey aliens. Her sweet brown eyes had comforted Lily and they'd made an almost immediate connection. Later, even though Lily was pregnant, Hunter had confessed her feelings for Lily. Now, studying the woman she had come to love more than life itself, her heart swelled anew, warmed by the memory.

Sage had served the meal and then disappeared from the kitchen, dusting spray and cleaning cloth in hand. Lanny had eaten way earlier, as was his wont, and he and the ranch hands were rounding up cattle and loading them into trucks for delivery to a buyer.

The kitchen was eerily quiet except for the calls of the ranch hands and Lily found herself itching for a cigarette. She had given them up during, and since, her pregnancy, but the desire for one had never been stronger.

"So, I take it we are going on a road trip?" she said, leaning forward and lacing her fingers together. She had directed the query to Birdie, but her eyes sought out Hunter, to gauge her reaction to this news. Hunter lifted her head and studied Lily's expression.

Birdie carefully placed her spoon next to her bowl. "I think we have to, Mummy. I need to be physically with her for this next part."

"Part? What part?" Hunter had found her voice. "And what trip? I swear, you two are as thick as thieves sometimes, you know?"

Lily reached across the table and took Hunter's free hand. "Birdie and I have to take a trip down south, to Alabama, to seek out this Rosemary person who keeps calling to her. I'm not sure why. The powers that be aren't telling me much so I'm kinda working on faith here."

Hunter was petulant. "But why Alabama? That's a long way from here."

Lily shrugged. "I think that's where she is, right, Birdie?"

Birdie had taken a bite of oatmeal, and she nodded, then talked with her mouth full. "Yep, she lives in Redstar. Redstar, Alabama."

"Chew your food, Birdie," Lily said automatically.

"Redstar, Alabama." Hunter pulled out her phone and tapped the information into a search engine. "Holy cow, it's way down in the bayou, even way below Mobile. Not exactly an area known to welcome strangers. You two are crazy. There's no way." She shook her head for emphasis. "No way."

Lily smiled at Hunter as she took her hand again. "I love you so much," she said quietly.

"Yuck, you two," Birdie mumbled.

Hunter pulled her fingers from Lily's grasp. "I mean it, Lil. You can't just go traipsing into bayou country. Who knows what could happen to you guys?"

Lily sighed. "It can't be helped, Hunter. Do you really think that we *can't* go?"

Birdie took another spoonful of oatmeal and studied Hunter as she chewed. She swallowed before speaking this time. "It's okay, Hunny. It'll be safe. I can protect Mummy."

Hunter scrubbed at her face with both hands. "Look, if you have to go, then, by all that's holy, I'm going as well."

Birdie and Lily both stared at Hunter, mouths agape. "No way," Birdie whispered loudly.

Hunter scowled. "Look. I have a ton of vacation time built up. I'll take some finally."

"But your patients—" Lily began.

"Will just have to be covered by someone else," Hunter finished for her. She stood, stretching her small stature. "I'll take care of it today. When are we leaving and for how long?"

"Tomorrow, four in the morning," Birdie said decisively. She turned to Lily. "What do you think, Mummy? I think we'd better plan on ten days at least since we are driving there."

Lily shrugged and smiled at her wife. "There's your answer, I guess."

Hunter stretched out her arm and pulled Lily to her feet. "We'll make the best of it. It may even be fun." Still holding Lily's hand, she turned to Birdie. "Will it be fun?"

Birdie parroted Lily's shrug and sighed. "We'll be together, at least, and that's something."

"Yeah. That's something," Hunter agreed quietly, handing Lily's cane to her and pulling her into the main hallway.

"Wait!" Birdie called and they could hear her scrambling out of her chair. The refrigerator door slammed, and she was beside them, a blue vinyl lunch bag in her hand. "SaySay and me made this for you. It's veggies and dip and a veggie hot dog on a bun. Oh, and chips, lots of chips 'cause I know how much you like them."

Hunter let go of Lily and knelt in front of her daughter, taking the lunch bag. "Do you even realize how wonderfully special you are, my little bird? How empty my life would be if I didn't have you to take care of me?"

Birdie smirked and pressed into Hunter. She smoothed Hunter's dark hair with both her palms and kissed her on the forehead. "Yeah, I know," she said. "I love you, too."

Hunter patted Birdie's cheek and walked with Lily to the front door where she hefted her backpack. "So, we'll be okay, right? This is what we're supposed to do?"

"I believe so," Lily responded. "I had a brief conversation last night, and Flynn said we have to follow Birdie on this."

"All right, then, all right," Hunter said. She patted her pockets until she found her keys, then leaned toward Lily for a lingering kiss. "See you this afternoon, babe. I'll text you when I hear back from HR and get someone to cover for me."

Lily rubbed Hunter's back as she held the door for her. "Be safe out there," she said in her usual farewell.

Hunter grinned and stepped out into the day's already bright sunlight.

"She's worried, huh?" Birdie said at Lily's side.

It was strange how she moved through the house like greased lightning. It always caught Lily off-guard, even when she was somewhat prepared for it.

She pulled Birdie close. "Yeah, but she'll come around, she always does."

"She's like a cork floating on water, isn't she?"

Lily was puzzled. "A cork?"

"Yeah, no matter how many times you dunk her under, she comes up smiling."

Lily nodded. It was actually a pretty good description of Hunter. Even when Lily had been at her lowest, recovering in the hospital, Hunter had been a fount of positivity for her.

The two walked onto the porch. A stack of wide-brimmed hats rested on the back upright of one of the rocking chairs there and they each grabbed one as they passed by. Lily slapped hers against her jeans, in case a bug had crawled in or it was dusty. Birdie didn't bother, bopping it on her head and jumping off the porch.

Life outside the Good Neighbor Ranch's long, low main house was a different world from the cool calmness found inside it. Here the heat and sun were brutal, and there were few trees that could be used for protection. Beige and brown sand and rocks, of all sizes, stretched as far as the eye could see, dotted by dusky green pinon trees, pale Russian olive trees, some rabbit grass, and other low-lying shrubs. Some may have found the landscape dull and uninspiring, but Lily had loved it since first seeing it as a girl.

Her father, Denny Dawson, known by his peers as Ducky Dawson, was a lieutenant general in the United States Air Force. And unbeknownst to his wife, Sandy, and their daughter, he was also the Liaison between the United States Government military complex and the Collective. In concert with these hidden duties, he had bought the isolated ranch in the New Mexico desert and moved his small family away from the Washington DC they loved. Pulled away from friends and the city she enjoyed, Lily's mother, Sandy, had suffered. By the time Lily finished high school, the eventual rift and resultant drinking caused an almost amicable divorce. She and her mother had moved to Florida to manage a mobile home park.

Her father's untimely death had been the catalyst that caused Lily to return to the desert she had once loved. Reuniting with the Kya'nahs, Landon and Sage, had been more satisfying than she could have hoped. If only Sandy had come with her. Sandy, who was dead now, taken by the alien virus while still in Florida.

Lily gazed out over the west pasture and saw the black dots of grazing Criollo cows off in the heat-wavering distance and remembered how excited she'd been about moving from busy brownstone-bordered Washington DC streets to the wild, open desert outside Morris, New Mexico. As a child, she had often wondered why it was necessary for her father to move them to this remote outpost, though after she took on his position as Liaison between the IDBs and her own government, she'd immediately understood. The fewer people involved in her daily life, the better.

This was not to say she hadn't resented the move as she got older and had been faced with a bitter, often drunk mother separated from friends and her usual social events. Or a military father increasingly distant, swamped with learning how to work a ranch as well as dealing with the IDBs.

She spied Lanny walking back from the western pastures and smiled. Best of all, the move had brought Lanny and Sage into her life. They had become the parents she needed when hers became dysfunctional. SaySay had always offered ready arms to hold her, and Lanny had provided discipline and a calming masculine order to a needy child's life.

She noticed suddenly that her own child had disappeared from her side, so, not seeing her in the distance, she meandered toward the nearby bunkhouse and barn buildings. The aroma of burnt coffee greeted her. Today's blend was a strong pinon mix. Thinking back to her first taste of pinon coffee, stolen from the firepit by SaySay's mischievous daughter, Cibby, she wondered if she would enjoy its nutty rich flavor more now than then. Entering the bunkhouse, she saw that all the cubicle doors were closed, indicating that the workers were probably out and about, working the ranch. Knowing Birdie wouldn't go into any of them, especially with no one to visit with inside, she moved farther along the main hallway until the sound of voices reached her.

## Aili's Journal

### Now I Understand

The balance that must be maintained by the dance of matter and antimatter is at the root of everything that's held true. It is the fabric of space. Indeed, our very beings are crafted from this ever-changing balance of energy, of light and dark matter.

We were momentarily confused when our energy was shifted from our home universe into this one. After much memory research, it is believed that we had wandered too close to a collapsing star—light—that made the black hole—dark—pop into being. It pulled us through, away from our original heavily populated universe, and brought the dark and light energy response with it. A new lonely, empty universe was created from the debris of that collapsed star and it is the same energy that sustains the Collective.

Continuing as we have always done, in the beginning of this new universe we sought information hungrily and we travelled this growing, ever-expanding cosmos, seeking it. There was little to find, as this expanse was so new and the planets not yet formed, not yet ready to be seeded. We lingered or toured freely then. We watched planets form from rock and gasses, blended by magnetism and centripetal energy. We saw galaxies coalesce into beautiful spirals of light and dark as the constants of gravity, magnetism, and centripetal force created something new and different. And we left bits of ourselves and our energy on planet after planet.

Why? And why did some of us choose to seed Earth among so many others? Why Mars? Why create then take on human form so we could help settle the many colonies of what humans now call the Milky Way? Why this sun? Why other star systems that offer sustained life? There are no answers to these questions, other than how we sometimes simply seek to be part of the flesh of land-dwelling life as we had in our other cosmos.

In our prehuman and human forms, the Collective has passed through wave after wave of Earth history since this planet's formation. We were here during what modern humans call the Hadean Era, when the Earth was still molten and uninhabitable except by ourselves. We passed by again later and exhaled into the burgeoning ocean flesh of the new planet and helped it grow. Eventually, we began building huge monuments, laying the groundwork that would enable humans to want to live better lives. They needed something to strive for. We manifested into human form, gave them legends, creation myths, religion. And we watched them grow.

A catastrophic collision with a passing asteroid, in that early time, ejected our energy away from the flesh and back into the cosmos. But we came back once again. Enhanced flesh and built the god life again. Then another collision, by a passing planet in an unstable orbit, separated our energy and the flesh once more. But this time, except for some parts of us that splintered away to other galaxies, a part of the Collective was pulled into Earth's gravitational field, held by a new powerful magnetism from a now tilted globe. We watched patiently as our huge structural accomplishments were buried in the falling sand and debris from that collision.

So, we rebuilt and continued to reside here, above the atmosphere, gods to the humans who feel us. Many of us remain vested in the preservation and care of this planet and the humans who occupy it. We are somewhat settled nomads who continue to soak in all the knowledge from this, our new planetary home.

As an older human hybrid, I also have learned that, if one properly respects the light and dark energy and uses it skillfully, one can bend it to accommodate whatever one desires. And that it is a skill not only kept for our powerful communal, because any human can bend and use the fabric of the cosmos if they so desire. The Collective has even, long ago, enhanced higher Terran brains to more easily have this ability and those in their line have become strong, accomplished leaders.

Unfortunately, most modern humans have evolved away and lost the conscious skill to do it, although they often shift reality without realizing it, deep in their subconscious. Dreams have always altered the fabric of space. Which means I can age in decade-sized leaps of shifted energy in my current flesh. A hard thing to explain to those who cannot understand. My poor mothers.

I find myself wondering when it will happen again. Or if it will. Perhaps the Collective will have an answer, but I feel the answer may lie within me as I adapt to need.

# CHAPTER SIX

## *The Ranch and the Rock*

"It was just one piece," Margie said defensively as Lily stepped into her office.

Lily grunted and pointed to Birdie, who was chewing a massive piece of chocolate. "Cavities mean more dentist visits, right?"

Birdie nodded and threw her arms about Margie in a quick hug before speeding out the open doorway.

"She's something else, that girl," Margie said, gazing fondly at the door Birdie had disappeared through.

"Don't I know it," Lily agreed. "Listen, Hunter and Birdie and I are taking a little vacation. Gonna leave in the morning to go down to the Gulf for a few weeks. You think everything will be hunky dory?"

Margie glanced at her calendar. "Right as rain," she said musingly. "Nothing coming up that needs your attention. How the devil is Hunter getting away?" Her deep brown eyes studied Lily expectantly.

Lily shrugged. "I was as surprised as you are."

Lily took a moment to admire Margie's Johnny Depp poster, front and center on the east wall. He was young, in non-actor garb, wearing torn and frayed jeans and a pale-yellow button-down shirt, mostly unbuttoned. He was gorgeous. A second poster, on the same wall, depicted him in his pirate outfit, with a reddish head wrap and dangling earrings. He was still gorgeous.

Turning in the other direction, she noted the Jimi Hendrix posters on the opposite wall, the largest being a close-up with the tips of his hair glowing red from backlighting. In the other, he seemed to be caressing his large, flat guitar. He was handsome as well but appeared fiercer in demeanor than playful Depp.

Lily grinned. The dichotomy of her heroes perfectly reflected Margie somehow.

Margie leaned back, her desk chair squealing in protest, and folded her strong arms across her ample belly and chest. "Do you both a world of good," she said. "I heard about that tree stunt. What were you thinking?"

Lily's mouth fell open. "How did you...? Never mind. I was thinking I was tired of deskwork. That's what I was thinking."

Margie grinned, her gold tooth bright against the darkness of her skin. "Ain't we all?"

Boots sounded outside and Lanny poked his head into the office. "Click and Eddie took the trucks on to the Borrows's place. Make sure you get the payment and the receipt when they get back," he said.

"Will do," Margie said. "Thank you."

"Thank you, Lanny," Lily echoed absently as he nodded and ducked out.

"Before you take off, can you check these over and sign off on them?" Margie handed Lily a sheaf of paperwork.

Lily sighed and took a seat on the chair opposite the accountant. After perusing and signing them for the next quarter of an hour, she breathed a new sigh, one of relief this time. Margie did a consistently good job of keeping the books for Good Neighbor Ranch. Each expense was impeccably presented, and Lily knew that each ranch income and expenditure was also dutifully recorded into the computer. She laid the paperwork on the desk and sat back. "Have I thanked you lately for the excellent job you do?"

Margie pulled her hefty body straighter in her chair, suddenly defensive. "Wait. Are you firing me?"

"What?" Lily was honestly perplexed by the question. "Where did you get that idea?" Lily remembered how upset Margie had been when she had planned to sell Good Neighbor. Did she still feel insecure about her home there?

Margie was quiet for a long beat. She glanced down at her hands, clasping them atop the desk. Her voice was subdued. "It's just, you know, always the same. Things begin to change. Then it's, 'Good job, Margie, now hit the road.'"

Lily pressed her hands down hard onto Margie's hands. She wanted to make sure she had the accountant's full attention. "You listen to me. You are family. *Family.* You don't fire family, for God's sake. I cannot even imagine Good Neighbor without you and Click here."

Margie tucked her head as though embarrassed, but she did squeeze Lily's fingers.

"Okay," Lily muttered. "I'm gonna walk the ranch, but you remember what I said. I mean it."

Margie glanced up, a rueful expression on her face. "I will, boss. And you enjoy that vacation. Y'all certainly deserve it. And I mean that."

Lily patted Margie's hands as she extricated her fingers. "Sweet words, but I'm listening to you."

Margie grunted and sat back. "Best had."

Lily grinned and shook her head side to side with indulgent exasperation as she grabbed her hat from the desk.

Once outside the massive wood-sided bunkhouse, Lily took a deep breath of the heated desert air and surveyed her land as she leaned her weight on her cane. Twenty-two hundred acres stretched as far as she could see. Far off in the distance, where the desert lay fallow and undisturbed, little glints of light appeared and disappeared in random shards of brightness. Some were so far away their pinpoint flashes could barely be seen.

A year or so after Birdie was born, Flynn had inexplicably requested that Lily install tall panes of framed glass at key points on her land. The IDB had prepared a map of the Good Neighbor acreage with the specific locations marked, which made her job infinitely easier. And Lanny had overseen her new pet project, which she called a creative art installation, with no question, the ranch crew, per her specific instruction, mounting each pane on pivot settings that allowed the mirrors to be moved side to side by the wind.

Seeing them now gave her a sense of security. Yes, she was worried about this possible threat that Birdie was leading them toward, but she knew each sparkling pane of specially tempered glass was a sentry point, checked often by the Collective. They may not be able to help her with this new personal issue, but at least the ranch was being well looked after. The viral threat the Greys had wrought several years ago had lit a new fire under the members of Code C, the international governing board that was responsible for monitoring the relations of Earth and the Collective, and the Collective had graciously offered a new level of protection all around the world. Lily assumed the panes of glass were part of this, especially as she was the US Liaison with them.

Clapping her hat back onto her short blond hair, Lily set off to the right, heading toward the huge mesa that towered in reddish glory behind the low, flat ranch house, which was framed by the two-story barn and the long, low bunkhouse. She glanced from side to side, searching for Birdie as she traversed the distance. The girl often roamed the ranch freely and Lily didn't worry overmuch. She knew Birdie understood the possible dangers of the scrubland, and she knew that all the hands had Birdie's best interests at heart and would look out for her.

She didn't see Birdie but kept going. There was an enormous boulder at the foot of the mesa, and Lily often went there to overlook the grazing lands, to satisfy her curiosity. She had complete faith in Lanny and the crews who maintained the property but couldn't resist a bit of woolgathering in the guise of an overview inspection of the land. The visual evidence of the excellent management always soothed her, and her thoughts seemed to line up more orderly as she perched on the boulder.

The reddish soil was loose beneath her feet as she trudged up the incline. Her eyes caressed the huge granite boulder ahead. It had fallen from the top of the mesa and rolled to its present location eons ago, and its bottom was encircled by a tangled thicket of gray-green scrub. An opening had been cleared in the undergrowth, and Felix and Click had shoveled the rocky soil along the more sheltered side of the granite, making a sort of ramp that Lily could use to ascend to the top. With her left hand smoothing along the rock's hot surface, her right hand supported by the cane, she made her way along that ramp.

"Hey, Mummy."

Lily was surprised to find Birdie perched atop the boulder, arms wrapped around her calves, chin on her knees.

"Well, hello, little bit. What are you doing up here?" She rubbed Birdie's back as she hoisted herself into a seated position next to her. "I figured you'd be out pestering Lanny."

Birdie frowned at her mother. "I don't pester him. I help out."

"Umm hmm," Lily said, grinning. "I'm sure you do."

"I do! Even he says so," Birdie protested.

They grew silent and Lily allowed the dusty scent of hot granite and sandy dirt to fill her nose and lungs. She loved the heat of western New Mexico. It was very different from the suffocating, humid heat of southern Florida. The sun seemed hotter at this high altitude, but the air was clear and dry. And the insect population was almost nonexistent except for the occasional horsefly. In Florida, fighting mosquitos, biting flies, and huge flying cockroaches was a never-ending battle. She did not miss that. And the thought of heading back south, to Alabama, was bringing the memory of those struggles roaring back.

She cleared her throat. "It looks like this place, Redstar, in Alabama is way south. Like in the bayou maybe?"

Birdie nodded as she tapped an index finger lightly on the toe of her white athletic shoe. "She lives on the water. Been there her whole life."

"And what's her family like? Do you think they'll understand why we are there?"

Birdie sighed and squinted at her mother from beneath her floppy brimmed hat. "Some will and some won't. I think her mama has passed away."

"Oh, that's a shame," Lily said. "No one should have to grow up without a mama."

"Yeah, she's pretty sad about it."

"Did she tell you what happened?"

Birdie lifted the leg of her jeans to scratch idly at her calf. "I don't think she really thinks about that. She was little. But I have an idea."

Lily pulled up her own knees and rested her cheek on them, her eyes on her daughter. "You do? Tell me."

"I think it has to do with the Collective. I think we made her die."

Lily sighed and lifted her head to gaze out across the desert. "Oh, that's horrible. Was it an accident like mine?"

Birdie shook her head and patted the back of her neck, her hand disappearing in the wet heat beneath her thick braid. "Not exactly. She didn't deal well with having a daughter like me."

Lily could hear the sadness in her voice. "I'm sorry, kiddo. I guess sometimes people don't realize how valuable and special their loved ones are." She studied Birdie as she patted her knee.

Birdie sighed. "Yeah, I'm really glad you and Hunny think I'm special. And are okay with it."

Lily thought of her conversation with Margie and about how families are often chosen and not always born. "You're our baby and all babies are special. You just have a…a few extras and we love it because it is all a part of you. Families can be made up of a ton of elements."

"Hmph," Birdie grunted. "You should try dealing with my Collective family. Talk about a ton of elements. It's more like a hundred trillion at the very least."

Lily laughed and pulled Birdie close. "And the best of it is right here by my side. Let's go pack and get ready for our great adventure. You ready?"

Birdie grinned and nodded as they stood and made their way carefully down the sloping dirt path.

## *Aili's Journal*

*War*

I don't think I understand what the Collective is telling me. I'm supposed to be packing for the trip, but I can't focus. They keep knocking at my head, sending images of war. There are tanks and guns and bombs. Humans running in fear.

None of this makes any sense. We are not those people—our existence promotes peace and practices it. Have some humans fostered stupidity and started yet another conflict? One that would require Collective intervention?

I thought of past wars, remembering what had been passed to me in several large lozenges of historical knowledge. Hitler had been a horrific black hole in space and time, eventually removed by the Collective after years of worldwide bureaucratic nonsense. As had other brutal despots, Stalin, Mao, Genghis Khan. Was this the change I felt so keenly, an upcoming war under yet another tyrant?

I want to ask them but need to get things together for my trip. Hunny had texted Mummy and me, saying she had gotten the time off all organized, so I knew the trip was imminent. What should I wear to meet Rosemary? It would be hot in southern Alabama, so shorts seemed a given. Maybe I would wear my favorite Einstein T shirt, the one where his eyes twinkled. I tried to remember what colors looked good on me, but my mind blanked out on even that topic. I was trying to avoid the scenes of war that kept pushing into my brain. I sincerely hope Rosemary has been spared these horrific visions.

# CHAPTER SEVEN

*Under the Microscope*

Leaving Birdie to pack her own bags, Lily made her way to the office and shut the door. Pressing a button built into the top drawer of the desk, she seated herself and waited patiently as the secure screen rose from behind her desk blotter. A muted ring sounded, and Uncally's dear face appeared, his dark green eyes worried.

"Hello, peanut. Everything okay?"

Lily smiled, pleased and comforted to see her godfather, Colonel Alan Collins, as always. "I dunno. Birdie has been in contact with the Collective and she is dragging us off to a town way down south. Redstar, Alabama."

She waited as he jotted down the name. "It's by Mobile, I think," she added finally.

"Any idea why?" He studied her as he awaited an answer.

She sighed. "There's a girl there, like her. They need to meet."

He sat back. "Hmm, is that wise?"

Lily shrugged. "At this point, we seem to have little control of it. Flynn says we need to go, too. It's gotta be important, right?"

He fell silent, rubbing his chin, obviously mulling the topic. Finally, he took a deep breath. "I guess. You realize that I'm a little out of my element here."

"I know." She nodded. "We all are. Flynn said we have to trust, and we know, from past events throughout all Earth history, that they do have our best interests at heart. I think I'm okay with it."

"We both will have to be. I'll need to file this, though, with the higher ups. Have you told Wendell?"

"I haven't. Would you please do that for me? The three of us are driving down starting tomorrow morning, early, and I need to get ready. We should be there in a couple days."

"Sure. And I'll tell him to text if he has any questions."

"Thank you, appreciate it."

"No problem, peanut. Do me a favor and check in every other day. Everything else going okay?"

Lily smiled, realizing anew how great her life was these days. "It's all good. The ranch is even turning a profit."

Alan grunted. "Thanks to Lanny, no doubt."

"Hey!" She tried to sound indignant even though both of them knew it was true. "I help, too."

"And Hunter, and Lunan, Felix's family and Click. Sage and Martha."

She nodded agreement. "We're quite the family here at Good Neighbor."

"Hey, are they still doing okay, after that first shock? You know, Birdie's thing a couple years ago?"

Lily sat back and blew air at her bangs. "Ahh, you mean the age thing? They've all accepted it. They did almost right away, you know that. Lanny still thinks she's an angel straight from heaven, though, and I often see him still crossing himself from time to time when he spies her."

Alan chuckled. "And the others?"

"There was a conspiracy of denial, I'm thinking. No one wanted to believe such a thing could happen. If they didn't discuss it or acknowledge it, then it wasn't real."

"And then there's the charm factor," Alan pointed out.

Lily laughed and leaned forward, resting her forearms on the desk. "For sure, she's everyone's darling. Margie is going to make her fat with all the chocolate candy she gives her." She paused and tapped an index finger on her bottom lip. "They all, no matter how busy they are, make time for her. I see these wizened old guys stop whatever they are doing to patiently explain stuff or to listen to her go on and on about a better way to do it. It's pretty amazing."

"She's an engaging little girl," Alan offered. "It'll be interesting to see what happens next, as she matures."

Lily nodded. "Yep. I'm still torn about the journal though. I don't even read it."

"As I've said before, we'll have to see them all eventually."

"It's too much like putting her under a microscope, Uncally. I still feel that way." Her voice had risen, grown louder.

Alan's voice was resigned but forceful. "Lily, we've discussed this. As a human and IDB hybrid, we have to study her. Suppose more of them appear? It could very well turn into a type of threat. Like taking over the people of Earth and replacing them with hybrids. It could happen. POTUS David has mentioned it more than once. He watches a lot of science fiction apparently."

"As if they would do something so crazy, so threatening. Obviously, you don't remember how apologetic Flynn was about what happened to me. And it was trying to save my frickin' life."

"Now, Lily, don't get worked up about this." His voice was low and calming. "Birdie will have a say in what we read. I believe she understands about us studying her kind."

Lily nodded again. "True. There's not much she doesn't understand. Did I text you that Schoolboy Robbins can't teach her anymore?"

"The tutor you found for her? No, what happened?"

"She has surpassed him. He said that there was nothing else he could teach her. They've been just looking up things on the computer, which she does at home anyway."

"So, he felt guilty getting paid, I bet."

"Bingo."

"Her intelligence is kinda creepy. What are you going to do now?"

Lily sighed and shrugged. "I dunno. I guess we'll let her decide our next step. I feel like she, because of her IDB side, will be a lifelong learner. She's like a little knowledge vacuum, sucking up info."

She sighed and stretched out her arms. "Guess I'll go get everything ready for our weird trip. Did I tell you Hunter is going?"

"Miss Workaholic herself? That's hard to believe." He chuckled and shook his head.

"Yeah. I'm kinda excited about it. We've never really vacationed together, even after almost three years of living together."

"Wow," Alan said. "It'll either be excruciatingly painful or blissfully wonderful."

Lily grunted. "Hmm, no in-between ground, I guess?"

"Well, it is sort of a working vacation," he pointed out. "I guess that will be the determining factor."

"Killjoy," Lily muttered.

Alan laughed until his eyes watered. "Have a good time, kid. Love to the fam." He used a bent finger to swipe at his eyes. "You know where I am, if you need me."

"Love you, Uncally. Big time!"

"Back atcha, kiddo."

They signed off and Lily fell thoughtful as she watched the screen lower into the body of the desk. She was thinking about Birdie being a test subject of the US Government. The intellectual part of her brain knew how necessary it was. Birdie was her baby, though, no matter her strange origins, and the maternal side of her wanted the government to simply butt out.

## Aili's Journal

*Leaving Good Neighbor*

Will I ever come back here? I don't know why this question

has been plaguing me so. I feel such sorrow at the prospect of leaving. I so want it to be temporary, only a vacation, but tears spill from my eyes as I finish loading my bag. I grabbed my teddy, Quantum, off my bed and stuffed him inside. He looked up at me with one eye, the other buried in the bag. *I'm your connection to home*, he seems to say as I zipped him securely inside.

I study my bedroom. Mummy had made it beautiful while still making it mine, with a mobile of this solar system and a large chart of periodic elements on one wall. The color scheme was dark and light purple, which represents endless space to me. I will definitely miss it.

A notion came to me, and I realized suddenly that Mummy was telling our plans to her governing body. The United States of America. I shake my head and smile. The need for order from chaos was so important to humans. It seems necessary for humans' very survival. This is why they need their gods, to feel that someone was in control at all times.

But as mathematician Edward Lorenz said, when coining the term butterfly effect, chaos is when the present determines the future, but the approximate present does not approximately determine the future.

Randomness is a pattern that is never fixed.

# CHAPTER EIGHT

*Sandy's All You Can Eat Buffet*

Birdie was nervous. The tension practically radiated off her, even as she played games or surfed the web on her cell phone and tablet. Lily, sitting in the front passenger seat, had already turned and checked in with her daughter at least a half dozen times. Each time, the child soothed her mother's worries, but they unfortunately didn't abate due to Birdie's continued anxiety.

Hunter looked at Lily questioningly, and Lily interpreted it as the concern it was. She shrugged at her own helplessness and studied the road ahead.

"Maybe some food?" she suggested finally.

Hunter glanced at her watch and nodded. "Sounds like a great idea. It's past lunchtime."

"Japanese?" Birdie said hopefully, eyes still on her phone.

"Central Texas, hon," Lily said with a sigh. "Rural. Unless you want a burger, ribs, or brisket, you're out of luck."

"Shoot!" Birdie replied. "French fries?"

"Hey, there's a buffet," Hunter said suddenly. "It's a steak house, but they usually have good veggie options."

"Sounds good to me," Birdie chimed in. "I bet they have good desserts, too."

Lily smiled, exceedingly glad Birdie had something to focus on now besides fidgeting with what had to be apprehension.

Hunter pulled off the interstate and into the huge parking lot of Sandy's All You Can Eat Buffet. They parked and securely locked the SUV.

Inside, loud country music surrounded them, and a fresh-faced teen named Tandy seated them and placed overlarge menus in front of them.

"I thought this was a buffet," Hunter grumbled as she opened the dark brown menu that was decorated with a huge longhorn steer head on the cover.

"Top of page two," Lily muttered. "Eighteen ninety-five for each."

"Sheesh! Highway robbery much?" Hunter said.

"Highway," Birdie said with a snicker.

Lily laughed just as the middle-aged, motherly server, Florence, came to take their drink order.

"Y'all doing the all you can eat?" she asked after jotting down their beverage choices. Her voice held the heavy twang of a native Texan.

"Yes, I think we will," Lily said. "Does it have lots of veggies?"

"Oh yes. It's a good spread. There's prime rib, ham, and brisket, too. Some chicken. Everything you could want."

Birdie opened her mouth, no doubt to share some pertinent vegetarian nugget, but Lily placed her hand on her daughter's forearm to still her.

"That sounds wonderful," she said.

"How old are you, sweetie? Children twelve and under get half price when a parent gets the full buffet," Florence added.

"I'm twelve going on thirty, my mummy says," Birdie answered.

Florence laughed. "Well, I think you'll qualify, even though," she said as she walked away. "Y'all help yourselves. Plates are on the buffet."

Sure enough, the numerous mounds of food covered a forty-foot expanse of sneeze-guarded hot steamer trays. Plenty for any all-you-could-eat gourmand. They spent a good hour gorging themselves on surprisingly well-prepared vegetables, fruits, and rolls.

"That's me," Hunter said, patting her stomach and covering the war zone of her final plate with a paper napkin.

"Me too," Birdie agreed, copying Hunter's action.

Lily just studied the two people she loved most in the world and took another bite of surprisingly sweet watermelon. "That should hold you two for a while."

Soon they were on the road again, Hunter back at the wheel, and Lily found herself drifting into a peaceful post-prandial slumber. Though the air conditioner was on full blast, the heat radiating from the window felt like being in a warm, but dry sauna.

As she dozed in half-sleep, her mind drifted back, to the fierce smothering heat she'd felt after the Greys had kidnapped her from the Acoma lands four years ago. The Greys had taken her when she was dropping off Sage and Lanny so that Sage, suffering from the viral Polar Purge, could get treatment from the pueblo's wise man. Because they knew the IDBs communicated via glass and crystal, the Greys had imprisoned her in a small, room-sized, metal-only box in a hot and remote desert location.

She had only survived because an Air Force major, betraying his country and working with the Greys, had left his sunglasses behind. She'd been able to use them to contact Flynn, who had rescued her by pulling her out through the Collective abode, a radiation-rich space and time vacuum, something that had damaged her physically and inexplicably left her pregnant with Birdie.

A sudden wash of intense heat and light splayed across her, the heat crisping the exposed hair on her body, reminding her of that earlier time. Her eyes snapped open as the car swerved sickeningly. Blinded by bright light, she snapped them closed again, feeling the nauseating motion as Hunter tried valiantly to maintain control of the veering vehicle. Praying that no other cars were nearby, she awaited the shocking crunch of a collision but took a deep breath of relief when Hunter successfully pulled the car to the wide, grassy shoulder of the road and turned off the engine. Slowly, Lily's vision began to return.

"Holy shit!" Hunter muttered, rubbing her hands across her face, obviously trying to clear her own eyes. "What the hell *was* that?"

"Birdie?" Lily cried, turning to see if her daughter was all right. "Are you okay, honey? Do you know what has happened to us?"

Silence fell heavy in the car. Lily blinked repeatedly to try to clear the spots she was still seeing. "Hunter? Hunter, do you see?"

Hunter, sensing her alarm, swiveled in her seat. She gasped.

"I'm so sorry, Mummy," Birdie said. She was absently pulling at her shredded clothing as she stared tearfully at her mothers.

"She's so…so beautiful," Hunter whispered in amazement.

Lily took in a deep, trembling breath as she unlocked her seat belt. "Oh, honey. It's okay. It's nothing you did."

She checked traffic, which was oddly sparse at the moment, and stepped from the car, holding onto it, moving around to her daughter's side to open the door. "Let's get you some clothes. Hold on."

She opened the back hatch of the SUV and rifled through her suitcase. She came up with a pink tank top and a pair of shorts, plus a sports bra and panties. She handed a beach towel across the back seat.

"Here, Birdie hon, wrap up in this, and come back here with me," she said.

Birdie soon stood next to her mother. She was slightly taller than her mom now. Lily reached up and, using her thumbs, brushed the girl's tears away. "Look at you," she said, smiling warmly, their gazes comingling. "How does it feel to be so grown up?"

Birdie's fragile smile was a wren with a broken wing as she murmured her answer. "Kinda weird, Mummy. Kinda weird."

Hunter opened her door, letting in some fresh, calming air, as Lily helped Birdie dress under the cover of the beach towel. Moments later, she was able to fold the towel and place it atop their suitcases.

Lily studied her daughter, marveling at the transformation. Birdie was now a good five foot ten and, though thin, looked the picture of health. Her hair was even more white-blond than before and was a good six inches longer. It fell in a straight silvery waterfall along both sides of her heart-shaped face. Wide cheekbones gave her something of an exotic air, but the crystal blue eyes above those cheekbones were all American. Swedish American maybe, but not overly foreign. Her lips were full and rosy, the lower lip more full than the upper, which led to a cute pout of her resting face.

Those lips spread in an embarrassed smile as she acknowledged her mother's interest.

"How do I look?" she asked, nervously catching that full bottom lip between gleaming straight teeth.

"Perfect, almost too perfect," Lily replied with a deep sigh.

"I think it must be time for more knowledge," Birdie said in a new, slightly deeper voice. "I guess I needed to be older."

Lily hugged her arms about her own waist. "I guess," she agreed absently.

"Everyone okay back here?" Hunter asked, tentatively approaching them.

Birdie looked at her Hunny with sad eyes, so Hunter immediately drew the young woman close, cupping the silver-haired head against her shoulder with one hand, no longer an easy feat when Birdie was so much taller. "It's all good, baby bird. It's all good."

They stayed that way for a long beat as Lily repacked the cargo area and closed the hatchback. When Birdie stepped away from Hunter's embrace, they continued holding hands and Hunter led Birdie back to her seat.

"It's burned," Birdie said sorrowfully as she spied the area where she'd been sitting. "I'm so so sorry."

"No problem!" Hunter said. "Let's just get in on the other side."

Once Birdie was settled, a subdued set of parents climbed into the front seats, each thinking about this new circumstance and how all three of their lives would be affected by it.

## *Aili's Journal*

### *Understanding Change*

It happened again. I was once more bathed in a disorienting, yet much more powerful bath of heat and light and I am suddenly older again. Much older this time, maybe not in years but certainly in knowledge. It poured into me, like an endless waterfall, and I abruptly understood the possibility of an upcoming war and what it would mean to my human family.

I also knew Rosemary, really *knew* her, on a visceral level, and I was no longer afraid. I knew we would be allies, leaders in the imminent conflict. I knew we would love one another for the eternity that had been given to us.

I felt suffused with new power, my energy suddenly limitless. I sensed their thoughts more clearly now and feared for my darling mothers, about how they would understand and react to all the changes. This one and the future ones caused by the Greys' culture. This fear reigned supreme in my mind, overshadowing the huge glut of knowledge just given to me by my stronger connection to the Collective. My other family.

# CHAPTER NINE

## *Birdie's New Skills*

They stopped southeast of Dallas, opting to splurge on a Hilton for security's sake. Still silent and subdued, they loaded everything onto a luggage cart and locked the car. Upstairs, they unloaded the cart just as silently, still processing what had happened.

Lily left Hunter and Birdie alone to return the cart to the lobby area. Taking a moment for herself, she placed her cane on the floor and collapsed into one of the lobby chairs, wistfully eyeing a crystal lamp base and wishing she could discuss this monumental new change with Flynn.

What was her role in all this? she wondered, feeling more helpless and confused than she'd been since Birdie's birth. She wondered whether she needed to do something, say something, that would be important and useful.

Birdie was now a young, stunning woman, not too many years younger than her mothers, and Lily knew, intellectually, that the best she could offer would be guidance…and friendship. These would be what Birdie needed most as she navigated this new chapter of her life. Lily had no doubt that she would provide these things. There was a fear, though, almost a premonition, that this meant she would lose her beloved child. This child, who was so much bigger than any simple or complex life on Earth, was also bigger than life on Good Neighbor Ranch.

Lily felt gut-punched as she thought about this. Tears sprouted in her eyes and her skin flushed hot, even in the heavy air-conditioning of the hotel lobby. She rocked slowly to and fro. How could she lose this darling child, flesh of her flesh, the beacon of her soul? What cruel twist of fate had chosen her to experience this monumental loss? She grew angry. She wanted to rail at fate or God or whoever had orchestrated this cruelty. She hated the Collective, hated their unavoidable manipulation of her life and the lives of others on her home planet. She wished that she didn't know about them, wished that she could be taken back in time, to her life in Florida before she had any inkling that they existed.

Then Birdie's face appeared before her, not the twelve-year-old face, nor her new twentysomething-year-old face, but her adorable, beguiling four-month-old baby face. If Lily had never been presented with the IDBs, with Flynn, she would never have had Birdie. Would never have even met her. And that was unthinkable.

She straightened her spine and forced herself to become resolute. She pressed the heels of her hands to her eyes to remove the tears brimming there. Birdie was hers to love. To forever love, and, no matter what the future brought, that was one thing that would never change.

Returning upstairs, she was met with the sounds of quiet conversation. Birdie and Hunter were lying together on top of one of the queen beds, earnestly discussing something that must have been important. They hadn't even turned on the television.

Lily sat on the other bed and regarded them. She smiled. "So, what are you two cooking up?"

"Just menstruation and stuff," Birdie replied. "I already hate it."

Lily laughed. "We all do, hon, but it's what makes us human, I guess. Do you think you'll have to deal with that?"

Birdie sighed heavily. "I have no idea. I'll have to ask Flynn and the others." She wriggled her toes and stretched her feet out. "Feels weird to be so big."

"I bet," Lily agreed.

"She's taller than me," Hunter added with a frown.

"Everyone is taller than you," Lily said, grinning.

Hunter lobbed a pillow at her partner. "Smart aleck!"

Birdie laughed and slammed a pillow into Hunter's belly.

The fight was on. Twenty minutes later, all three were sprawled throughout the room, panting from the exertion.

"I think you left a bruise!" Lily berated Hunter from the floor, where she rested against the footboard. She held out her arm so Hunter, sprawled on her back on the bed, could see.

Hunter rose to a sitting position and peered at the arm. "You'll be okay," she said. "There's some arnica in my bag."

"I'll get it!" Birdie said, hopping off the opposite bed. She flicked on the television before searching out and retrieving the ointment. She handed it to her mom and, muting the volume, she switched to a non-station and pressed both hands to the screen.

"Uh oh," muttered Hunter as she rolled onto her side and covered her head with one of the well-pummeled pillows.

Lily pulled herself from the floor and sat on the bed, tailor-style, rubbing her arm, applying the arnica ointment. She watched her daughter with curious eyes, still amazed by the transformation. She thought about this other child, Rosemary, and wondered whether she would appear as a child or as a young adult like Birdie.

Operating on faith had always been hard for Lily, and this adventure they were on... On the one hand it was enjoyable as a vacation, on the other it was shrouded in frustrating mystery. Flynn's advice to trust resurfaced in her mind, and she realized that she did trust Birdie. And Flynn. And the Collective. She just hoped that the three humans could continue to live some semblance of a normal, everyday life.

"Nope, no monthly menses," Birdie told them, switching the television station to a cooking show. "I'm a true hybrid in every sense of the word. No procreation for me or the others like me. We can still divide within the Collective should we so decide, but no human procreation."

"Well, you dodged a bullet there, kiddo," Lily said. "But I'm sad I won't have any grandbabies to spoil."

Birdie sat in the desk chair and pulled her long legs up against her body, feet on the chair seat. "You never know, Mummy. Maybe I'll surprise you with an energy baby." Birdie chuckled and hugged her knees.

Lily grunted in reply, wondering what a pure energy baby would be like. "I think an energy baby would kill any humans that got close. Flynn warned me away early on in our relationship, saying being too close would damage my heart."

"Probably would," Birdie agreed nonchalantly, eyes fastened on the TV. "I could make that," she said suddenly.

Lily jerked her head up and looked at the screen. "What? Is it potatoes?"

"Yessss," Birdie said excitedly. "Fondant potatoes. I'd use mushroom gravy instead of beef gravy on them, of course."

"Of course," echoed Lily. "Maybe you can make them when we get home."

*If we get home*, she thought silently.

"Look what I can do," Birdie said. She lifted one hand and waved it in a twisting motion.

Lily was perplexed. "What did you do?"

"Captured it. The video of the potatoes," she replied.

"You mean you have it now? You can play it back?"

"I think so," Birdie replied. "Here."

She took her mother's arm and images suddenly filled Lily's mind, pushing her own thoughts into the background. She saw the show that she had just been watching with Birdie, the images showing clearly how to peel and cut the potatoes before cooking them in the oven. The video stopped immediately when Birdie released her arm, leaving behind a mild headache.

"Wow," Lily whispered. "Is that new?"

Birdie nodded. "Now that I'm bigger, I think I'll be able to do a lot more," she explained.

"Wow," Lily whispered again.

"And, Mummy, you'll get home okay. Don't worry."

But Lily felt worry rise anew. First that Birdie had seemingly read her mind, and secondly, Birdie had said that she, Lily, would get home okay. Not that all of them would. A shiver raced along her spine.

## *Aili's Journal*

*Hotels*

I have discovered that I love hotels, though I am not sure why. I think it might be the order enforced in all these types of businesses. It's very different from anything else in the universe. Even twin suns vary in appearance and matter.

I've discovered by remote views that hotels use the same towels, bed coverings, and decorative features in every room. They buy in large quantities, varying by business chains, of course. Doing so enables easy replacements when things are damaged, like sheets, blankets, and bedspreads. Or used up, such as soap and shampoo. It allows the same cleaning methods to be used on all linens. There's less confusion on all fronts. There is a persistent corporate control, fighting chaos. It feels delicious in my psyche.

Plus, I love to touch the orderly, cleaned linens with my human hands. I enjoy the roughness of the towels against my skin.

Rosemary thinks I'm a little crazy, though she, too, enjoys the tactile beauty of her much more chaotic bayou home. She especially likes leaving her human body and becoming part of the fauna of the bayou and experiencing the rampant life at and under the water. It was something she'd learned to do after this most recent aging. I wanted so badly to be able to do that, too, but had not been able to. Yet. Rosemary had promised she would teach me how when I was with her in Alabama.

# CHAPTER TEN

## *Big in Biloxi, Mississippi*

The southern United States was vastly different from arid, wind-battered New Mexico. This landscape in Mississippi was positively seething with life. Lily took a deep breath of heavy, humid, swamp-scented air and noted how different it was from how the air in Florida had been. It was just as humid there, sure, but the air had been redolent with the scents of citrus blossom and grasslands. Even the swampland there had been less smelly than it was here.

They had stopped to stretch their legs and get snacks at a gas station outside somnolent, seemingly deserted Biloxi, Mississippi. A few elderly souls sat outside, butts holding down the bench beside the double glass doors of the station, but Lily, Hunter, and Birdie seemed to be the only other customers. There were a few cars backed up at a red light on the tributary road from Highway 10 but that was about it for traffic. Even the air, though odorous, seemed to have an unexpected empty quality.

The weedy, swampy areas running alongside the tributary road were the only exception. They seemed filled with all sorts of bayou life. Large birds took flight as others landed, no doubt fishing the stagnant water for food. The hoarse bellow of a gator sounded suddenly, and Lily pushed off from the brick wall of the station. It was time to get a move on.

She nodded to the old gents as she passed them and entered the coolness of the station's modest store.

"We got a whole case of bubbly water," Birdie said, coming up behind her.

Her fully grown appearance still seemed so very strange to Lily. Her gaze roamed across her daughter lovingly. "Oh, good. What else?"

"Chips, sandwich stuff, well, PB&J, anyway," Hunter said, passing by them with a full carry basket. "What else do we need?"

"Candy bars," Birdie said. "I'll get them." She hurried off.

"Let's get some paper plates and napkins," Lily suggested. "Utensils, too?"

"You got it." Hunter set the laden basket on the counter and disappeared. She reappeared moments later, arms full. "Had to get paper towels. They didn't have napkins."

Lily was studying a rack of corn chips flavored with red chili. "Can't even spell chile right," she muttered.

"I think it's different in the East, Mummy," Birdie said from behind her right shoulder. "Anything else you can think of?"

She studied the haul as she approached the counter. "I think this will hold us for a while." She nodded to the middle-aged man behind the counter. "Afternoon."

"Afternoon to you, ladies," he replied. "Where y'all headed?"

Hunter bristled, but Lily limped closer to her. "Just south, going over into Alabama."

"Mobile?" he queried as he studiously jotted down each of their items on a paper sales pad.

"Um, just south of Mobile. Visiting friends," Lily replied.

"Mmm." His eyes never left the task at hand. "That's down there then."

"Yep, bayou land." Hunter spoke up suddenly.

The cashier raised his gaze finally. "Yep, them there call it livin' on the water. Some people been there forever, seems like. Your friend a native, then?"

Hunter just nodded and moved in front of Lily. "What's the tally?" she said pulling her wallet out of her back pocket.

"Nosy fucker," Hunter whispered to Lily as they walked to the car moments later. Birdie had gone on ahead, raising the hatchback and stowing her bag of goodies. By the time they got to the car, she was curled up on the back seat unwrapping a chocolate candy bar.

"He was," Lily agreed as she rearranged things in the back, making room for the case of soda water and for her paper grocery bag. "Let's get out of here. Those old guys are giving us the once-over, too."

"Say no more," Hunter said. She opened the passenger door for Lily, then clambered behind the wheel.

"Sure you don't want me to drive?" Lily offered.

Hunter checked the side mirror before pulling out onto the cracked and buckled asphalt. "No, I'm good."

"I could drive," Birdie said, leaning forward and emitting a waft of chocolate breath. "I'll need to learn eventually. I bet I could do it now."

"I'm sure you could," Lily said. "Let's get you used to being fully grown first, okay? And maybe get you a license?"

"Hmph!" Birdie exclaimed as she flopped back against the seat.

Silence grew as they left Biloxi behind, but it was a comfortable one. Birdie was reading on her e-book reader and Lily watched the scenery become ever lusher and more pervasive. Soon both sides of the highway were teeming with overhanging trees or shrubs and they were passing over bridge after concrete bridge spanning dark, sluggish water. Spotting gators lounging on muddy creekbanks, Lily knew that anybody living nearby with a pet or small child would have to be on high alert all the time. "I just don't know if I could live here," she said finally, pensively.

"Why, hon, what's wrong?" Hunter said, glancing at her.

"It seems really dangerous here. So many alligators."

"And venomous snakes, too," Birdie chimed in. "And the forests have puma. Don't forget the flesh-eating bacteria in the water."

Lily turned to look at her daughter, but the young woman had spoken with her attention still firmly enmeshed in her book.

"Thanks for that, Miss Cheerful. What are you reading?"

"Just a book by this psychic guy who's talking about the prevalence of hidden psychic ability among humans. It's pretty interesting. According to research he's done, most people *are* psychic, but they just ignore it. We already knew that."

"I kind of figured that, too," Hunter said. "The things I've witnessed in the hospital...well, I believe in it, big time."

Birdie leaned forward, setting aside her reader. "Like that woman who left her husband in the hospital but came back right before he died because she knew he was going to?"

Hunter peered at Birdie through the rearview mirror. "How did you know about that? I never told that to anyone," she retorted angrily.

Birdie touched Hunter's shoulder, causing her to calm visibly. "I'm not sure, Hunny. I...I'm sorry."

"It's okay," Hunter said, clearing her throat. "It *was* strange."

"Lots of strange goes on where people are transitioning," Birdie said. "You know, I seem to be able to see it more now that I'm big."

"Why do you think that makes a difference?" Lily asked, curiously. "Now, versus when you were younger. Littler."

Birdie's face twisted in thought. "When I was a baby, I was really helpless. Then, as an older child, I knew more but not enough, really. I think I'm full-grown now, this time, and it's like all the doors to the Collective have opened to me. I see and experience new things every hour, every minute. One is perceiving what others are thinking about, especially if it's poignant or memorable. It's all part of gathering knowledge."

"And you were able to save that cooking show," Lily agreed.

"What cooking show?" Hunter said.

"Oh, you missed it," Lily said. "Had your head under a pillow at the time, I think. She was watching a show about potatoes and managed to record it and play it back for me. In my mind."

"Oh," Hunter responded, pressing her lips together into a thin line.

"It's okay, Hunny. I'm still me," Birdie said, wrapping Hunter's right arm with both of hers and laying her head on her other mother's shoulder.

Lily watched them, her eyes fond. Her mind betrayed her, however, as it screamed *yes, she's still her, but for how long?*

## Aili's Journal

*Trees*

I absolutely love being on the road. I think this must hail from being part of the Collective—who were nomads of the universes until becoming united with this planet and the others in this galaxy. America is amazing, but it seems to be unsettled in a lot of ways. As soon as you leave a major city, you're surrounded by wooded land that seems to stretch on forever. Part of me wishes to see it all developed into housing for humans, learning facilities to expand their minds, and maybe entertainment to please them, but I have been told repeatedly how that would blight the landscape and cause human angst and depression.

Trees are important and, of course, I realize that. The problem with the trees that live on the sides of the major highways and in the medians is that they are suffering. Far removed from the majestic pristine forests where they belong, such as those that cover other continents like the European one, American trees are suffocating, barely surviving. This is evidenced by the rampant, exhaust-filled undergrowth that has taken control of their habitats. It makes me sad. There is no dichotomy of nature to protect and preserve their lives from this onslaught.

The trip has been eye-opening in other ways as well. I got to see a number of sleepy little towns that are much different from Morris, New Mexico. These towns seemed lethargic, filled with a type of languor engendered by the heat and the oppressive humidity. Every time we stopped to eat or fuel up, I found myself missing the crispness of desert air. Humidity makes breathing difficult. And many of the waterside towns reeked of old ocean scents, marsh scents that I found discomforting. I mentioned this to Rosemary. She assured me that I would get used to it and eventually find some value in the marshy, waterlocked land.

Rosemary. I am still a little nervous about meeting her, which is ridiculous. She is already a part of me, via the Collective. We both have our human aspects, however, and I guess that is the daunting part. How can I know what to expect from that part of her?

# CHAPTER ELEVEN

## *The Seafood Capital of Alabama*

A little more than an hour later, they entered into the quiet little waterfront town of Bayou La Batre. Lily smiled when she spied a sign proclaiming the town the seafood capital of Alabama. Obviously, the townsfolk made a living harvesting fish and other seafood from the Gulf of Mexico.

"It was a Spanish land grant in the seventeen hundreds to a guy named Joseph Bosarge," Birdie told them. "It was the first permanent settlement on Mobile's mainland, named from a fort, called a battery, along the shore. Maintained by the French. Hey." She waggled her phone at Lily. "*Forrest Gump* was filmed there. I love that movie."

"You saw that movie?" Lily asked, remembering certain scenes that might not be child appropriate.

"Oh yeah, years ago. On streaming." She fell silent then, studying the information on her phone.

"There's about twenty-five hundred people there," she said finally. "There was a lot of shipbuilding before Hurricane

Katrina. They built the pirate ship here for the *Black Pearl* movie. How cool is that?"

"Very cool," Hunter agreed, studying her in the rearview mirror. "This isn't where Rosemary lives, though, is it?"

"Nope." She scooted forward and rested an elbow on each of the front seats. "We have to go south from here."

"South? Holy cow, we'll be in the Gulf," Hunter exclaimed.

"Pretty much," Birdie agreed. "We need to take 188 to the mouth of the Fowl River, then south into the Bayou Lisse."

"I think the interchange is right ahead," Lily added. "It shouldn't be much longer." She turned to Birdie. "Are you excited, hon? You know, to finally meet her?"

Birdie nodded, chin resting on her clenched hands. "I think so. Nervous, too."

"How old do you think she'll be?" Lily asked thoughtfully.

"She's like me," Birdie answered quickly. "We need to be this age for the next thing we need to do."

"What thing?" Hunter interjected. She slowed to go up the access road to the smaller road that would take them east then south.

Birdie sat back and looked at her phone again. "Just something we need to do. Don't worry about it."

Hunter glanced questioningly at Lily, who only shrugged her shoulders and resumed examining the landscape.

Highway 188 was a much quieter stretch of highway than Highway 10 had been, and the surroundings were lower and more water-specific than anyplace they'd been since leaving home. Now, bogs full of thin, feathery mangrove trees appeared, with alligators sunbathing along their murky tributaries. It was different from anything Lily had seen, and she was fascinated. There'd been alligators and mangroves in Florida but seemingly on a larger scale, more spread out on more waterways. Alabama was more concentrated and seemed more dangerous somehow. The ramshackle houses built right up to the edge of some of the bogs were suicidal in her opinion. Who knew what kind of creepy creature would come up out of that water? She'd seen

*Creature from the Black Lagoon*, but she bet those families living there had not.

"So, where does Rosemary live exactly?" she asked finally. "A lot of these houses seem like they are right on the shores of the rivers here."

"She says she lives above the water. She has a family of river otters that live underneath her house. One had a baby this past spring."

"Otters. They are so cool," Hunter said. "Maybe we'll get to see them while we're here. Any idea where we're staying, by the way?"

"No clue," said Lily. "Totally taking this trip on faith alone. Birdie?"

"Not sure, Mummy, but I feel that it's not something that should concern us."

"There's probably some bearable motels nearby," Lily agreed.

"You need to turn just ahead, Hunny. On Courtship Road. See that sign that says Bayou Lisse, three miles? Just past that."

Soon they were on a poorly paved road that was covered completely by green, Spanish moss-laden, interlacing branches. Although it was pretty, like a photo in a *Southern Living* magazine, Lily found it rather spooky. She scooted to the edge of her seat and scanned the roadway as they progressed along. She wasn't sure what she was looking for, but she wanted to be ready. No danger appeared, just a lone tan-colored doe eating grass along the side of the road. The deer watched them pass, her mouth munching on a mass of verdant green.

"Omigosh. She's so stunning," Lily said, looking back as they passed her. "Birdie, did you see?"

"I did. Hey, Hunny, we need to go left here, on this crossroad. Left on River Run."

"Okey-doke. Are we almost there?"

"Almost," Birdie replied. "Not far now."

They travelled along in silence, venturing deeper and deeper into areas with overgrown asphalt and concrete bridges over small and large offshoots of water. At one point Birdie lowered her window and breathed in the humid air. Lily looked in her side mirror and was amazed at how much her daughter seemed to be enjoying the hot air bathing her face. She was a beautiful young woman now, with sharp angles bordering her clear, almost glowing visage. Lily sighed, thinking that she was missing Birdie's most important formative experiences, the teen angst, the first dates, the school prom, her first love, her first heartbreak. A certain amount of melancholy accompanied these thoughts. Then again, on a subconscious level, Lily had known this might happen even during her pregnancy, when Birdie was still a complete mystery.

"Take a right here, onto Deco Road," Birdie said suddenly.

Hunter complied and they pulled up in front of a rambling, weathered, wooden structure. A worn but professionally painted sign above the door declared the business to be Deco Bait and Tackle. Display racks bearing magazines and ranks of fishing poles filled both sides of the wooden-framed screen door that led inside. A huge deck extended out to the left, where, for as far as Lily could see from the car, tree-bordered bayou water stretched almost to a gulf horizon.

"She's here. She's waiting," Birdie said nervously.

Hunter sighed and put the car in park before switching off the engine. "I guess this is it, then." She looked at Birdie in the rearview. "You okay, BirdBird?"

Birdie straightened her shoulders and took in a deep breath. "I guess I have to be," she replied thoughtfully.

## Aili's Journal

### Heroism and Its Cost

I think about all the heroes of Earth history. I think of the Buddha, Socrates, Lorenzo de Medici, Susan B. Anthony, George Washington, Thomas Jefferson, Gandhi, Martin Luther King, Jr., even Florence Nightingale. Then I think of Rosemary, who will be a next great hero. And it frightens me. Disappoints me. I don't want to lose her to this heroism. Or to lose myself to the difficult call of duty and responsibility…

There's a looming threat to her. Joan of Arc comes to mind. Was my sweet, soon-to-be companion in serious danger?

I only hope I can take her place, take the danger from her. I know, when the time comes, I will want it to be so.

# CHAPTER TWELVE

*Rosemary Deco*

The sunlight of the southern day disappeared as soon as they stepped into the dimness of the bait shop. The store was cluttered with shelves, some bearing groceries as well as many holding myriad sporting supplies. The three stood inside, waiting for their eyes to adjust. Within moments, though, a subdued glow, emanating from behind the worn, pocked Formica checkout counter, filled the deserted shop.

Birdie pushed her mothers aside and stepped forward, her own body beginning to glow with a new, unfamiliar radiance.

"You're here!" a husky voice said. Then they saw her.

Draped in sparkle, a young woman stepped from behind the counter. She moved diffidently to stand in front of Birdie. The contrast of the two young women struck Lily into numbness.

The two were of similar height, but while Birdie was silver-blond and fair, Rosemary's complexion was a creamy brown, and her long, braided hair was black ebon except for the streak of white along the length of the left side. She was as thin and lanky as Birdie, and when she glanced at Hunter and Lily, they saw her eyes were the same bright blue in color and sheen.

"Oh, my God," Hunter whispered next to Lily's ear. "She's so gorgeous."

Lily nodded her agreement.

The girls extended their right arms at the same time and each placed a palm on the other's shoulder, resting it up close to where the neck met the clavicle. The glow radiating from them increased, and a low hum sounded.

"Get away from her!" a loud male voice shouted suddenly.

A middle-aged man had emerged from a back curtained-off area behind the counter. He stood watching the interaction, his dark visage twisted in anger. His breathing was harsh and loud in the room. "Get away!" he repeated.

Both Birdie and Rosemary turned their glowing eyes upon the man, and Rosemary raised her free hand, pointing her open palm at the man.

"Demon child!" he gasped out, even as he cowered behind the counter.

The two young women released one another, and the still, quiet air made it seem as though nothing had been different.

Lily studied the man, not really seeing a resemblance to Rosemary but deciding he had to be her father. She wasn't quite sure how to approach him. Or Rosemary. Luckily, Hunter took the reins on this one.

"Rosemary," she said, walking forward and extending her hand. "It's great to finally meet you."

As their hands met, Lily saw Rosemary's eyes light with a bluish gleam, but it was gone in an instant. "Hello, Hunter. It's really good to meet you, as well. Birdie has talked about you endlessly. She admires you greatly."

Her voice was low and melodious. Sexy, even, if attached to an adult.

Lily moved forward then. "May I give you a hug?" she asked shyly.

"Of course!" Rosemary replied as she pulled Lily into an embrace.

Lily's breath stopped as the girl pulled her close. The power emanating from Rosemary was almost as powerful as what

Lily had experienced in close proximity with the IDB Flynn. A proximity that was discouraged as it could stop a human's heart. Lily wasn't afraid, though. She sensed that Rosemary would never allow her to be harmed. Eventually she was able to make her lungs work again and they parted.

Lily was surprised to see that Rosemary's crystal blue eyes were bright with unshed tears. Instinctively, Lily reached up and pressed Rosemary's sweet face between her palms. "It's so wonderful to meet you. We're going to be very close, I'm sure."

Rosemary, who seemed to be unable to speak, just nodded.

Lily heard voices and saw that Hunter had approached Rosemary's father and was introducing herself.

"This is a fine bait shop you've got here," Hunter was saying.

The father had removed his angry gaze from the two young women and was focusing now on Hunter, one eye squinting as he examined her.

"Are you named Deco or is that just the name of the store?" she asked, trying to draw him out.

As Lily expected, the man preened under the attention.

"Theo Deco," he said, shaking hands with Hunter.

He had a strange accent and pronounced his first name as ta-yo with emphasis on the first syllable. The last name he pronounced as it appeared but it was said with a long crooning sound, *daycooo*. It would take some time before she could readily understand his thick drawl, she sensed.

"This store been in my family for t'ree generations now," Theo said proudly. "We haven't changed much about it, just some updates and whatnot, you know, to keep up with the times."

*Yeah, the eighteen hundreds*, Lily thought, amusing herself.

She stepped past Birdie and Rosemary and approached Theo. She extended her hand. "Mister Deco, I'm very glad to meet you. I'm Birdie's mom. She's been talking about Rosemary nonstop."

"We drove all the way from New Mexico so the two of them could meet," Hunter added.

"You're from Mexico?" Theo asked, raising his eyebrows, thinner than expected in his somewhat round face. "That's a long way!"

Lily grinned "Well, almost as far as Mexico. *New* Mexico is just this side of Arizona, so not quite as far."

Theo nodded as though he understood, but Lily could tell he wasn't well versed in American geography.

Rosemary and Birdie, tied together by held hands, pushed past them, with Rosemary in the lead, and disappeared through a back door. The screen door slapped shut with leisurely intent.

"Birdie," Lily called, alarmed that the girl had disappeared so suddenly.

"You two best go on t'rew," Theo said. "Simmy's out there so they be safe, and y'all can get comfortable on the porch and rest a spell."

He indicated that they should follow Rosemary and Birdie.

"Thank you, Mister Deco," Lily said. "Sorry we're taking Rosemary away from her duties."

"Theo," he corrected her. "I've got the store so's they can visit." His voice had grown impatient again, and Lily realized that he really didn't like his daughter. If indeed Rosemary was his child. He hadn't said.

Theo's porch was more of a huge wraparound dock with an arm that extended more than eighty feet out over the sluggish inlet of bayou water that bordered the back of the store. Seated at the far end of the pier were a handful of grizzled men and one young teen boy chewing the fat while the lines from their long fishing poles, like the strings of so many tea bags, steeped bait in murky, unmoving water.

Rosemary and Birdie sat at one of the many umbrella-shaded tables placed along the store half of the dock. They were animatedly talking to a tiny, wizened Black woman whose hair was wrapped in a bright orange headwrap. As the door closed behind Hunter and Lily, she glanced their way and beckoned them closer. Rosemary stood and welcomed them with an open arm.

"Miss Dawson, Lily, this is my *Sha* Meemaw, Simmy Pascal."

Lily returned the grin of the elderly woman who took her hand.

"Good to meet you, *cherie*. You've a beautiful daughter. She so well-mannered, not like most of these hoodlum girls coming up today. Does my heart warm to see such."

Her accent was almost as strong as Theo's, but her demeanor was much more welcoming.

"Meemaw, this is Birdie's other mother, Hunter Moon," Rosemary said, stepping aside and pulling Hunter closer.

"And you have de magic of de moon riding on dem well-named shoulders," Simmy said, holding Hunter's hand in both of hers. "Welcome, welcome to Bayou Lisse."

"Thank you, Missus Pascal, I appreciate it," Hunter said.

"And there's dem good manners again," Simmy said, shaking her head as though in disbelief. "And you call me Simmy, you hear. It's Cimmaron for fancy, but Simmy gets my attention quicker."

She turned to her granddaughter. "Now, Rosie, you and this darling girl go get cold iced teas all around. Get 'em from the back of the cooler now, so's they be good and cold," she added, pulling at the neckline of her bright blue T-shirt. "It's hot and still as blazes out here today."

Rosemary indicated that Lily and Hunter should sit at the table with her grandmother, so they seated themselves as the two girls made their way back into the store.

"That Birdie gal says y'all hail from the desert. What brings y'all over here to us water peoples?" Simmy asked, one hand straightening one of the breeze-ravaged beer advertising pyramids that adorned the centers of each table.

"Umm," Hunter sighed. "It's kind of a weird story..." she began.

Lily helped out. "It seems that Rosemary communicated with Birdie, and she asked us to come here so the two of them could meet."

"Oh." Simmy nodded thoughtfully. "Through that Collective thing, I reckon."

## *Aili's Journal*

*Rosemary's Sorrow*

I can find nothing of Rosemary's father in her. Not surprising as she is actually a child of the Collective and a human female. He is shorter than she and bigger boned, also coarse in a way that she is not. She speaks much like him, though, their cadence and pronunciations similar but that is the only parallel I can discover. Nurture versus nature.

Her life with him, after her mother's death, has been difficult. His distaste of her is disturbing. I feel the pain of a lost child with only the Collective for solace. Her grandmother stepped in, thankfully, and has deflected the brunt of her father's drunken verbal belittling. Yet it exists and Rosemary has felt it keenly, especially when she was younger.

I saw Rosemary's mother, shared from her childhood memories, and they are much more alike, both refined and sensitive, gentle in ways and thought. The sorrow Rosemary feels for the loss of this mother is palpable, backlit, of course, by the regret of the Collective for having been at the root of her suicide. Even accidents are mourned.

# CHAPTER THIRTEEN

## *The Energy That Made Rosemary*

Lily felt as though she'd been gut-punched. "You know about the Collective? How...?"

Birdie and Rosemary approached their table, arms laden with glass bottles of iced tea.

"Man, that's cold," Birdie said, carefully placing the bottles on the table and shaking and rubbing her bare arms to warm them. She passed out three of the bottles and lifted two as she and Rosemary moved across to sit at the next table. Rosemary grinned and pulled two candy bars from her shirt pocket. Birdie laughed out loud.

Lily cleared her throat as Hunter opened a tea and took a deep gulp.

Simmy raised one hand as though negating Lily's disbelief. "Oh, that gal...she tells me nigh on everything. *Mwen pa konnen, repete souple!*"

Lily laughed. "So, you're saying she talks a lot?"

"Lordy, yes, and there's no other mama but me so's I gets it all."

"And Theo? He's her daddy, right?" Hunter asked, rolling the cold, wet bottle between her two palms. The soft susurration of its base against the wooden table blended perfectly with the incessant insect chatter and the soft slap of bayou water against the dock pilings.

Simmy waved one hand in disgust. "Ahh, Theodule. He's thick as a cypress knee, that one. I warned my Jeanne not to marry the idiot, but they were so in love, she said, so happy together. Hmph." She leaned back and sipped from her bottle.

"You don't sound like you believe they were truly happy," Lily said.

Simmy eyed her with a sideways glance. "Let's us say that in the trey years just before Rosie was born, I never saw it. I saw my Jeanne, a bright shining star, her spirit beat down by that ogre of a man. All has to be his way wit no considerin' what others want. It took my Jeanne from me, even before she passed."

Lily reached and took Simmy's hand, rubbing her thumb across the back to impart comfort.

"What happened?" Hunter asked quietly.

Simmy glanced toward the other table where Birdie and Rosemary were chattering away, their foreheads close together.

"Well, Theo drinks a bit and to get on away, Jeanne had taken to walkin' the bayou at night. She say to dig the worms and just to enjoy her own company and get away from his endless talk, talk, talk, all about hisself. She grew up on the water and knowed about the gators and the snakes and the wild boar that roam the lands here. I didn' worry overmuch."

"Did one of them attack her?" Lily asked, her voice almost a whisper.

Simmy shook her head, and she pinched the bridge of her nose, closing her dark brown eyes momentarily. "It was worse," she said in a low whisper.

She straightened her shoulders as though fortifying herself. "She come home one night all shook up. She call me late on de cell phone askin' to meet for breakfast. We went to the Denny's near town and I say, she look so bad. At first I thought the bastard done burned her 'cause her hair was all burnt and her face and arms too rosy. She claimed no, that the Will o' the Wisp had got her. Den she tell me de story."

She quieted as the two girls passed close by on their way out toward the end of the long pier. Birdie trailed one hand across Lily's shoulders as they passed.

Simmy continued as soon as they were out of earshot. "She tell me she was on de water side of a log, diggin' bait worms there alongs the water, just woolgathering, when a gator come shootin' out de water toward her. She jump up to run and tripped off dat log right into a big patch of swamp light. They's legends here about the demon spirits who decorate like dey good light and wanderin' the bayou lands at midnight. She said de demon light's what burned her."

"Light?" Hunter mused, and Lily grew still and quiet.

"That what she say," Simmy said with a helpless shrug. "It pull away after she fall and it float away, but she left layin' there, barely able to breathe cuz it so hot, her heart just squeezin' in her chest. Took her hours to get back home, her skin burning something fierce."

"She told you this that next morning?" Lily queried quietly.

"She did."

"And then she was pregnant with Rosemary," Lily stated with some certainty.

Simmy studied Lily for a few long moments. "It was the light, wadn't it?"

Lily nodded, eyes seeking Simmy's gaze.

Simmy looked away, at the fishermen on the dock, at the bright undulating water. "I thought maybe…is it dem aliens, you reckon?" One finger nervously pointed to the sky.

Hunter looked at her lap.

"Not exactly," Lily began. "They're older than our universe. Just beings made of energy, the Collective. Jeanne was lucky to survive the encounter."

"She didn't." Simmy's voice was flat, emotionless. "After the babe was borned, she knew right on that there was something wrong, something different. And those bright blue eyes! I tol' her it was Theo's bad seed and she got mad at me." She smiled tearfully.

"So, what happened?" Hunter prompted gently.

Simmy sighed and her face fell. "When that first agin' happened, I thought Theo was gwine kill my Jeanne. He beat her with a black eye and a split mouth, wanting to know why she lay with Satan hisself. It was then he turn against Rosie. Wouldn't have any more to do with her. It was all just too much for my girl."

She paused and sipped from her bottle of tea. "One morning, I get no answer when I call her. Finally, I call and call and get dat record for a message. I figure Theo done kilt her and I feel dat loss. He claim no, but she been gone for two day. So, after then all the men of the parish gather to look fo' her. They find her dead and half eaten on the edge of the water. Turns out she take some pills and breathed her last. Guess Rosemary wadn't enough to keep her here."

Lily looked toward the girls who were sitting on the edge of the dock, feet dangling above the water. She sensed that they were talking to the otters in the water below but wasn't sure. As she casually watched them, she noticed that they had each lifted one of their hands and were touching fingers, one at a time, almost playfully but with some kind of intent. They weren't talking at that point, but Lily could imagine that a network of information was passing back and forth between them. Like a light signal passing through fiber optics. She watched this for quite some time as Simmy and Hunter discussed how the bait business was managed. Then, suddenly, both girls turned their heads at the same time and looked at her. Their eyes were glowing a surreal blue and Lily felt afraid.

## Aili's Journal

### Right is Right

There is a shift in the Collective and it weighs heavily on my shoulders. There is another hybrid child who lives in Houston. Her mother is dying of cancer engendered by offshoots of space radiation from the Collective. This is also an accidental exposure, but the collective sorrow of the energy beings is no less painful.

An idea has been brought forth and has spread like an out-of-control wildfire across the Collective. Some, due to the emergency we are facing, want to table this idea, something that is very much non-Collective in implementation. There is right and wrong, dark and light, cold and hot, being and not being, so tabling an issue goes against everything we are. Is the idea right? Then so be it.

I voiced my approval of it, as did Rosemary. We knew it was only right for the mothers of the hybrid children to be incorporated into the energy collective that spawned their children. After they pass from their human lives, of course.

Rosemary and I shared the sadness of this idea coming too late for her mother, Jeanne, whose soul and energy had already cycled through the narrow hall of souls and had probably already been revolved back into something new in nature. The knowledge of this, that her mother would always live on in some manner, did nothing to temper the fact that a reunion with her was unlikely. If her mother had been bound to the Collective, she would have remained close and at Rosemary's side, always. The new idea is a good one. Right, not wrong.

# CHAPTER FOURTEEN

*The First Night—Finding God*

Theo had gotten a good deal on a shipment of citronella torches, and now five-foot-tall Tiki torches outlined the entire border of the extensive dock outside the Deco bait store. Miraculously the flames and smoke kept mosquitos and other flying insects away and the two families were able to visit late into the evening. The bayou itself was alive with insect sound, however, highlighted by strange splashings and sonorous froggie sounds of contentment.

Theo's intense, disapproving regard of Rosemary and Birdie was the only uncomfortable aspect. He swigged beer while watching them, and Lily, watching him, worried about his penchant for violence, especially after hearing Jeanne's sad story. She remained diligent, her periodic glances assessing him for signs of dangerous inebriation.

"So, when did you change again? Grow older, I mean," Hunter asked Rosemary.

"Hmph! Was just yesterday," Simmy interjected. "She was in de shower and steam just blowed all through the house before she come stumbling out all growed like she is now."

Rosemary nodded her agreement. "I was way surprised, but I felt that Birdie had just gone through it. So…." She shrugged.

"I burnt up the back seat," Birdie added. "Did you burn the shower?"

Rosemary shook her head and grinned. "Guess the water helped."

Theo grunted suddenly and loudly.

"Theo, what do you think about all this?" Hunter asked pleasantly.

"Not much," he said, his voice low and gruff. "Never seen the like. You should take both of dem down to the Baptist and leave dem on the steps. Let the church handle deys ungodliness."

Hunter laughed and looked away. She shook her head before speaking. "Ungodliness. You know, Theo. I'm a member of the Acoma people's family. Back in New Mexico. Our god is very similar to yours, but our creator god is associated with the sun. Actually, going farther back, our creator gods were two women, born of the earth but nurtured by the light and energy of the sun."

"And the trees of Earth brought them closer to the light of the sun," Lily added. "The communion of this god light allowed them to flourish as a people."

Theo grunted. "What make you t'ink these two speak for God? How can dey?" He popped the top on a new bottle of beer and took a deep swallow. "Ain't nothin' godlike or even plain natural about them."

"Unnatural just somethin' that ain't yet been seen, you damned fool," Simmy said, uncrossing her legs and leaning forward. "There's nothing wrong with these gals, beyond bein' deviled by your ignorance, that is."

"What do you know, you ol' swamp witch? You and Jeanne probably danced naked with the devil. Both of you!"

Simmy rose to her feet, hands shaking with abrupt anger. "Don't you ever say trash about my good girl, you flamin' ass! You wouldn' know good if it come an' hit you in the face!" Her chest was rising and falling as it tried to contain her anger.

"*Pere*," Rosemary said in her low, dulcet voice, quietly drawing everyone's attention.

The two young women rose as one unit and stood on either side of Theo. They each laid a palm on his shoulder and a slight glow emanated and surrounded the three of them. At first Theo resisted, but soon his eyes widened and his gaze fixed on Simmy who was slowly sinking back into her chair. Seconds seemed like hours as Hunter, Simmy, and Lily watched the bewitching scene. Lily focused on Birdie's face. Both she and Rosemary had their heads leaned back, eyes and mouth pressed tightly closed as they seemed to focus on the generation of the strange energy cloaking them.

They stepped back, and Theo rose shakily to his feet. His face was slack, eyes wide but vacant. Lily wondered what he was seeing. Had seen. Was it the strange mix of light and flux that Lily had witnessed when she'd been rescued by Flynn and thrust into its world, or was this something different?

Birdie took Rosemary's hand, and they watched Theo.

"Theo?" Simmy queried.

Suddenly Theo turned abruptly and looked at the two young women. "Jehovah!" he croaked. "You...you." He swallowed with difficulty. "I didn't know. I didn't..."

Rosemary wrapped her free arm about her father, still holding Birdie's hand. "No one does. So, do not fear for I am with you always. He who sees me..."

"Sees de Father," Simmy whispered.

Theo pulled Rosemary close, and his tears made a few dark spots on the back of her shirt.

"I'm so...so very sorry," Theo muttered, standing back.

"You were afraid," Rosemary said quietly. "There is no need."

Theo nodded, releasing her and turning to regain his chair.

Lily found herself wondering what he had seen to have caused such a monumental change in his opinion of Rosemary. He was in his seat, Rosemary kneeling next to him, one of her hands wrapped in his larger paw.

"We are the god force, the original. We created, or encouraged you to create, the Judeo-Christian God that you follow." The voice speaking in her mind was Birdie's.

"No thank you," Lily responded aloud, causing Simmy and Hunter to eye her curiously.

"Jehovah means that we brought into existence everything that exists," Birdie persisted, causing Lily to experience a slight headache.

"Well, I do thank you for that," Lily whispered, rubbing the left side of her head.

"Are you okay?" Hunter queried, gently touching her shoulder.

"Miss Lily?" Simmy said, brow furrowed with worry.

"It's just Birdie in my head," Lily explained. She held the coolness of her tea bottle to her crown. "Talking about God."

Simmy sat back. "That must be an interesting conversation."

Lily sighed deeply. "The Collective was first. Before the god we know. They helped us create him."

Simmy sucked her bottom lip between her small, crooked teeth. She shook her head. "I don't know how comfortable I am with that," she mused.

"No need to ponder that too much," Lily said quickly. She lowered the tea bottle. "So, it's getting late. We'd best be getting on. Do you know of a good hotel nearby?"

"Hotel? Well, *Chez* Simmy is a good bet." She smiled impishly.

"*Chez* Simmy? Is that a real place," Hunter asked, her voice dripping with doubt.

"It is," Simmy replied in a firm tone. "Located right there, right smack dab on the beauty of the bayou."

Both women looked in the direction she had pointed and saw a small square house on the other, far side of the bait shop.

"Not too big but comfy. I think y'all will be just fine in my room. Theo and Rosie sleep in the rooms backa the bait store, but I asked old Scotch Barnaby to build this place here for me."

Hunter eyed her warily. "Are you sure we won't be inconveniencing you?"

Simmy laughed. "Ain't got no gentlemen callers here lately so no reason not to share. Save you some hotel spendin', too."

"Well, thank you. You are too generous," Lily said, patting Simmy's arm. "As far as I know, we're just here for a few days, so won't be underfoot too long."

"You stay as long as you like," Simmy responded. She rose to her feet and straightened her headwrap. "Let's get your t'ings from de car and get you settled."

Rosemary stood and pulled her father to his feet.

"We'll get the cases, Mummy," Birdie said, moving to stand next to Rosemary.

"I'll help," Theo said. He hadn't touched his beer since communing with the girls and the Collective and he sounded almost sober.

Hunter stood and brushed off her shorts. "Me, too," she said.

The four walked around the wraparound dock in the direction of the parking area and disappeared into the sweltering bayou night.

## Aili's Journal

*Simmy's Life*

The tiny child cot in Rosemary's bedroom in the back rooms of Deco Bait and Tackle was way too small to hold both of us, especially since we were almost twice the size we'd been before. So, we opted instead to sleep in her grandmother's crowded spare bedroom. Rosie slept there often, anyway, seeking a closer proximity to Simmy during lonely nights.

Besides the double bed, shoved into one corner, the room was cluttered with Simmy's stored possessions. It was a treasure trove for us. We knew with certainty that her grandmother did not mind the intrusion, so we eagerly explored the heavily perfumed boxes filled with outdated clothing, framed sepia pictures of blurry ancestors and photo albums filled with photos of a young vibrant Cimarron Pascal cavorting with friends and family with the fecund bayou as a backdrop. There were photos of Rosemary's mother, well-marked by Rosemary's fingerprints, as well as photos of Simmy's late husband, a handsome man of color wearing a dark suit and string tie in most of the pictures. In early depictions, his hair was parted on one side and heavily slicked down. In later photos, his appearance found more freedom and his hair sprang forth in a corona of glory, his clothing more relaxed and contemporary.

Rosemary's mother, Jeanne, was a blooming bayou flower. In a few of the photos, when she was young, her dark hair was longer and artificially straightened, her face carefully made up, her smile wide but shy. In one she held a ribbon-tied cluster of greenery. It was hard to tell but I surmised it was rosemary. Of course.

In later photos, as she posed sullenly beside Theo, her hair was cropped close and her face cosmetic free. The progression seemed tragic as I pieced together the images I had received from Simmy's memories. I wondered how much joy Jeanne had experienced in her short life. Rosie mourned her death but in truth we both knew that even had she lived, she might have had to endure a walking, talking death of her spirit.

I spend a lot of time looking at Rosemary. Not that I need to because I already feel her as part of me. It's a guilty pleasure that I indulge in. She's so beautiful and I find her beauty absolutely enchanting. She's like a Disney princess, lithe and graceful. And, like Snow White, she's able to communicate with animals, actually all of nature, with a special connection. She knows everything that it is possible to know about our earthly environment and I stand awed by her wisdom. It's not a particular interest of mine, I lean more toward nutrition and food sciences but I learn amazing things about nature from her by the osmotic relationship we have.

The other part of Rosemary that fascinates me is her inherent sunny nature. Even when she is sad about losing her mother, or dealing with her father's anger, that innate joy is still there, lurking, peeking from around a corner. I like that so much and the glow of approval that emanates from the Collective sometimes makes us giggle.

# CHAPTER FIFTEEN

### *Breakfast on the Bayou*

The next morning Lily woke to the very confusing fragrance of bug spray mixed with frying bacon. She snuggled closer to Hunter's back and buried her nose. This smell was better, Hunter's natural scent reminded Lily of New Mexico. She inhaled deeply and felt Hunter's body shake with laughter.

"Getting a snootful, are you?" Hunter asked, rolling to pull Lily into her embrace. "Be careful. I have wicked morning breath."

Lily grinned and pressed her lips to Hunter's. "I don't even care."

"Weird, huh?" Hunter asked quietly.

Lily knew immediately what she was talking about. "We always knew having a Collective baby was going to be strange."

"Yeah, but reading minds and glowing? Didn't expect that."

Lily cupped Hunter's slim hip in one palm, caressing along the length of her hip and thigh. "Mmm. You feel good," she muttered.

"Keep doing that and we'll see if you can feel just as good," Hunter said huskily. Her hand found Lily's breast, and she teased the tip into a peak of raw sensation.

Lily gasped and her lips found Hunter's, their kiss quickly growing into a maelstrom of need and pleasurable tonguing. Lily moaned and pressed her body against Hunter's.

"Is Birdie still with Rosemary?" Hunter whispered.

"Yes, and you know she'd knock," Lily replied absently. She was preoccupied by licking and sucking the bare breast she had exposed by lifting Hunter's sleep shirt. Hunter moaned in her ear, and Lily slowly, tantalizingly, slid her hand into the front of Hunter's panties. She let her fingers slide easily into her wife's slick folds.

Hunter jumped as Lily's finger found its mark. "Just a…just a quickie," she gasped.

"Yes, a quickie," Lily agreed as her hand found a good, steady rhythm and she sucked hard on each of Hunter's nipples. She paused and curled two fingers deep inside Hunter, pressing upward, finding just the right pressure point her lover enjoyed. Soon, too soon, Hunter arched hard away from the mattress and her moan of pleasure was low and long. The walls of her vagina clenched hard, trapping Lily, who enjoyed the sensation more than she would ever admit. She closed her eyes and rested her forehead against Hunter's collarbone, pleasurably awaiting release from those tight muscular walls.

Moments later, Hunter had recovered and was kneeling above her, hands cupping her breasts, thumbs teasing the nipples. Her knee pressed against Lily's now erect, responsive clit, and she moved that knee to and fro, the soft cotton of Lily's sleep shorts adding another layer of sensation.

Hunter released a low sigh of pleasure as she lifted Lily's shirt for a nice visual display. Both breasts were rosy and puckered with anticipation. She leaned, and teased one nipple with the tip of her tongue.

Lily, eyes partially closed in high arousal, used her hands to push her breasts closer to Hunter's tongue. Hunter helped her out, using her tongue as a fuck tool, as if hoping that Lily would feel it clear down to her clit. She reached a hand down, a shudder shaking her violently as she felt Lily's wetness and swollen need. She plunged her fingers deep inside, stroking, thumb lashing hard against Lily's engorged nub until Lily screamed silently, biting a knuckle as she fell over the cliff of orgasm.

"Yoohoo! Y'all gals want some breakfast?" Simmy called as the screen door slapped open and she entered the house. "We got bacon an' eggs and Rosie made some a her killer pancakes."

Hunter muffled a giggle as she rolled off Lily.

"That sounds great," Lily called out, breathing hard. "We'll be right out."

"Okay," Simmy said, tapping the bedroom door one time. "We're outside on the dock. Birdie got the gas grill going to keep it warm."

Another slap of the screen door marked her departure.

"Sheesh! That was close," Hunter whispered.

"But, oh, so good," Lily responded, curling into Hunter's embrace.

Hunter pulled her closer, kissed her forehead, then lightly slapped Lily's bottom. "Up you go. But I get the shower first!"

She leapt from the bed, throwing the top sheet and light blanket over Lily's head.

Lily pulled the covers down and smiled at the ceiling as the rickety shower came to life.

The two young women and Simmy were sitting around the same table they had used the previous evening, stuffing their mouths and laughing at goodness knew what, as Lily and Hunter approached.

"Good morning!" Hunter said. "Sorry we're so late. Didn't know early breakfasts were a thing in Bayou Lisse."

"Not really," said Rosemary. "We just woke up early."

"And woke me," Simmy grumbled.

"Did you do okay on the sofa?" Lily asked. "We feel terrible kicking you out of your bed."

"Oh, pshaw," Simmy said, lifting a butter knife to cut her pancake into small bites. "I generally sleep there anyways, fallin' asleep with the late-night movies on."

Rosemary spoke with her mouth still full of pancake. "This is true," she said. "And I can hear her snoring all the way into my bedroom in back of the store."

Birdie laughed and pointed a food-laden fork at Rosemary as appreciation for the comment.

"Y'all help yourselves," Simmy said pointing to the large, covered grill nearby. "It's still hot under that top."

Hunter and Lily found a veritable feast of eggs, bacon, and pancakes on the griddle top of the large grill, and they loaded the thick paper plates waiting nearby. Hunter carried the laden plates to the table, where they settled with satisfied sighs.

"You girls sleep okay?" Lily asked as she loaded her mouth with eggs.

"After we eventually dozed off," Birdie said with a loud sigh.

"There was so much to discuss," Rosemary added with a sage nod.

Hunter frowned as though perplexed. "Such as?"

Rosemary and Birdie shared a furtive glance.

"Just catching up," Birdie replied finally. "We're still getting to know one another."

Lily frowned and pressed the side of her fork into a pancake. She knew, deep down, that all private information had already passed between the two girls almost as soon as they met. So, what were they hiding from them all? Suspicion grew in Lily's breast, and she felt oddly uneasy. Her sweet Birdie was changing after meeting Rosemary and not in a good way. She'd become distant, sly, somehow superior. Was it the age change or was being in closer proximity with Rosemary exerting an unsavory influence?

She stared at her pancake, filled with indecision and doubt. She realized suddenly that the past three years may have been the calm before a new and perhaps destructive storm. She swallowed hard, filled with an uncharacteristic, certainly unrealistic, fear.

"What do you think, Mummy? It could be fun."

Birdie was speaking to her and Lily realized she'd missed most of the ongoing conversation. "What's that, hon? I was woolgathering."

Birdie rolled her eyes, drawing a snicker from Rosemary. "Going into Redstar. Just to see what the town is like."

"We *are* on vacay," Hunter chimed in, lifting a glass of orange juice.

"Of course," Lily agreed, hoping the excursion would improve her sour mood. "Sounds like fun."

"You going with us, *Sha*?" Rosemary asked her grandmother.

Simmy rubbed her hands as though they hurt. "I don't think so, *bebe*," she answered. "I'll stay and help your father in the store."

Rosemary frowned, her beautiful smooth skin wrinkling. "Oh, I should stay and help. That's my job."

"Don't be silly, *cherie*." Simmy took Rosemary's hands in hers. "You got company. Show dem what our little town has to offer."

Rosemary grinned. "I'll tell them not to blink or they might miss it," she joked.

Simmy just tutted in response as she turned back to her breakfast.

## *Aili's Journal*

### *Sleeping with Rosemary*

Her skin was like fine silk cloth, her smell like carrots in hot sunlight. Not that I had ever encountered silk or growing carrots, but those images had somehow come to mind via the Collective. We had lain naked, side by side, pressed close, passing packets of energy back and forth between us. I entered her soul and she mine as we shed our human skin and coalesced into the starlight of our Collective halves. The sensation had been exquisite, even without the five human senses we'd grown up with. Her body of light touched all my most erotic places, entering my body and filling me with heat and substance until I cried out for mercy.

This merging of our beings was new, but I knew right away why the Collective existed as it did. This assimilation was the logical progression of humanity. Reclining in bliss, Rosemary and I pondered whether the Collective had evolved from another creature, another humanity, forming into the energy conglomeration as it now existed. We knew, with the inner knowledge gleaned from our Collective, that the question was moot and unanswerable. The Collective just was and had always been, in time before time. It is starlight. We are all starlight eventually.

# CHAPTER SIXTEEN

## *Touring Redstar*

Unloading Rosemary and Birdie from the back of the SUV drew several curious stares from the passing townsfolk. Hunter grinned and rolled her eyes at Lily.

"Stranger danger," she whispered.

Lily smiled. "You don't look *that* dangerous," she teased.

"Get me alone," Hunter countered. "Then we'll see."

"This is the library," Rosemary was telling Birdie as she pointed to a tall, antebellum building that sat on a triangular aspect to the wide boulevard called Stella Avenue. It appeared as though this one long boulevard was pretty much the extent of Redstar. Lily could see the interstate ramps in the distance on both sides. A few side roads branched off Stella but, as far as Lily could tell, Redstar was one of the tiniest towns she had ever seen. There was no lack of people, however. It seemed as though the entire populace was surreptitiously surveying them while ambling toward the line of businesses near where Hunter had parked the car.

"Guess we're the biggest news of the day," Lily muttered.

She glanced at the two young women with them and realized anew how strikingly beautiful they were. Then, of course, she and Hunter could be being perceived as obviously lesbian, and she was walking with a cane. She sighed. And they weren't regular town residents, always an attention getter. She decided to make the best of the situation.

The businesses lining Stella Avenue, Lily saw, were like other businesses in small-town America strip malls. There was a nail salon, a hair stylist, an insurance firm, a florist, and, at the very end, a bakery called Tina's Sweets & Treats.

"I wanna check that place out," she said, grabbing Hunter's arm and pointing.

"You and your sweet tooth, I swear," Hunter replied, shaking her head. "I want to go across the street to look at the tools."

Lily turned and saw a computer repair business, a hardware store, and a drugstore on the corner of Stella and a street called Mangrove Row.

"We're going to Tina's shop, okay, Mummy?" Birdie asked. "They have cupcakes!" The final word was spoken with special emphasis that brought a smile to Lily's lips.

"Tina's is fine," Hunter said next to her ear. She indicated, with a sideways nod of her head, a group of three men who had gathered and were leaning against the brick wall of the insurance business.

Their eyes had fastened on Birdie and Rosemary, and the way they were looking at them made Lily distinctly uncomfortable. "Sounds good to me," she muttered.

Hunter positioned herself between the insurance storefront and the girls, and they all headed past the nail salon and the florist. Before entering the bakery, she looked back and pressed the fob on her keys, making sure the doors of the SUV were securely locked.

The scent of spun sugar assailed Lily's senses as they entered the warm, welcoming business.

A plump woman, with short, curly brown hair, rose up from behind the display case and greeted them. "Well, hello, newcomers! Welcome. What can I get for you?"

Rosemary had pulled Birdie toward the display case and was whispering animatedly, sharing the merits of this or that confectionery goodie.

"I think cupcakes are in our future," Lily replied, indicating the clamoring girls.

"Do you have coffee?" Hunter asked.

"We sure do and it's fresh, from a good local supplier. Will you be wanting hot or iced this morning?" Her perkiness was somehow young and endearing though she appeared to be approaching middle age.

"I think we'll go with iced. A latte sounds good."

"Make that two," Lily added.

"Do you have soy milk?" Birdie had appeared at her side.

"They do," Rosemary offered. "Tina has it on hand because I always ask for it."

"Oh, cool! Let's make those four iced coffees, with soy milk, then."

A sudden, pregnant silence caught all four women unaware. They lifted their eyes as one and noticed a look of confusion marring Tina's features. It changed, as they watched, into something resembling horror. "Do I know you?" she asked Rosemary, gaze roaming across Rosemary's features. "I thought maybe…"

"We should leave," Hunter whispered against Lily's ear. Lily cringed, realizing quickly what the issue was. They should have anticipated this.

"Oh no, of course not," Rosemary replied. "I misspoke. My cousin Rosemary Deco told me about it. My uncle Theo runs the bait and tackle outside town."

Relief flickered slowly across Tina's features, but it was tinged with doubt. "Oh. So, you're new in town," she said, moving toward the espresso machine. "I'll have your coffees right out."

"Let's get a table," Lily said, spotting several empty ones in the front of the room.

"Should we?" Hunter asked in a worried tone. "I mean…"

"I think we'll be fine," Lily responded. "Check out that table in front of the window."

Hunter looked across and smiled. "Sisters!"

"I think so."

Lily studied the two women. One was small in stature, similar to Hunter, but with short, dark-blond hair, blunt cut. The other was bigger and had a glorious long mane of thick, champagne-colored curls. As Lily watched discreetly, the one with the longer hair expertly gathered that hair together and tied it up into a messy bun using a thick blue hair tie. Both women were dressed in knee-length denim shorts and faded T-shirts. They must have sensed Lily's interest because they both turned and the taller one waved and smiled.

"I say we stay," Hunter agreed suddenly.

Within a few minutes, the four were presented with a tray of four coffees and six cupcakes, chosen by the expert hybrids. Lily paid as Hunter and the girls chose a table next to the two women. Rosemary's head was down as Lily approached.

"Rosie? Are you okay?" she whispered as she slid into her chair across from the girl.

"We know them, Mummy," Birdie explained. "She's worried they'll recognize her."

"Oh." Lily nodded understanding. "We can go if you want to." She reached out and laid her hand on Rosemary's.

Two chairs suddenly appeared next to Rosemary and the two women joined them.

"As I live and breathe, it is you, isn't it?" the taller of the two said in a low whisper. Her deep brown eyes examined Rosemary with avid interest.

The smaller woman held out her hand. "Delora November. And this is my wife, Sophie."

"Nice to meet you," Lily said as she shook their hands and introduced herself and the others.

"So, it is you," Sophie said, leaning even closer to Rosemary. "What happened? How can this be?"

She turned to Hunter, eyes wide. "I delivered this child," she explained. "About four years ago. I saw her a month ago and she was just a kid."

Rosemary glanced fearfully at Lily, clearly wondering how to explain the circumstance of her aging. A deep silence fell.

## *Aili's Journal*

*Limitless*

In the Collective, we are energy and as such, we are able to shift the particles of our being into endless shapes and essences. We can travel at will on the Collective bus, even to that tiny planet at the end of the Earth's universe and become the slimy tentacled life that exists there, a Collective experiment from eons ago. Or become the frigid multi-celled creatures on one of the watery moons of this solar system. We can become any form we choose, at any time. My human side finds this disturbing, but the energy forms take it in stride, without a second's hesitation.

We hybrids are bound by the flesh, true, but the core of that same energy burns brightly within us. This gives us powers beyond the normal human. The adjustment of living with this core of power should be difficult for a child born of a human, but in all actuality, the difficulty lies not in accepting the star energy but in the flesh holding us back.

Sadness is still an emotion I feel, and I am sad for my amazing mothers. As I age, I can sense that emotions are stepping aside as the Collective energy grows within me. I worry that I will become distant, mentally and physically. They will be disturbed by what may be coming. They cannot understand the extent of the Collective energy. If not bound by compassion and empathy and détente, we could crush the Earth like an overbaked cookie.

# CHAPTER SEVENTEEN

## *The Bayou Holds Many Secrets*

Lily sighed and took a swallow of the surprisingly good coffee. "There's not much I can tell you," she said quietly, leaning in close to Sophie and Delora. "It has to do with a government program, so it's really hush-hush. I work with a special science unit and you really need to keep all this to yourself."

Sophie leaned back and crossed her arms, eyeing Lily suspiciously.

"Who're we gonna tell," Delora said, one hand brushing futilely at her long bangs. "We live in the deep bayou."

"I'm just saying," Lily said, spreading her hands wide. "This is pretty serious."

Delora leaned close and whispered, gaze traveling to the counter to see if anyone was listening. "So, it's like a growth serum? Some kind of experimental drug to make kids grow faster?"

"Government program, huh?" Sophie leaned forward again, and her eyes found Rosemary. "They doin' all right by you, Rosie? Does Simmy know what's goin' on?"

Rosemary lifted her chin finally and smiled, eyes sparking bright blue for a few quick seconds. Sophie jumped as though she'd been jolted by electricity. Her eyes widened, and Lily wondered what information had been imparted to Sophie's mind.

"She does," Rosemary replied. "I promise you that all's good. There's nothing for you to worry about."

"There's nothing for us to worry about," Sophie repeated as though reassuring herself of the fact.

"So, Delora, what do you do for a living?" Hunter asked before taking a huge bite of cupcake. White frosting formed a thin mustache until her tongue captured it in a majestic sweep.

"We're healers," Delora replied, pulling her troubled gaze from her wife. "Sophie and me, we take care of the people who don't want to be beholden to a doctor or hospital."

"Oh, like house calls," Birdie chimed in. "Are you two country doctors?"

Sophie laughed and turned to Birdie, seemingly less troubled now by Rosemary's apparent age. "It's more a type of natural medicine so no, we don't have medical degrees. I have a bachelor's in nursing, though, and Lora is studying for hers."

"We call them swamp witches," Rosemary added. "In an endearing way. They work almost magical cures for all the people of the bayou."

"We serve as midwives, too, which is how Sophie and Rosemary met," Delora added.

Sophie frowned at Rosemary. "You really did grow up, didn't you?"

"I did, too," Birdie added. "At about the same time."

"I know what you are telling me is impossible," mused Sophie. "But I have always believed that there is more to our lives than just this physical plane. The healings I have seen, people brought back from the brink of death, forever changed by the experience…" She shook her head. "The bayou holds so many secrets."

"What brings you to Redstar?" Delora asked Lily.

"Mostly a vacation, but also so Birdie and Rosemary could meet face-to-face. They've been communicating for some time now. It was time for them to actually meet."

"Ahh." Delora nodded and sipped her coffee. "So, where are you from?"

"New Mexico. Western part," Hunter offered.

"I so want to see New Mexico," Delora said, shifting in her seat. "My friend Hinchey went there to live with a gal he met online. They are so happy now. And she's pregnant. Check this!" She pulled out her cell phone and showed them a photo of a sonagram. "It's a girl. How cool is that?"

"Oh look! She's sucking her thumb," Birdie exclaimed, practically climbing across Rosemary to get a better view.

"Where are they in New Mexico? Albuquerque?"

"No." Delora looked lovingly at the photo one more time before stashing the phone in her pocket. "They're in a little town in the north, I think. It's called Alliance."

"I know where that is," Hunter said. She turned to Lily. "There's Montez Pueblo there."

Lily nodded.

"You're Native, aren't you?" Sophie said, taking Rosemary's hand in hers and intertwining their fingers. "I thought so."

"Acoma Pueblo, though I live at Good Neighbor Ranch with Lily and Birdie," Hunter replied.

"SaySay and Lanny live there, too," Birdie added. "They're from the same pueblo."

"That must be cool for you, living with so many people from the reservation," Delora mused.

Birdie and Rosemary turned as one to give Delora a disdainful look.

"Yes, it's cool, because they are really good people. They are my family," Birdie said slowly.

Delora looked as though she had awakened to her own words suddenly. "Oh, that's what I meant," she amended.

"How long are you guys going to be in town?" Sophie asked, lifting her cup and draining it.

Lily looked at Hunter and then they both looked at Birdie.

"Probably a few more days," Rosemary answered for them.

"Maybe you guys would like to come to Salamander House," Delora said. "Our friend Clary makes a mean gumbo."

"That sounds like fun," Rosemary said. "They live deep inwater, right on Cofe Creek."

"Can she make it without meat?" Birdie asked, as Rosemary nodded eagerly.

"Oh, I'm sure. The shrimp goes in last anyway, and she doesn't usually add chicken unless she has some left over from another meal," Sophie explained.

Lily shrugged. "Sounds great to me. We don't have any other concrete plans while we're here." She looked to Hunter, who nodded assent.

"Good. That's settled then. How about tonight? Say, seven?" Sophie eyed them expectantly. "Bring Simmy along, too. I know Clary would love to catch up."

Rosemary grinned. "I bet she would just love to visit Salamander House again."

Delora rose and lifted her to-go cup. "Well, we'd better get back to work. We have two more cases this afternoon. No rest for the wicked."

Sophie handed her phone to Lily. "Can you put your number in so I can send you directions to the house?"

"Absolutely!" Lily took the phone and created a new contact with their full names, adding both her number and Hunter's, just in case.

Sophie took the phone and stood next to her wife. "Looks good. We'll see you this evening. Y'all have fun during your ten-minute tour of Redstar," she joked.

After the two women left the coffee shop, the four remaining women looked at one another with wide eyes.

"Well, that was something," Lily said to no one in particular. "Wasn't it?"

"A little scary there, for a minute or two," Rosemary offered. "I've known Miss Sophie my whole life."

"It's really weird when you change so fast and so much," Birdie agreed. "You should have seen me trying to make all the hands at home accept the new me when I had the first aging."

Rosemary nodded and chewed on the straw protruding from her latte. "My dad went ballistic. I think he saw me as some evil thing that my mom had spawned."

"He hated me," she added softly after a short pause.

Birdie took Rosemary's hand and clasped it to her chest. "It's okay. He understands now."

Lily leaned forward, emotionally stirred by the girls. "So, what's next? What else does Redstar have to offer us?"

Rosemary grinned. "I think we should go out toward Spinner's Fen. The houses along that road are so gorgeous. Beautiful antebellum architecture. I think you'll like it."

"Spinner's Fen, it is," Hunter stated as she rose and stretched.

Tina was still eyeing them doubtfully, so they wished her a great day and waved cheerfully as they stepped out onto the main thoroughfare.

## *Aili's Journal*

### Redstar Folk

The little southern town of Redstar is so shuttered. Rosemary has loved living here and associating with the people here and thus, so must I, but truthfully, the town wears like a leather shirt. Too tight and unyielding. Watching the people interact has been a lesson in hopelessness. Being born here has given the residents a closed mind. They cannot see beyond their cookie-cutter homes and families. Beyond their illicit affairs and the subtle machinations that falsely empower them.

It's like nothing exists for them beyond the borders of the town, as well. The residents do go to a nearby, larger town, Goshen, to get and see what isn't available here. But opinions of Goshen are negative, many of the older humans thinking the city too racy, too forward. They seem to embrace the strict borders of their existence. Even finding superiority in it. If only they realized how truly small they are. Each spark of life is important, true, but that spark is only a launching pad. What happens after is a decision.

# CHAPTER EIGHTEEN

*Salamander House*

Lily's first sight of Sophie and Delora's wood-sided bayou home took her breath away. The small, well-maintained, white frame home fronted on a wide tributary, resting on eight sturdy pilings. A generous wooden verandah, also painted white, wrapped around the house, ending where the base of the house met solid land. A sweeping grass lawn, bordered by an herb garden, raced downward to meet a weathered wooden building jutting out above yet another, narrower, body of water.

"Wow," Birdie whispered as she stepped from the car.

"I agree," Hunter said. "Getting lost twice was worth it to see this place."

Lily bestowed a wry look on Hunter and poked her in the ribs.

What?" Hunter said. "It was confusing. All this bayou."

Birdie and Rosemary had gone ahead to meet up with Delora and Sophie, who had come out onto the porch to greet them.

"This place is amazing," Lily said, approaching the two healers. "You must absolutely love living here."

Sophie grinned. "Shoot, I couldn't even imagine living anywhere else. My mama, who lives in Florida now, keeps trying to get me to come live down there. But there ain't no way!" She laughed at the absurd notion.

"The population in the state of Florida is almost twenty-two million, a good percentage older than sixty-five," Birdie offered. "Not sure you'd want to live there. The whole state of Alabama only has five million."

"No matter where you live in the state of Florida, you are never more than sixty miles from the ocean," Rosemary added. "So, it is sort of like southern Alabama."

Sophie snapped her mouth closed, obviously awed by the knowledge of the two younger women. "Well, I was born and bred here and plan to stay."

"Your family has always lived here?" Hunter asked.

Sophie nodded and gently touched Delora's neck for no apparent reason other than sheer affection. "Yep, my grandmother's father, Wassel Fox Cofe, built this place back in the forties. We've been here and healing the people of the water ever since then."

"Wow," Lily mouthed.

"Well, you guys have all certainly taken good care of it. Not an easy task, down here on the water," Hunter murmured.

"You got that right," a new voice interjected. "My Salty has been here twice already this year, patching up the floorboards. The water combined with the humidity just makes them rot."

"This, ladies," Sophie said with a short laugh, "is our dear Clary. We couldn't function around here if she didn't take care of us."

The screen door parted, and a beautiful young woman of color stepped through. She bobbed her head and shook each of their hands in turn. "Welcome to Salamander House. It's so good to have visitors and the downtime to enjoy them. Come in, come on in, please!"

She stepped aside, ushering them all across the verandah and into the well-furnished living area. Lily's mouth fell open.

The large, wood-paneled room had walls completely lined with shelves, shelves packed with gleaming glass jars, many repurposed, as well as numerous, well-worn books.

"Oh my gosh," Birdie whispered. "This place is great!"

Rosemary took her hand and pulled her toward one of the shelves next to the unlit fireplace. They proceeded to examine, with eyes only, the many jars aligned there.

"I apologize for their rudeness," Lily said, shaking her head in disbelief.

Clary just laughed as she moved to the spacious, open kitchen area. "No such a thing. We live by 'an' it harm none, do what you will' motto in this house."

She lifted the lid of a large Dutch oven and released anew the delicious scent that permeated the home. The smell of perfectly toasted Cajun spices washed across them all, making Lily's stomach growl in eagerness.

"Y'all come sit down at the table," Delora said, pulling out mismatched chairs from a huge table that had been fashioned from polished wooden planks. She stilled and studied the visitors with dark, wideset eyes. Her hair was cropped close, but she still managed to pull loose a curl and twirl it around one forefinger.

"Wow," Hunter said, drawing her hand appreciatively across the gleaming surface. "This is a beautiful piece."

"Oh yeah, we love this table. Uncle Tassidy got together with some of the other men of the Light of Holiness Church and made this for us about ten Christmases ago."

"And it's seen its share of family drama," Clary said with a short laugh.

The group sat at the table and one by one they joined hands.

"We thank you, Mother Earth, for this nourishment that we are about to receive," Sophie said in a low voice. "Blessed be to all."

"Amen," Clary said, and the others repeated it, quietly.

"Well, pass those rolls over here, Birdie," Delora said. "Clary makes the best homemade refrigerator rolls. Her loaf bread is something, too. I just wish I had that kind of cooking skill."

Clary chuckled as she dished up bowls of gumbo from the large pot in the center of the table. "Now, why on earth would you say that? I'm certainly not going anywhere."

"Thank goodness," Sophie said as she passed a full bowl to Hunter.

Silence fell as the women set themselves up and began eating.

"Oh, my heavens, this is so good," Lily said finally. "You're coming back to New Mexico with us, right?"

"Oh, no, no, no," Sophie said quickly as Clary laughed.

"Just glad you're enjoying it, Lily," Delora said.

"Meemaw sends her apologies," Rosemary said as she buttered a roll. "She wanted to come, but a brush fire on the Raymon tributary called Dad away. She stayed on and minded the store for him."

"Oh no, hope no one was hurt," Sophie said. She laid a hand of benevolence briefly over her heart.

"You tell her no worries when you get home," Clary said, pointing a soft roll toward Rosemary. "I'll get all the news and a nice visit with her when I see her on Sunday."

Lily listened quietly as conversation moved around the table and realized that she felt better than she had for the past few days. She was suffused with warmth, happy to be included into such a loving and caring group. Her guard had to remain up, of course, but she was still able to relax and enjoy the pleasant visit.

## *Aili's Journal*

*Fleeting Happiness*

I feel a close familiarity with this part of the deep bayou through Rosie's many memories of her short childhood here. It's interesting how she has bonded so completely to her human side, although as I reflect on my life, I realize that Good Neighbor Ranch has a similar hold on me. Our human half is certainly shaped by location and by those around us who nurture us. I find myself wondering what influence, beyond the thirst for knowledge, has been imparted by our energy halves.

We adore watching my flesh parents interact with other humans, especially humans meaningful to Rosie. We touch digits and playfully pass the joy of this thought back and forth. And we question—do they even realize how important they are? That the circumstances of allowing and fostering our births may eventually save this planet from possible destruction? I am beginning to comprehend that my mummy has come to some understanding of this. It could be her bonded relationship with the Collective through the energy entity she calls Flynn that has given her this insight. Rosemary concurs. After all, the Liaison should know more than the human populace should ever know.

# CHAPTER NINETEEN

## *That Second Night*

"We had the best time," Birdie said that evening.

The four of them had joined Simmy on the back deck, and they were regaling Rosemary's grandmother with tales from their time at Salamander House.

"And oh, the gumbo! It was amazing." Rosemary kissed her fingers Italian style.

"That Clary. She always was a really good cook," Simmy said. "There was a passel of kids at her house and a lot of the cooking fell on her."

"Well, it paid off," Hunter said, rubbing her belly. She pushed a covered bowl and a foil-wrapped packet toward Simmy.

Simmy grinned and lifted her eyes to Hunter. "From Clary?"

Hunter grinned back. "She said to tell you she'll see you at church."

"I'll get you a spoon, *Sha*," Rosemary said, rising and heading toward *Chez* Simmy.

"Bring a napkin, too," Simmy called after her and proceeded to peel back the foil from four rolls oozing melted butter. She smacked her lips.

"That's the way we felt, too," Lily said, chuckling.

Rosemary returned, handed the spoon and napkin to her grandmother and sat once more. They all watched expectantly as Simmy reverently opened the bowl. She leaned and inhaled the intoxicating aroma, then dug in, loading her mouth with the hearty rice stew.

"Rosie," Lily asked suddenly. "Are you going to miss going back to school in a few months?"

Rosemary cocked her head to one side. "Oh, I know there's no way I can go now. Sometimes school is redundant anyway. That's been the case with us. Also, they all always picked up on my differences."

Lily sighed in agreement.

"She thickened it with *filé*," Simmy said quietly. "My favorite. No shrimp, though."

"You win some, you lose some," Rosemary teased as Birdie giggled.

"It's vegetarian," Birdie explained. "She did it special for us."

Simmy shrugged. "Is still perfect, though." She patted her stomach, then reached for a second roll.

"We had a weird situation that you may have to address next time you see Clary," Hunter said, leaning forward and catching Simmy's attention. "Sophie and Delora wanted to know why Rosie had aged so much. Clary probably will, as well."

"Ah," Simmy said and nodded. She used the buttered roll to swipe the gumbo gravy from the bowl. "I wondered about that when y'all went to town. The customers have asked after it, too."

"What did you tell them," Lily asked.

"That's she's a cousin on Theo's side and that Rosie was away at youth camp."

"Sheesh," Hunter said, burying her face in her two hands.

"I know how hard it is," Lily commiserated. "We had ranch hands who'd known Birdie since birth. It was pretty weird until she won them over."

"I figured you'd be around here," Theo said, approaching around the side of the bait shop. He was filthy, no doubt from fighting the brush fire, but Lily was happy to note that he wasn't inebriated. Maybe his days of drinking too much were through.

"Look at you," Simmy said.

"So, no one was hurt, that's good," Rosemary said.

"How did you…?" Theo crossed himself briefly and pulled another chair to the table. He stared at his daughter, then turned to Simmy. "What's dat I smell? It smell so good."

"Gumbo sent from Clary, but none lef'," she replied. "You eaten?"

"I did. We'd burgers and beer at dat chain place in Goshen. Ate outside so we didn't smoke de place up."

"Smart move," Rosemary said, holding her nose and causing Birdie to laugh.

"There's a roll left that I ain't room for." Simmy pushed the foil packet toward Theo.

He lifted it, his hands smudging the baby bottom surface of the roll and took half of it in one bite. "Dat Clary," he muttered in appreciation around the bite.

A comfortable silence fell as night settled around their shoulders. Fireflies danced above the bayou water and tree frogs accompanied the dance. Otters splashed a downbeat under the boards of the deck, and Lily found herself tapping her foot in four-four time.

Her thoughts flew to the future and the necessity of separating the two girls. She wanted to broach the topic but was reluctant to break the peace of the evening. Helplessness washed across her. How could the two be parted? Would communicating via the Collective be enough in the future? She was still confused about the purpose of this trip and vowed to ask Birdie again as soon as she could and demand answers from her.

Hunter seemed to sense her thoughts and reached to clasp her hand in both of hers. Those beautiful deep brown eyes searched her face lovingly. She squeezed Lily's hand, so Lily smiled reassuringly.

The two joined in small talk, sharing the Salamander House visit with Theo until, after a couple hours, Simmy stood and said it was past her bedtime. The others followed suit, and Lily, after rising, paused at the railing to look out across the bayou. She would miss its sultry, beguiling beauty, so very different from her home in New Mexico.

"What are we going to do?" Hunter said, once they were dressed for bed and lying atop the coverlet together. "I have to go back to work, and you need to oversee things at the ranch. We only have one, two more days at most."

"I know," Lily whispered. "We'll have to address it in the morning. I'm dreading it."

"I won't leave Birdie here," Hunter said petulantly. "I don't care how old she looks, she's still our baby."

Lily nodded and tucked her head into Hunter's shoulder. Hunter pulled her tight.

Hunter, feeling the chill of the damp night air, rose during the night to pull the coverlet over them. She tucked the blanket securely around the slumbering Lily, but a glow from beneath the door caught her eye and drew her away from the bed. She cautiously approached the door and rested her palm against it, wondering if the cottage had caught fire. The door was cool to the touch, though. Looking down, she noted that the glow was blue, not red or yellow, and her thoughts flew to Birdie and Rosemary. Gingerly, she cracked the door and peered through.

Simmy was on the sofa, curled on her side facing the quietly murmuring television. The glow was emanating from the bedroom the girls occupied. Hunter opened the door all the way and took two steps forward but paused. She wasn't sure that she wanted to see what was happening in that room. She was daunted by the idea of how the two hybrid girls might make love. Then horror movie imagery paraded through her mind. *Village of the Damned*, *The Hole in the Ground*, even *The Invasion of the Body Snatchers*. No, she wasn't brave enough to open their door. Closing the door softly so as not to disturb Lily, she rested her back against it, relaxing as she saw the blue glow at her feet ebbing. She returned to bed and gratefully snuggled next to Lily. It was some time before sleep claimed her, though.

# CHAPTER TWENTY

## *The Owl*

A strange sound woke Lily in the early morning hours. She was on her left side, one arm around Hunter. She roused slowly, ears finely tuned, struggling to make sense of what she was hearing. The noise repeated. It reminded her of the susurration of birds' wings as they settled in and roosted for the night. As her thoughts became clearer, she wondered why birds would be so close. It sounded as though they were actually in the bedroom with her. Her mind lurched into high gear. Something was wrong.

She shifted the light coverlet and turned onto her back to survey the room. There, at the foot of the bed, talons grasping the old-fashioned footboard, rested a huge white owl. Gigantic dark eyes studied her, and its heavy pale beak opened as though it wished to speak to her. Lily, oddly enough, sensed malevolence in that unblinking stare. Her hand stretched out, and she pushed at Hunter's slumbering form.

"Wake up! Hunter, wake up!" she hissed urgently.

Hunter rolled toward her, eyes blinking sleepily. She followed Lily's rapt gaze and lurched to a sitting position, pressing her back hard against the tall wooden headboard.

"What?" she gasped sleepily. "How did…?"

As they watched, the owl spread its massive white wings— and was replaced by the figure of one of the Greys, the small aliens that had once kidnapped Lily. It jumped down next to the bed, and the dry wing noise of earlier changed to a wet, shifting sound as it moved its small feet. A smell similar to charcoal washed across them.

Rampant fear swamped Lily as memories of her kidnapping resurfaced. She swallowed the scream that rose in her throat as paralysis swept through her body. The bulbous head on the small, wizened body moved closer along her side of the bed, its oval tilted eyes filled with hatred as they studied her, and its small mouth twisted. Horrified by her helplessness, Lily pined for something, even death, to free her from the sight of that menacing alien face.

She heard Hunter gasping for air and knew she must be experiencing the paralysis as well. Her thoughts next flew to Birdie, and rage replaced her feeling of helplessness. It was one thing to threaten her, but when the alien bastards began threatening her family… Well, it was more than she could bear. She had to keep the monsters from hurting them and she had to act fast.

Lily struggled to form a fist and, after what seemed like hours, regained some control of her body. She grunted loudly and managed to swing one fist at the creature. Her hand encountered hard, unyielding flesh and glanced off the alien's mouth. The creature recoiled, lifting a three-fingered hand to its face, and grimaced at her as a strange vertical slit began to develop in the wall behind it. The alien turned to look at it, then turned back to the bed. It cast a threatening glance at Hunter and Lily, and a creepy smile formed on its little gash of a mouth. It stepped through the slit, which shrank to the size of a small dot that then popped away into nothing.

The paralysis took almost a minute to dissipate. Lily looked at Hunter, who was deep in the throes of a panic attack.

"Oh, oh honey," Lily soothed, pulling Hunter into her embrace, heart breaking that her love had ever had to experience the alien's evil presence. "It's gone, it's gone now."

Hunter was struggling to breathe through her terror, and she pulled away from Lily, gathering her knees to her chest and wrapping her arms around them. She rocked to and fro. "They're real," she muttered. "Real!"

"Shhh, shh, I know, I know," Lily soothed. "Listen, I've got to go check on the girls. You stay here. I'll be right back."

"The girls," Hunter said. She cleared her throat and rose carefully to her feet. She took a deep breath and amazed Lily with how deftly she reclaimed her calmness. She was a trouper.

Lily lifted her cane, moved to the door, and slowly opened it. She glanced at Simmy as she crossed to the girls' bedroom and was alarmed to see her still in a sleeping position, on her side, but with her eyes wide open. She was staring at the TV but obviously unseeing.

Was she dead? Oh, God, was she dead? Lily's heart lurched in fear. "Can you…can you see to her?" she asked, eyes seeking Hunter's face. "I'll check on the girls."

Hunter looked down at Simmy, fear again highlighting her features. She nodded.

Lily strode to the bedroom door and cautiously opened it. The sounds of the awakening bayou were loud in the room. The window was wide open and its curtains were moving sluggishly in the humid swampy air. The room was empty. The girls were gone, their blankets peeled neatly to the foot of the bed, Birdie's teddy bear, Quantum, perched on the pillows. There was no evidence of a struggle.

"Birdie?" Lily whispered as she moved to the window, hoping they'd just gone for a stroll. She peered out. "Rosemary?" She found herself looking down into the inlet. The girls would have had to swim to leave via the window.

"Birdie," Lily wailed. "Oh, Birdie!"

Hunter and Simmy stepped into the room.

"Rosie?" Simmy questioned in a hoarse voice.

Lily took a deep, calming breath, wondering how she could explain to the elderly woman what had happened. As she studied Simmy's sweet, alarmed features, tears swamped her vision and pain swelled in her heart.

"They're gone?" Hunter said, moving to the window. Lily stepped aside so Hunter could see what she had seen. Hunter's eyes grew wide as she turned her bewildered face to Lily.

"What do you mean gone?" Simmy scoffed. "Ain't no way. I woulda hear them coming past me. They ain't that quiet!"

Lily pushed past Simmy and entered the front room, scanning it for clues. The front door was closed and locked with the security chain still intact, the windows were barely cracked open. They had not gone out either of these ways. Alarm bells clanged in Lily's brain. She thought she knew where they had disappeared to and she had no idea on how to get them back.

Falling into a nearby chair, she wept bitterly, hugging herself and rocking while Simmy rushed to the empty main bathroom, then by Lily to unlock the front door and step out.

"Rosie! Rosemary Deco, you come here this minute, my girl. You won't be worryin' me in such a way!"

Hunter stood in the middle of the room, hands twitching powerlessly at her sides. Lily sobbed as she looked up at her. "Oh, Hunter, they have them. The bastards took our girl."

"I don't...I don't understand," Hunter muttered, lowering slowly to sit on the sofa. "The girls are gone?" She eyed Lily expectantly, hopefully, as though her wife had all the answers or maybe different ones.

# CHAPTER TWENTY-ONE

*Heartbreak*

It took some time before Simmy gave up calling for the girls. She had called for them as she wandered up the road in front of the bait store and then back to the end of the fishing pier. She even studied the surface of the water, as though they'd gone in for a swim and just couldn't get out.

Theo lumbered out of his rooms behind the store when her shouting woke him. Upon hearing the girls were missing, he jumped into his truck and drove the nearby roads searching for them or some evidence that would explain their abrupt disappearance.

Simmy ended up in a chair on the deck, in her pajamas, her curly, disheveled graying hair uncharacteristically unbound. Her face was haggard and awash with silent tears, but Lily could offer no solace.

Hunter stood at the edge of the deck where it met the fishing pier, white-knuckled hands gripping the railing as she stared out across the water. The sun had risen but was still low in the sky, creating intriguing shadows of dark and light across the bald cypress trees that framed the inlet water.

"Someone's done took 'em," Simmy sighed finally. "There's white slavers hereabouts and they done took 'em. They done sold our girls for de money."

She stretched out a hand and clasped it on Lily's arm. "The dream I had. There was an owl. The Natives say they bring death. That they're a bad omen. Oh, God above, don't let our girls be dead."

"No, no," Lily agreed. She pressed her lips together and limped briskly away from Simmy and into the house, ending up in the guest bath. She slammed closed the door and pressed both palms to the ancient glass mirror of the medicine cabinet. "You'd better come to me, you bitch," she snarled at her own face. "Flynn! Flynn!"

Her arms tingled almost immediately and Flynn, as a silver woman, appeared in the mirror.

"Where the fuck are they?" she whispered hoarsely. "I know you know, you alien bitch. What have you allowed to happen to our daughter?"

"Lily, calm down—"

"What! I'm not going to freaking calm down. Birdie is gone!"

"We know," Flynn said. "It had...had to be this way."

Lily laughed in disbelief and pushed her face closer to the mirror. "No, it fucking did not. I want her back now, Flynn, or so help me, I'll..." She broke off, her breathing heavy and fractured.

"Lily. Lily, the girls have a...mission. Our war against the Greys has been...escalating. They have destroyed one of the sister planets that we...built and now threaten your world's very existence and...we cannot allow that to happen. So—"

"So what?" Lily snarled. "You send children, *children*, to deal with those monsters? What the hell?"

"They are women now, Lily. Women...warriors who gather information for the Collective."

"That doesn't matter. Why didn't you send me? You still can. Bring them back and send me. I can gather whatever information you need." She hated the pleading note her voice had taken on. The thought of her Birdie with the aliens was almost more than she could bear.

"They are our...peacekeepers and are linked to us as... communication vessels. You could never...never withstand the energies they are dealing with nor ask the questions that...we need to ask."

Lily wailed once as she dropped her head. "Send me, send me," she whispered.

"Lily," Flynn said calmly but forcefully. "Lily."

Lily lifted her head.

"We will...keep them safe, Lily. Let this happen. Accept. We believe all will...all will be well."

"I...I don't think I can," Lily said, her voice low and filled with pain. "I'm not that strong. What if it's not well? What if they get hurt? What will the bastards do to them?"

A knock sounded at the bathroom door. "Lil, you okay in there?" Hunter queried.

"All will be well," Flynn said as it vanished from the mirror.

Lily pressed her palms harder against the glass. "Flynn! Flynn!" she hissed. It did no good. The IDB was gone.

"Lil? Hon? What's going on?"

Lily dropped her chin to her chest as she fought for control. "Okay, hon. It's okay," she said hoarsely as she dropped to the covered toilet seat.

"I'm coming in, Lil, okay?"

The doorknob turned, and Hunter's beloved but worried face peered around the door. Her brown eyes were swollen and puffy, and Lily knew she'd been crying, too.

Lily rose and moved toward Hunter. She took Hunter's hand and led her back to their bed.

She sighed as they sat side by side. She placed her free hand on top of their clasped hands.

"I'm not supposed to tell you exactly what I do, my love. My position with the US Government is need-to-know."

"Yes, I know that, Lil, and that's always been all right," Hunter said. "But what—"

She squeezed Hunter's hand. "And you know about the Collective, right?"

Hunter looked puzzled. "Well, yeah, I know that you had Birdie because of them. They're like aliens, right? But not like that horrible—"

"No," Lily hastened to reassure Hunter. "They're nothing like the Greys. In fact, the Greys are often a threat to us, and they are held in check by the Collective. Do you remember when we met? At the airport, during the plague?"

"I do," Hunter mused. "The Greys were the ones with the virus, right?"

"Right. And the IDBs, the Collective, gave us the antidote."

"Ahh," Hunter said. "But what's happening now? Did they take the girls?" Anger rose fiercely in her voice.

Lily dropped her head, so she wouldn't have to look at her beloved partner. She nodded. "The Greys did."

Hunter rose and pulled Lily to her feet. "Well, we need to go get them. What do we need to do?"

Lily pulled her hand away. "I just talked to Flynn, to the Collective. There's nothing we can do."

"What do you mean?" Hunter queried angrily. "There has to be something!"

Lily shook her head sorrowfully. "They have made the girls into peacekeepers. They have been given a mission. They are talking to the Greys as emissaries of the Collective. We have to allow this to happen, Hunter."

"But I…but we…" Hunter stammered.

Lily drew Hunter into her arms and wept uncontrollably.

"I was a coward," Hunter hissed suddenly. "I woke up at one point before…I saw light, blue light under the door, but I couldn't, I just couldn't go, go see."

Lily choked back tears and rubbed Hunter's back. "Shh, I understand."

"But if I'd gone in there, if I hadn't been afraid. Maybe I could have prevented this. Scared those little monsters off." She took in a deep, trembling breath.

Lily drew back and swiped at her eyes. She sighed. "It wouldn't have mattered, Hunter. Those little demons are almost unstoppable. Believe me, I know. Humans have little power against them. I mean, come on, they paralyze us in our beds. We're helpless without the Collective looking out for us."

Hunter held Lily's hands tightly. "There has to be something we can do, though. There has to be," she whispered.

"All we can do is wait," Lily said between harsh sobs. She pulled Hunter close again. "All we can do now is wait."

# CHAPTER TWENTY-TWO

## *The Void That is Left*

The girls' disappearance weighed heavily on everyone. A much-subdued Theo kept his business open, but the regular customers crowding the fishing pier annoyed them all as they wallowed in their misery.

Simmy had taken up permanent residence out on the dock. Lily sensed that she was waiting for Rosemary to find her. She was steadfast, only taking bio breaks and bringing tidbits of food and drink back to that chair, that table. Her gaze was vacant and her mien gaunt as she waited for her dear granddaughter to return.

Hunter stayed in bed the morning of the second day after their vanishing. Her head was under the blankets, and she was hugging Birdie's teddy bear, Quantum. Hunter had never laid abed since Lily had known her. Even with a severe cold, she'd always been the first to rise and greet every day.

Lily watched the anglers, their fishing lines barely twitching in the sluggish currents of the bayou, and she wanted to scream at them. None of this was their fault, of course, but the very fact that they were idling away the hours happily fishing when her Birdie was gone, well, it was hard to watch.

She leaned her forearms on the railing and stared mindlessly at a snowy white egret foraging among the high cypress knees. She needed to make some decisions and had no one to turn to for help in making them. Flynn wasn't responding and Hunter was holed away in her own personal hell. She scowled at the distant bird. Should they return home without Birdie? Hunter needed to go back to work, but the ranch could probably survive a while without Lily, especially with Hunter back there. The truth of the matter was, she needed New Mexico, she needed the ranch to help alleviate her pain and grief. Bayou Lisse was beautiful, an undeniable fact, but it wasn't her home. She needed the desert, its ever-cleansing wind and the cry of the coyote at night. She was homesick.

She dropped her head down and shook it sorrowfully. How would Birdie find her when she returned? Would she return to Rosemary's home? Find her way back to Good Neighbor? These new questions made her earlier fear about separating the two girls seem ridiculous. Swamped with grief and indecision, she wept quiet tears of frustration, hot, stinging droplets escaping her cheeks and dampening the front of her T-shirt.

Some unmeasured time later, arms wrapped around her from behind and she recognized Hunter's familiar scent and stance.

"Hello, sweetheart," Lily sighed. The phrase was punctuated by a heavy sob.

"We're going home, Lil," Hunter said. "The girls would want us there."

Lily swiped at her eyes and turned to face her love. "Are you sure? I mean, in your heart? Do you know this?"

Hunter nodded. "Yes. Yes." Her eyes were still swollen, the whites bloodshot and the lids heavy with grief. Lily's heart hurt to see her dear one suffering such sorrow.

Hunter took in a deep, shuddering breath and continued, "The Collective knows where we are at all times. We know this, right?"

Lily nodded and chewed on her bottom lip. "This is true, but what if she comes back here? And we're not here, one of us at least."

Hunter gazed steadily at her. "Will it matter, Lil? At this point? We don't even know if they will come back at all. Or in what form that could be. Suppose they changed again, giving up their human forms."

Lily felt a flash of anger. "Or maybe the bastard Greys have kidnapped and imprisoned them. Suppose they are being tortured, their human sides feeling every little dig, every little cut? Every blow?"

"Shh, shh." Hunter pulled her closer to comfort her. After a moment of silence, she continued. "You know, the people of the plains tell a story about the world flooding in the early days, deluged with miles and miles of water to punish those who spoke too much untruth, those disrespecting Mother Earth and her gifts. Much like the biblical flood for those who had sinned. The waves grew daily, forcing mankind to seek dry land at the highest points they could find. Decades passed as the hungry, starving people watched and waited for the water to recede. Finally, an elder had a vivid dream and she supplied this truth—to return Mother Earth, they had to prove their respect and rescue her. They needed someone to dive and bring back sand and rock so the earth could multiply and return to normal, beating back the water. She called a fire, but no one in any of the family groups volunteered for the task."

Lily sniffed and swiped at her nose. She drew back so she could see Hunter's face as she continued with the tale.

"After a day and a night, a young boy, a brave boy, approached the elders and said that after much soul-searching and dreamwalk, he felt called to do the deed. The people celebrated, presenting the boy with what meager treasures they had left. They carved him an elaborate spear to ward off water monsters. They fashioned a fur loincloth from their own clothing and the dream mother made him a bag for his waist so he could bring back the seeds of earth from under the water. Finally, one bright sunrise, he was ready. The whole of the people gathered at the edge of the water, and they cheered his bravery for this risky endeavor. He'd never felt so loved."

Hunter paused and Lily watched her expectantly. "Well? What happened?"

"He found his way home, of course," Hunter said, trying to smile. "The Earth is whole again thanks to the heroism of this little one."

"So, what does that mean?" Lily asked petulantly.

"It means our girl is a hero. She knew what needed to be done, and she, and Rosemary, are gone to do it."

Lily took in a deep breath and new resolve filled her. "We need to trust. Birdie is exceptional. If anyone can survive the Greys, it is our girl."

Hunter nodded and swept Lily close again. They stayed that way for a long, long time.

# CHAPTER TWENTY-THREE

## *The Poison That Wasn't*

Lily couldn't sleep. She chased it hard, knowing their trip the next day would be long and tiring, but peaceful slumber proved elusive. She finally rose, careful not to wake Hunter, and lifted her clogs and cane from the floor. She passed through the bedroom door and moved through the front room to the locked outside door. Carefully, silently, she disengaged the security chain and turned the lock on the doorknob. Simmy stirred but slumbered on, exhausted by her daily vigil of sorrow.

The door creaked on its hinges, so Lily moved in slow motion, opening it in time with the swelling croaks of the tree frogs outside.

Even though it was the middle of the night, the heat was still unyielding. A good thing as Lily was wearing only sleep shorts and a T-shirt. She eased shut the door and took in a deep breath of the muggy air. She walked quietly to the railing and watched the water swirl with underwater life for some time before slipping on her clogs. She strolled quietly along the railing, one hand trailing along its rough, sun-worn surface. The bumps of the nail heads felt good as they pulled against her palm.

Rounding the store, she stepped across the dirt parking area and onto the asphalt of the country lane, her cane trailing at her side. There were no streetlights here, so she walked along in the dimness of a waxing quarter moon, walking blindly down the center of the road, thoughts of despair roiling within her.

She'd known, since Birdie's birth, that the Collective might reclaim her, but the thought had been a hidden one, buried somewhere deep into her subconscious. It didn't bear thinking. Not back then. Now, though, the day had come, and Lily was heartbroken. How could Flynn, who she'd come to see as a friend, or at least an ally, do this to her? To Hunter. Hunter, who had accepted Lily's unorthodox family completely and without question. Hunter who loved Birdie as much as her own birth mother did.

Tears clouded Lily's vision and she paused to swipe them away. The road dipped close to the water there, and she stepped to its side to peer into the depths, leaning heavily on her cane. Lacy trees on each side dipped night-darkened branches down to kiss against the oddly sparkling water. Studying the branches, she thought how easy it would be to succumb. To just slide into the water and let it carry her away. She could return to nature and be done with missing Birdie. The idea, though appealing in many ways, also terrified her.

Lily wrapped her free arm around herself and wept soundlessly. Wailing would disturb the normal night sounds surrounding her and she had no desire to do that. Tears would have to be enough.

She stood there for some time, trying to find the kernel of steel within her that she could use to fashion new purpose when her whole life had been demolished. She knew the strength was there. She had fostered its growth many times in her life. She took in a deep shuddering breath and dried her tears with the neck of her T-shirt. She'd have to be strong now, for Hunter, for Simmy, and even for Theo. They'd all lost someone important to them and somehow Lily had to help all of them get past it. It was up to her now. She was the strongest. Letting the sluggish, thick water carry her away was a weakness she could not allow.

With new resolve, she turned to walk back to the bait shop. Abruptly, with lightning speed, something solid and heavy slammed into her weaker leg and hung on. Unbalanced, she crashed onto the rocky side of the road, her shoulder erupting with pain as it impacted hard asphalt, rocks, and debris. Panicked, she tried to see what had hit her, immediately thinking alligator. She saw nothing at first but then, looking toward the bayou, she spied a long thin tail disappearing into the water, a cloudy swirl marking its exit.

She painfully pushed herself to a sitting position and watched as a gray-striped snake, with a long body as thick as her forearm, wriggled its way across the water.

"Oh no," she whispered. "Oh no."

She had to get help. Or did she? If she could find a more comfortable place to lie down, like that grassy patch she could see off to her left, well, maybe she could just allow things to happen. She wondered if there would be pain when the venom percolated through her system.

Oddly calm, she examined her calf to see if she could find the injury. Her shoulder screamed in pain every time she moved it. And then she saw it, a darker spot just below her knee. In the dimness, it looked like a bruise, but she felt a gush of fluid— blood or venom—leaking from it when she drew a finger across it.

Would she die? The possibility seemed very real. Did she *want* to die? She didn't know. She really didn't. She thought of Hunter. And of their special relationship. She envisioned Hunter's dark eyes, lovingly studying her. She thought of those eyes, swollen with tears and pain, and she knew suddenly that she could not die. She would not, could not, be the cause of more pain.

With difficulty, she got to her knees and, using her cane to steady herself, rose to her feet. There was no pain from the snake bite, but she was not surprised. Since her exposure to deep-space radiation several years ago, and her subsequent treatment in the hospital, that leg was mostly numb. She felt unsteady and light-headed, however. Was it a result of the venom flowing through her veins or the shock of being attacked? Either way, she needed to get a move on so she could get some help.

Luckily, she hadn't walked too far along the road, and she was able to get back to the bait shop within minutes. Her breathing was ragged and labored, but some sixth sense told her it was from exertion and panic, of course, and not the venom attacking her breathing mechanism. Somehow, she remembered to remove her muddy clogs and leave them outside the door of *Chez* Simmy. Holding her cane up in her hand, she stepped inside silently, opening the door a crack at a time until she could slip through. She closed it, holding the knob and letting it go so it wouldn't click.

In their bedroom, Hunter slept on, unaware of her absence, so she moved to the nearby bathroom, shutting the door before turning on the light. She sat on the toilet and examined her leg. The site of the bite was already bruising but oddly enough, there was no swelling, just bleeding. Gingerly, she wet a cloth and pressed it to the wound, sopping up the blood. Several pellets of gravel fell off and bounced on the tile floor. She sighed and tried to twist her body sideways enough to have a better look. The bite was low down on the outside of her calf, below the knee, not easy to see. She growled in frustration. This was not a good week!

# CHAPTER TWENTY-FOUR

## *The Snake That Bites*

"Lil, hon, you all right?" Hunter asked sleepily, just outside the door.

Lily rose up and leaned to open it. "I'm sorry for waking you, sweetheart. I just couldn't sleep—"

Hunter's eyes widened and she stepped into the room. "What's that on your face? What's—" She looked down and saw the bloody washcloth curled on the floor. Her eyes flew back to Lily's dirt-stained face, and she grabbed her shoulders, causing Lily to cry out in pain.

Hunter leapt back, pulling her arms away. "What the hell?" Her gaze raced across Lily, and she spied the spot on her leg. "Lily? What is that?"

Lily sighed and closed her eyes. "It's from a snake. I was down by the—"

"Holy shit! I'm calling—"

"Hunter. Hunter!" Lily said in a low, steely voice. "Bring me my phone and be quiet, for Pete's sake!"

"But—" Hunter began, but seeing Lily's determination, she moved to the nightstand and unhooked Lily's phone from the charger. She brought it to the bathroom. "Nine one one," she insisted.

Lily flipped through her contacts and found Sophie's number.

"Hey, Sophie, I'm so sorry to wake you. It's Lily."

"Hey. I'm still up. Just delivered a baby. A big old boy. We just got home. Are you okay?" Her voice flattened with concern.

"Well, stupid me went outside and got snakebit," she said sheepishly.

"I'll be right there," Sophie said. Lily could hear her bustling about, Delora's voice in the background. "Was it near the water?"

"Sophie, listen, don't come. I'll go to the hospital if you'll tell me where it is. I just don't want to bother Simmy and Theo. They've had a kinda rough day."

Sophie fell silent and seemed to still. "Lily? I can come over there."

Lily felt Hunter probing her leg around the bite.

"Can we wait 'til daylight? It's just a handful of hours. That's why I called, to see what you thought."

Sophie seemed to be mulling the question. "What does the bite look like? Is it swelling?"

Lily looked down at her leg. "Doesn't seem to be. It's bleeding a lot, though."

"Bleeding. That's a good sign. Is Hunter around?" Sophie's voice lifted in tone as she asked the question.

Lily handed the phone to Hunter.

"Yeah, I think the bleeding is easing some. Just water to clean it so far. No, but let me look."

Hunter handed Lily the phone and lifted her leg so the light would be better. She took the phone back. "Scratches mainly and bruising. I'm sending you a photo. It looks way different than the rattlesnake bites I'm used to. More like a huge garter snake."

Hunter lifted the leg again and used the phone's camera to take a photo. She sent it to Sophie. "Check your text. Do you see it?"

Lily watched Hunter expectantly. The bite was starting to sting a little, so she laid her palm across it. She gingerly took the phone back with her injured arm and spoke to Sophie.

"It was a big, long snake. I saw it go into the—"

"Tell me exactly what happened," Sophie interrupted soothingly. "Where were you?"

"Well, I was having some trouble sleeping," she began, launching into an account of her time outside. Hunter shook her head in disbelief, and Lily caressed Hunter's shoulder as she continued.

"So, it was kinda long, with narrow stripes going across its back? Some reddish, maybe?" Sophie asked when she finished.

"I didn't get a real good look at it. It was dark and it went in the water right away, but I guess you could say that."

"It didn't look like almost solid black? Short, thick body?"

"No. It was long. I'm sure it had some bands across it. I watched as it swam away," she answered.

"And there's not much swelling?"

"It's kinda hard for me to see, where it's at." She tapped Hunter on the arm. "Is it swelling?" she asked her.

Hunter took the phone from her again. "Not much, Soph, though there's a lot of bruising. No, she doesn't seem to be in much pain."

She listened a minute. "Just about three years ago. She was chasing Birdie and slammed into a fence nail. Okay, I will. Eight hours. We'll see you in the morning then."

Hunter disconnected the call, then pulled up the photo she'd taken earlier. She showed it to Lily.

"Yuck," Lily said as she pinched out the photo to make it bigger. "It's oval shaped. What are those scratches below the bite?"

"Okay, see here? See that line of tooth punctures on either side of the oval there? Sophie told me to show you this. She says that if it was a moccasin there would be two pretty big puncture marks, like from a rattlesnake back home, almost no bleeding, and lots of immediate swelling. She says this looks like the bite of a regular Alabama water snake, not the bad kind with venom. The moccasin skin doesn't scratch because they just bite and go. These scratches are from the water snake's scales, because they're known to wrap against you for leverage as they bite."

"So, I'll be okay?" Lily studied Hunter's face, seeking reassurance.

Hunter shrugged. "I believe so. We'll just keep it clean and within eight hours, if there's no swelling, neurological symptoms, or signs of bite site necrosis, we'll know we're in the clear."

Lily absently stroked her sore shoulder. "Well, that's good news. I guess we'll just watch it. So, what was that thing about me chasing Birdie?"

"Tetanus shot," Hunter said, rising. "What's with that shoulder. How did you hurt it?"

"I lost my balance when it bit me," Lily explained.

Hunter probed the shoulder, ignoring Lily's evident pain as she manipulated it. "It's not broken or dislocated. I think you just bruised it. I don't think I'd do too much with it the next few days."

"We should be in a car the next few days," Lily said firmly. "We're still heading home, right?"

"Right, but it depends on how that leg looks. If it gets worse, we're going to the hospital."

Lily yawned, fatigue finally settling in. "I'm glad it doesn't hurt worse."

"Me too," Hunter agreed. "The herpetology course I took in med school told us about this kind of bite. It can seem harmless, but they can get nasty, especially as a lot of the nonvenomous snakes will chew when they bite like this. Some even leave a few of their teeth in the wound. As doctors, we're supposed to dig them out." She grinned at Lily.

Lily drew back, dismayed. "That sounds awful," she said finally.

Hunter dug in her toiletry bag and brought out the tube of antibiotic ointment she always carried with her. She smeared a good layer across the bite mark and scratches. "I don't have any bandages in my bag," she said musingly. "I know Theo has some in the store. We'll grab some when he opens in the morning."

Lily stood and grabbed her cane from the floor. She walked carefully to the bed and placed her suitcase on the counterpane. "Let's get some shuteye," she said quietly. "I'll just prop my leg up on this so we won't mess up the sheets."

Hunter flipped off the bathroom light and crawled onto the bed. She lay next to Lily, holding her hand. They stared at the ceiling, lost in thought and some fear, until sleep finally claimed them.

# CHAPTER TWENTY-FIVE

## *Going Home*

The bite looked much better in the morning, and they were packed and ready to leave shortly after rising. Though it was still early, they found Theo and Simmy sitting silently at one of the small round plastic tables inside the bait store. The scent of coffee warred with that of bait and prepackaged sweet rolls as Lily and Hunter entered through the back door.

Simmy jerked one thumb toward the coffee urn, and Hunter helped herself to a cup as Lily took a seat at the table. She held Simmy's hand in both of hers.

"We're gonna head back," she said.

Simmy nodded. "I knew," she whispered.

"Y'all can't leave," Theo said tonelessly. "They won't come back, you ain't here. I done told Simmy."

Hunter sat and sipped from her cup. "It won't matter, Theo. You know that."

Theo fingered the bill of his worn ball cap. His gaze was distant, his brown features blank, and Lily worried how he was handling the craziness that had infiltrated his life. He didn't respond to Hunter.

"How long will it take?" Simmy asked.

"Well." Hunter rubbed her chin. "I'd say about twenty hours total and we generally stay overnight in a little town west of Dallas."

"Well, I guess I'd better use the bathroom then. Old bladder." She rose and Lily noticed the medium-sized suitcase that had been hidden behind Simmy and Theo.

"You're…I mean—"

"You really think Rosie won't be with BirdBird?" Simmy asked as she strolled toward the restrooms.

Lily stared wide-eyed at Hunter as the front door to the bait shop opened. Sophie came in, stuffing a keychain into the pocket of her jeans. Her frizzy blond mane was tamed today by a red fabric-coated hair tie, and a worn backpack was slung over one shoulder. "Good mornin', all," she said cheerfully.

"Mornin'. Help yourself," Theo said, nodding toward the coffee urn. "There's a box of donuts open."

Sophie ignored the donuts but poured herself a cup of the coffee. "How you feeling, Lily?" she asked as she stirred in two spoons of sugar. She strode across and pulled a chair close to Lily, dropping the backpack to the worn wooden floorboards.

"I'm good," Lily said. "The shoulder hurts worse than the snake bite."

Sophie raised an eyebrow at Hunter.

"She took a tumble when the snake hit her. Lost her balance," Hunter explained. She rose and grabbed a donut from the box using a nearby napkin. "It's not broken or dislocated, so I think she's just got a pretty bad impact bruise," she added, returning to her seat.

"She snakebit?" Theo asked, rising and peering across the table. "I swannee. Is she gwine be all right?"

Sophie nodded at Theo, then frowned at Lily. "You had a helluva night, I'd say. Let me have a look, leg first."

Lily turned and unnecessarily lifted the hem of her shorts so that Sophie could see the bite even as her eyes found Hunter, sweetly begging. Hunter shook her head in amusement, mouth full, and rose to fetch a donut for Lily.

Sophie studied the bite closely. "Yeah, no bad boy here. There are more of the brown-banded water snakes hereabouts than cottonmouths, but I still say you were mighty lucky. What in the world possessed you to be wanderin' around the bayou at night? Even the water peoples are put off doing that. We know better."

Theo rose and shook his head as though exasperated with the city folk. He disappeared into the back.

Simmy came up behind Sophie as she pulled bandages and ointment from her backpack. "Slavers done took our girls. We all torn up about it."

Lily and Hunter stared at Simmy, mouths open in shock at her disclosure. This was going to be hard to explain.

Sophie studied Lily with keen eyes. "What's this about?"

"Well," Lily began, spreading her hands wide. "It's not slavers. We...we think it's espionage. You know, because of the program the girls are in."

"But they've been taken? Kidnapped?" Sophie frowned with worry as she treated, then bandaged Lily's leg.

"Yes, they've gone missing," Hunter explained as Simmy took her seat, head bowed.

Sophie studied them all as if they'd taken leave of their senses. "Well, you've got to call the police! Have you done that?"

"Actually, it's an FBI matter, if they've been taken out of state," Hunter offered.

"Yes, and we're heading north today to see what's what," Lily added firmly.

"I'm going with them," Simmy added as she lifted her coffee cup.

Sophie calmed somewhat, as if glad some action was being taken. "Do you think they're okay?" She sat and took Simmy's hand in hers. "How are you holding up?"

Simmy shrugged and a deep silence fell. It was sad and tinged with confusion.

Finally, Sophie stood and began checking Lily's shoulder. She sighed as she lifted Lily's arm and pressed the tender spots, seeking a disabling injury.

"I think this will be okay," she said, reclaiming her chair. "Just rest it and take acetaminophen every four hours for the pain."

She studied Lily closely. "The FBI will get them back, right? I mean, they'll be okay?" Her voice was hopeful and fearful at the same time.

"We think so," Lily replied reassuringly. "We're just awaiting further information."

"Is there anything we can do?" Sophie asked hopefully. "Anything?"

"No, but thank you. We've searched already and believe we know where they are. We'll let you know when they're returned to us," Hunter answered.

"You do that," Sophie said. She remained sitting in silence a good while, commiserating with them. Helplessness swamped all of them.

Finally, Sophie emptied her cup and glanced at her watch. "I'll need to go check on the Carsen girl, but Lora wanted me to make sure and tell y'all she's sorry she couldn't come with me. She has a class at the community college in Goshen. Test day so she couldn't miss."

"Will you tell her goodbye from us?" Hunter asked. "We're sorry we missed her."

"Have we got a baby yet?" Simmy asked. "That gal was ready to pop. She come by with her granda two weeks ago and I was seriously worried how she was getting' around."

Sophie shook her head as though in disbelief. "Yep, a big ol' ten-pound boy last night. Both doing well."

"That's good news," Simmy said, her mouth still in a grim line.

Sophie sobered and took Simmy's hand in both of hers. "Our Rosie, and Birdie, will come back to us, *Sha*. You ease up about that, okay? You just let us know whatever you need, and we'll make it happen." She eyed Simmy, her eyes radiating anger and power. "You know we will. Anything you need. I mean anything."

Standing, they all hugged Sophie and made their sad farewells.

The three women sat as though shell-shocked after Sophie left.

"Everyone will know now," Hunter said, eyeing Simmy reproachfully.

"Sophie won't tell," Lily offered. "Not about this. She might ask a few questions, certainly keep her eagle eyes open for clues, but no, she won't gossip."

Simmy nodded in agreement. "She's good people."

Lily stood. "Let's load up the car. We've got a long road ahead of us."

# CHAPTER TWENTY-SIX

*Sandy's All You Can Eat Buffet Redux*

Simmy had obviously never strayed far from the bayou. As the landscape changed from thick, verdant southeast to the wide-open plains of Texas, she could barely contain her excitement and wonder. At the motel near Big Spring, Texas, she'd spent most of the evening peering through a slit in the curtains, watching the young urban professionals pass by as they enjoyed their vacay.

"Look at all the dry," Simmy muttered repeatedly from the back seat once they were back on the highway the next morning.

Simmy's wonder fell into the background as Lily worried about Birdie and Rosemary. She sat silent in the passenger seat, floundering in her apprehension and misery. The thought that kept resurfacing, and the one she tried again and again to squelch, was the unfairness of it all. How dare the IDBs take her daughter? Yes, Birdie was half Collective energy, true, evidenced by her off-the-charts intelligence and her ability to mold matter by aging the way she had, but she was also half human. That was what had been betrayed by the energy side of her. It was as though the IDBs discounted her humanity and magnified her Collective half just to suit their own needs.

A rational part of her mind always interfered. She understood, intellectually, why this had happened. It was to protect the Earth and its people. The Greys had already infiltrated enough. Though not known to any but a few at the highest level of the world's governments, they were in the popular news often, with people claiming to have been visited during the night. Claiming to have been abducted and experimented on. Writers had even penned books documenting their own experiences. The little demon spawn was everywhere. And they had tried time and again to hurt the people of Earth.

She stared out the window and remembered what Flynn had told her when she was grieving the most. That the Greys had destroyed another planet that the IDBs had created and seeded. Earth could be next and that was why the IDBs had stepped in. And allowed the Greys to take her daughter.

She shifted angrily, then tried to soothe herself. She knew Birdie, her beloved Aili. The girl had certainly volunteered to serve as a negotiator with the Greys. Though undoubtedly of the Collective she was also, *also*, human and as such would feel loyalty to that half of herself as well.

She thought of Rosemary as she chewed on a thumbnail. She wasn't so sure about *her* motivations. The interactions of the two girls had seemed suspect. Well, if not suspect, certainly a little creepy.

She shook her head in her silent dialogue with herself. This wasn't true, really. Rosemary was a sweetheart. The two of them were, simply, alien, only half human, and when together that alienness was more evident. Especially as their power grew exponentially with their age. That was what she had been picking up on, Lily told herself, reassuringly.

"Look at all the dry," Simmy once again muttered from the back seat.

Lily smiled and caught Hunter's eye.

"How do you s'pose peoples live with no water?" Simmy asked.

"You mean to drink?" Hunter asked, watching Simmy in the rearview mirror. "There's water underground."

"Yep, yep," Simmy said thoughtfully. Her gaze was fixed on the sprawling desert and Lily was amused, watching her amazed expression in the side mirror.

Simmy had spent the first part of the second day using a spray cleaner to clean off the soot from the seat that Birdie had burned when aging. The cleaner and dirty cloth now sat forgotten in her hands as she studied the unfamiliar landscape.

"What do you think of the desert, Simmy?" Lily asked. "Do you think you'll like staying here?"

Simmy looked at the back of Lily's head. "Is y'all's ranch like this? No kidding?"

"Pretty much," Hunter answered. "Maybe even more desert-like."

"Well, how do y'all fetch on peace like this? How do you thoughts come together? I do my woolgathering at the water. Make my decisions."

Hunter shrugged and indicated Lily should have a go at explaining.

Lily shook her head. "You're the Native. You explain it," she said.

Hunter laughed low in her throat, and it was a welcome sound. Lily hadn't heard that sweet sound since the girls had disappeared.

"Okay," Hunter began with a sigh. "You know how the water in the bayou is crowded by trees? Well, to me it's limited. The whole East Coast seems limited by the trees. Visibility wise, I mean. Your roads were made from animal tracks through the forest and mostly still are. Even the big highways are bordered by trees and bushes. The West on the other hand doesn't have the limitation of trees, only mountain ranges or old lava flows that we call mesas. We can pretty much see forever, miles and miles away. Like an ocean."

"Oh," Simmy said, her voice filled with awe.

"Yeah, so you see, when we look out across the desert, that's kind of our water. We have movement, just like water, by the constant wind and a shifting sandy environment."

"I think I understand," Simmy said.

Lily could see her nodding expressively in the side mirror.

"I think we should grab a bite to eat," Hunter said. "That motel continental breakfast just didn't last long enough."

As they pulled once more into the parking lot of Sandy's All You Can Eat Buffet, Lily felt a keen sense of loss, remembering their earlier trek with Birdie, when she was still a little girl. Her eyes sought Hunter's, their sorrow commingled in a shared glance.

Simmy's eyes were like saucers as she took in every detail of the enormous, busy room. She clutched her crocheted handbag close to her chest and seemed to shrink into herself as she followed Hunter to a polished wooden table.

"Lorry, would you look at all that food," she muttered eyeing the buffet. "Who's gwine eat all that food?"

Hunter chuckled. "You are, my dear. Or at least as much as you can stuff yourself with."

Her eyes seemed to grow even bigger.

A young waitress came to them and, without even looking at the menu, Hunter ordered three buffets. She and Lily ordered iced teas, but Simmy asked for coffee and a glass of water.

At the buffet, Lily pointed out some choice dishes to Simmy. There was an Italian section that didn't seem to interest the older woman, but when she found pinto beans and cornbread, she seemed excited. Lily handed her a bowl and a plate. "There's beef over there and they'll carve you off a piece," she said. "All you have to do is ask. There's also baked and fried chicken, some roast beef. Just about anything you could want. I'm going after those green beans and boiled potatoes."

"Lorry," Simmy muttered, as her gaze roamed across the offerings.

Hunter came by Simmy, her plate loaded with carrots, potatoes, asparagus, beans and a pile of puffy rolls. "Reckon these rolls are good as Clary's?" she teased.

Simmy eyed the plate doubtfully.

"Guess you'll find out fo' sure," she replied, hurrying off to find the bread section.

Lily experienced great joy watching as Simmy thrilled to each new taste sensation. She demolished the cornbread and butter, then, at Hunter's urging, went back for seconds.

"I can't believe they just let people go on up there and eat like they got no sense," Simmy said finally. "Looka that man. I done seed him go up there four times already."

Hunter glanced in that direction. "Well, he is a big guy and you know what they say about Texas."

Simmy looked at her and shook her head.

"Everything's bigger in Texas," Lily offered. "It's kind of a slogan."

When the trio made it to the dessert section, Lily thought Simmy was going to have a stroke and travel right on up to heaven. She smacked her lips and stealthily took one of each of the smaller desserts, placing them on a plate of apple pie, smooshing them close. Lily, smiling indulgently, passed a plate full of dark chocolate cake to her and watched her amazement as she stared disbelievingly at it.

Once back at the table, Simmy savored every bite as Hunter and Lily ate their own dessert slowly so they could enjoy every bite along with her.

When the server came with the bill, Simmy dutifully reached into her bag and pulled out a ragged change purse.

"Your money's no good here, Miss Simmy," Lily said. "Put your wallet away."

"Here now," she protested, opening the purse and revealing a mass of crumpled bills. "Surely you don't expect to pay for my food. Had to be a pretty penny for all that."

Hunter leaned across and snapped the purse closed. She laid her credit card on the tray and shoved it to the edge of the table. "You put us up, remember? Fed us all for days. That's all I'll say about it."

Simmy's face acknowledged Hunter's firm tone, and she slid the change purse back into the depths of her bag and silently sipped the last of her coffee.

"I can't thank y'all enough," she said when they got back into the car. She rubbed her flat stomach. "I just can't thank y'all enough. That sure was some good eating."

Lily smiled tremulously at Hunter. She was suddenly very glad that Simmy was with them. It made things easier somehow.

# CHAPTER TWENTY-SEVEN

*Good Neighbor*

It was creeping onto dusk when they finally arrived at Good Neighbor Ranch. Sage met them at the door, holding it wide as Lanny and Hunter carried the luggage in. SaySay was surprised by Simmy's presence but welcomed her graciously as the introductions were made. Her gaze searched for Birdie.

Lily hadn't figured out yet how she was going to tell the ranch crew what had happened. As Lanny opened the back door of the SUV, he too looked for Birdie. His rough, weather-worn hand drifted questioningly across the scorched back seat. He looked to the house, and Lily, who'd been watching from the porch, simply turned and walked inside, not ready to deal. Sage came from checking the guest room and welcomed Simmy into it. Lily could hear Simmy muttering about how nice the room was, as well as being spoiled by having her own bathroom.

Sage emerged from the guest room and motioned for Lily and Hunter to follow her into the kitchen. When they entered, she was already sitting at the kitchen table awaiting the powwow that was certain to happen.

Hunter sighed and took a seat next to SaySay, as did Lily.

"Well?" Sage questioned. "The trip was good?"

Lily decided not to lie. "Birdie and Simmy's granddaughter, Rosemary, aren't with us."

Sage leaned forward. "I see," she said. "When do you plan for them to come back home?"

"They'll be back soon," Hunter said firmly. "That's why we came back here now. To wait for them."

Lily nodded. "Yes. We're not sure how long it will take for them to return."

Sage looked puzzled. "But Birdie is a child. Are they with someone? To look out for her, for them?"

Lily nodded and went for the sin of omission. "Yes, with a good friend who's taking excellent care of them."

"Yes," Hunter agreed. "It's all good so no need to worry, okay?" She took Sage's hand and patted it reassuringly.

Simmy peeked around the kitchen doorframe. "Can I come on in there?" she asked.

"Of course," Lily said, rising and pulling out a chair. Simmy lowered herself into the seat with a heavy sigh. "That's a mighty fine bedroom y'all are letting me use," she said. "And thank you, Miss Sage, for that nice soft blanket you put at the bottom of the bed."

"Nights can get cold here in the desert," Sage explained. "You're from Alabama then? It's warm there all year?"

"Pretty much," Simmy said, and she started telling Sage about her home on the Bayou Lisse.

Hunter caught Lily's eye, and they both took in a deep breath of relief that Sage had, at least for now, accepted their story about the girls' not being with them.

Simmy's descriptions of her life on the bayou fascinated Lily, even though she'd been there for several days. It was evident how much she loved living there and how the ever-moving inlet behind her home was her personal North Star. Lily pressed her lips together and vowed to get Simmy, and her Rosemary, home as quickly as possible. If the Collective would cooperate. Or the Greys, she amended.

"That sounds so beautiful," Sage said. "I can't imagine so much water on all sides. The fishing is good?"

"You never seen the like," Simmy asserted. "We get de crawdad, de crab, de catfish, beautiful big ol' trout, and even de flounder. Most catched off our own pier at Theo's bait shop."

Sage smiled. "When I was a little girl, my *N'ai* would take me and my brothers fishing at the little Acoma Lake. We'd catch trout and one time my brother, Chewie, got a twenty-five incher. Sometimes we'd get smaller browns, or maybe a catfish near the junction. Every now and then, we'd get one of those hard to clean muskie fish."

"Don't I know it," Simmy agreed. "Ever now and then someone reel in a big one but cleaning and fileting dat beast, even dem real big ones, was a chore for sure."

Though enjoying the fishing tales, Lily knew she had to check in with Lanny. After eyeing Hunter and nodding toward Simmy, a silent message to watch what was said, she excused herself and made her way outside, cane tapping slowly along the long main hallway.

The sun was low, so she didn't bother with a hat, and she paused outside to revel in the scouring wind coming off the plains. She stood in the front yard for several minutes, eyes closed to the wind, heartily glad to be home. If only Birdie could be there with her, her happiness would be complete.

Rounding the front porch, she saw Lanny sitting in an old, weathered rocker near the firepit located between the house and the bunkhouse. Click was sitting next to him, enjoying a late day cigarette. She crossed to them and sat in an empty ladderback chair next to her ranch foreman and dear friend. Silence shrouded the three of them for many minutes.

"Are you going to start a fire?" Lily asked finally. She lifted a charred limb and tossed it into the middle of the sad, cold firepit.

"Do you want me to?" Lanny countered, turning his upper body to squint at her.

"No, not really. It's warm tonight," she responded.

Click sighed. "Are you gonna tell her or you want me to?" he asked Lanny, glancing at the older ranch hand.

"Go ahead," Lanny responded, sitting back in his chair and rocking slowly.

"What? What's wrong," Lily asked, alarm in her voice. "Is everyone okay?"

"Sure, sure," Lanny soothed with a wave of his hand.

"Someone's been causing trouble," Click explained.

Lily chewed this thoroughly, imagination running wild. "Okay, what do you mean? What kind of trouble?"

Click gestured toward Lanny, then flicked his cigarette into the firepit.

"Someone broke into the bunkhouse. Took Margie's gold and diamond bracelet she got for Christmas," Lanny said with a deep sigh.

Lily recoiled. "Who would do such a thing? Have you seen any outsiders?"

"I saw a woman a ways away. She had dark hair," Click said excitely. "I bet she was the one who left the east gate open, too."

Lily looked at Lanny. "East gate?"

"I shut it tight, but it was open next morning. A handful of cows got out and we had to round them up." He seemed engrossed in the denim covering his left knee.

"Don't forget the water," Click said urgently.

"No need to dump this on her now. She just got home," Lanny said in a mild reprimand.

"She needs to know," Click countered. "Who knows what mischief could happen tonight?"

"The water?" Lily prompted.

"Someone drained two of the water troughs. Just opened the tap and let them drain away."

"Man, I was hoppin' mad," Click added. "We can't waste like that here in the desert."

Lily stared thoughtfully out across her land. "Have they been filled back up? The cows all right?"

Lanny nodded.

"So, y'all haven't seen any cars or trucks that don't belong? Right?"

Lanny and Click nodded.

"We been lookin' though," Click said.

Lily took in a deep breath. "The way I see it is, we've got two thousand-some acres here. This woman, or whoever, has to be parking a vehicle somewhere. Lanny, let's back off the normal stuff, beyond animal care, of course, and get all the workers out looking for this person. All day every day, until he or she is found, patrol the fence lines." She rose and studied both their worried faces. "And look out for one another. We don't know how dangerous this person could be."

Lily was swamped with concern as she strode slowly back to the ranch house. How could something like this be happening at Good Neighbor? She needed to share this information with Hunter and see if she had any ideas on how best to move forward.

# CHAPTER TWENTY-EIGHT

## *One More Chance*

Hunter was clearly disturbed about the ranch sabotage when Lily shared the information after Simmy was settled and they were in bed that night.

"That's ridiculous," she said harshly. "Everyone here knows us, knows the ranch. We have a good reputation and we're good to our folk and to our neighbors. It makes no sense that someone would want to do us harm."

"I know," Lily agreed with a sigh. She turned on her side and studied her partner's confused face. "The main issue is how we are going to fix it."

"I don't know, Lil. We got the girls gone, and I need to go back to the hospital tomorrow...I think I'm just tapped out." Her voice carried the burden of sorrow. "Why now, of all times?"

Lily had no answers, so she simply lay quietly. She wondered who, in their immediate circle of friends and acquaintances, would bear them ill will. She knew there'd been no bad deals or bad faith, no arguments. Her mind strayed to the Greys, of course. It would be just like them to cause trouble, even in this limited fashion. For many years they'd found mutilated cattle on the ranch, even a dissected stray dog once. They'd been butchered in odd, no, bizarre ways, genitalia removed, eyes taken, even flaps of skin from the jaws and haunches surgically removed. The meat had been left, so it hadn't been done by poachers. Lily would have preferred that, actually. This wasteful flaying and removal of parts was creepy, somehow, experimental in nature. Seeing them had haunted her dreams. She knew that the Greys had been responsible, a fact firmed up by web searches and her own research.

Perhaps this was why the mirror outposts had been set up. So the IDBs could watch and monitor the Greys' presence on the ranch. The thought of those smarmy little creatures roaming her land caused anger to flare and she shuddered helplessly.

"You okay, Lil?" Hunter asked. She yawned deeply.

"I'm good, baby. I think I'm going to update some of the books. I don't think I can sleep. Maybe working on those dull spreadsheets will make me sleepy."

"And maybe you'll have some fresh subconscious ideas on what to do about the girls and about the intruder, if you take your mind off those things for a while."

Lily patted Hunter's hip. "Sleep well. I'll be back soon."

Once in her office, Lily seated herself and glared at the crystal statue on her desk. She spent a good five minutes wallowing in her anger before storing it away and reaching to caress the crystal.

Flynn appeared surprisingly quickly. Today, the IDB wore the guise of a small boy, one Lily had seen several years ago, before Flynn had first spoken to her.

"You're cute, I'll give you that," Lily said sullenly. "Are you trying to torture me? A child? Really?"

Flynn manufactured a chair, and by the time it sat down, it had become the silver woman Lily was more comfortable with.

"How are the girls?" Lily asked, her voice quavering.

"They are…being held, but the…talks go well," it replied.

"How…how much longer, Flynn?" Lily's voice was a sad whisper.

"We cannot know. Coming to an...agreement has taken... longer than expected."

Lily sat up straighter and spoke with a more businesslike mien. "The humans here are questioning their absence. This needs to be dealt with."

Flynn cocked its head to one side, silver eyes calm. The attitude angered Lily anew. "You've done well. The story is... believed."

Lily nodded. "True, but we need them back as soon as possible. They are too young—"

"Lily. They are older...than time itself. They are ageless as...are we."

"But not their human bodies. Their human bodies, Flynn."

Lily rose and moved to the window, but she did not open the blinds.

"We...we fill those bodies, Lily, and they...become us."

"I think I understand that. But knowing it doesn't make it hurt less." She turned back to Flynn. "Why did you give them to us? If you were going to take them away?"

"There was no...giving, Lily. The children...across the Earth, are random...occurrences. There is no...rule for us. We are the...fabric of your universe. You are here because we are here."

Unreasonable anger sparked in Lily. "Is that some kind of threat?"

Flynn looked bewildered. "You need to calm, Lily." It tilted its head, communicating with the Collective. "Human bonds... are amazingly strong."

Lily blinked, struck suddenly by the alienness of the Collective. "Look, we have a new issue—"

Flynn nodded. "Ah, the woman."

Lily regained her seat and leaned forward across the desk. "Who is she? What does she want?"

"It is being...discovered."

"Discovered? What does that mean?"

"We...spied her days ago. Then there is a dark gray... vehicle, car. We are checking the...numbers there to see who she is."

"The license plate?"

Flynn conferred with home base, then nodded. "Yes."

"When will you know? Hasn't it been enough time? She's doing some serious damage here." Lily hoped her exasperation with the IDBs wasn't evident in her tone. She was the Liaison for the United States of America. She needed to remain in control and be reasonable, even though her aching heart was filled with unreasonable emotion.

"Time is...different for us. It will be in a...suitable time span."

Lily was close to losing it and felt ashamed. These creatures were not human. She began a soothing mental mantra *not human, not human, not human* to see if it would calm her.

Flynn tilted its head again, probably confused by what it was picking up in Lily's thoughts. "There may be a...war," it said quietly.

"A war? Here, on Earth?" Lily was jolted back to a nonemotional reality.

Flynn nodded slowly and took in a deep, almost human breath. "You will need to inform your leadership that, if... détente cannot be reached, the Greys will begin to...harm the people and...places of Earth. It may...happen soon."

Heat suffused Lily and she was terrified. "No. That just can't happen."

Silence fell for a couple of minutes.

"Wait! Why can't the Collective just destroy the little bastards?"

"We will, after one more...chance."

"Why? Why another chance? They killed millions with the plague, including my mother. And didn't you say that they destroyed a world you made? How can you tolerate all that without striking back?" Lily quaked at questioning the Collective, but she was on a roll and couldn't seem to stop.

"Compassion is the one worthy human...emotion that we've adopted from your free will, Lily. Anger has been...dismissed, unreasonable fear...hysteria...disappointment. These are emotions you have...bred within the human mind. We give them...one more...chance because we can."

"Will you protect us? Earth?" Her voice sounded small and fearful, but she couldn't help it.

Flynn nodded, blinking its silver-orb eyes. "We are bound to Earth. You are our…protectorate. Other outposts of Collective have theirs. When the time is…right, the Greys will see little…mercy. Even their creators will destroy their worlds with little…compassion. Sleep tonight, Lily. Know all is…well."

Lily nodded and yawned helplessly. "So, you will let me know who the woman is?"

Flynn nodded slowly.

"One more thing. Please contact Birdie and Rosemary. Tell them of…" She paused and took in a deep, shuddering breath. "Tell them we love them and that we all, Simmy, too, are here at the ranch, waiting for them to come home."

"It will be done," Flynn replied.

# CHAPTER TWENTY-NINE

## *And the Days Passed*

Lily spent an agonizing time in the office the next morning, conveying the information Flynn had shared. Colonel Alan Collins, Uncally, was not happy with the possibility of war or with the person who was snooping around the ranch.

"You'll need to tell me who it is once you find out," he ordered.

Lily studied his dear face on the computer screen and was swamped with the magnitude of the job she'd taken on so many years ago. "You know I will, Uncally. But what about the threat of war? Isn't that more important? What should we do?"

"You mean, like nothing?" Uncally asked sarcastically. "We have no control about that. When the Collective tells us what we need to do, we'll do it. As of now we just have to cross the first bridge we come to. Having some random stranger on the ranch is dangerous. We are need-to-know and that person doesn't need to know anything, savvy?"

"Savvy," Lily agreed automatically, eyes downcast.

Silence fell and she looked up to see Uncally watching her with sad eyes. "I know this is hard, Little Lil, especially with

Birdie gone. And I know we're asking a lot of you. I wish Flynn hadn't chosen your father and then later, you. I wish it could have been someone else. Someone I didn't give a damn about. It's fallen into your lap, however, and I would like to say, as someone who has known you all your life, you are frickin' tough as nails, Lily. You got this and the US gov'ment has complete faith in your abilities. I wish you could have heard the POTUS going on about how cool you were, how smart."

Lily tried to smile. "I don't feel very cool or very smart right now. But I know I have to pull up my big girl panties and just deal as best I can. There's a lot riding on me, a lot of people depending on me to inform them and keep them safe. And I will." She stiffened her jaw and her back. "I will."

"That's my girl," Uncally said. "I'm signing off now, but you know I'm always a call away. And a military transport can have me there in no time. Just call or text me."

"I will, I promise," Lily said, squaring her shoulders.

Hearing a ruckus in the front hallway, Lily quickly lowered the screen into her desktop, then opened the office door to peer down the hallway. Lanny stood there, hat in hand, talking animatedly to Sage.

"It's damned hemlock," he was saying.

Lily hurried to his side. "What's happened?"

Lanny took a deep calming breath. "We found hemlock spread along the west fence."

"Wait, we check the pastures every year, I thought." She frowned at Lanny, then at Sage.

"Someone *did* it," Sage said quietly.

"You mean—?"

Lanny nodded, his eyes sad. "Lunan found it, piled up in one area in the west feedlot. I got all the guys walking the fences now, looking for more."

"It was brought there, deliberately?" She was appalled. Any rancher knew to keep the pasture lands free of hemlocks and lupine-type plants. These and many other desert plants were harmful to sometimes not-too-bright, but ever-hungry cattle, which were generally kept penned in safe ranges as a result.

Feed lots and pasture lands were regularly checked for those plants.

"Margie and me are going to clean up the poison, so we can feed them this evening," Sage added.

"Wear gloves. There's extra pairs in the bunkhouse. I'll come help. Lanny, let me know what the boys find, will you?"

He nodded and, clapping his hat on his head, strode out the front door and across the wide wooden porch.

"I'm going to tell Simmy to come back to the house and then get my boots. Meet you in the lot," Sage said, following Lanny out the door.

Lily suddenly felt very alone. She glanced down the hall of the empty house and tried to remember how it had been when filled with her father's booming voice and her mother's laughter. She was missing them so much right now. She could have used their guidance but, more than that, their company and their comfort.

Margie was already in the west feedlot when Lily switched off the four-wheeler and dismounted.

"Hey, boss," Margie called, straightening her back and using the back of her gloved hand to swipe at her brow. She watched Lily approach. "You know, it takes a mighty disturbed person to want to kill stupid old cows," she said.

Lily looked around at the piles of pointy greenery and the delicate lacy white flowers and wondered where the saboteur had found so much of the stuff. The toxins in the weed could paralyze a cow, from feet to head, until it became unable to breathe and died.

"She must have roamed a good way to find it," Lily responded as she donned her work gloves.

Margie handed a huge black trash bag to Lily, then bent back to her task. "I just hope the devil was bare-handed," she said. "He deserves to get sick from it, not those poor old cows."

Sage arrived, dropped off by Click in his faded blue pickup. He waved as he pulled away, and Lily waved back.

Sage had donned her heavy rubber boots, and she pulled on work gloves as she approached in her jeans and button-down shirt. She paused and shook her head at the tumbled row of wilted poisonous plants running along the fence line.

"Simmy all right?" Lily asked as she got close.

"I told her to lock the doors, just in case," she replied, accepting a trash bag from Margie. She got to work, bagging the noxious weed.

After about a half hour of the hot, sweaty work, they were joined by Edgar Munoz, one of the ranch hands.

"Are the other fences okay?" Lily asked him.

"Click and Lanny are still on the back lots, but the front lots were okay. Felix is still locking those lots up after we drove the cows in them," he responded, flattening out the wide brim of his hat and lowering his backpack to the ground.

"So, no cows were affected?" Lily asked. She accepted the bottle of water Ed passed her and passed it on to Margie. Ed handed one to Sage and then another to Lily.

"Not as we can tell," he responded. "Lanny said something about getting Doc Marsel out to observe, but that'd be a big job. I dunno." He looked at Lily as though seeking confirmation.

She shook her head slowly. "No, you guys would be able to tell. They'd be stumbling by this point."

"And they hadn't put them in the feedlot yet," Margie pointed out. She took a deep drink of water. "I guess the scoundrel was hoping you guys would move them in without checking."

Lily nodded. "We gotta find out who's doing this crap. You guys have any ideas?"

She was answered with heads shaken in the negative.

"Just makes no sense," Sage said, tucking her bottle of water in her pocket and reaching for another clump of weed.

# CHAPTER THIRTY

*Cleo*

Their late dinner was microwave lasagna, a frozen tray taken from the deep freeze, and a hastily composed salad. Lily could tell Sage was exhausted, as was she, so she pitched in alongside Hunter and Simmy to help Sage prepare the simple meal. The five of them sat silently after filling their plates, as though recovering from an illness and still too weak to eat.

Hunter sliced off a bite of lasagna but left it on her plate as she stared at the large landscape painting that adorned the opposite wall of the dining room. New worry had etched lines into her brow.

"We checked all the pastureland, crisscrossed it just to make sure," Lanny said finally.

"Thank you," Lily said with a deep sigh. "I can't even believe this is happening. If the calves had still been nursing and the dams had eaten it, it would have wiped out next year's herd growth."

"None did, near as we can tell," Lanny said.

"Thank goodness y'all caught it before feeding," Simmy said. "Got lucky."

"The eastern lot wasn't done like that, but I still got Ed and Eddie staying with them while they eat this evening. Lunan and Click are watching in the west lot. Y'all did a good job cleaning it all away. We fed them nearer the fence on the other side, but I didn't see a single leaf left where it had been," Lanny said. He finally took a bite of his cooling lasagna.

Sage just nodded as she chewed. She must have been hungry as her plate was almost empty. Her deep brown eyes looked troubled, though.

After helping clean up from the meal, Hunter and Simmy retired to the front room to watch TV and Lily went into her office. She sat at the desk a long time, too dispirited to call Uncally and tell him about this new bit of trouble. The idea that someone, somewhere hated her enough to try and kill her cattle was disheartening. Wracking her brain for an identity, or even a reason, did little good.

A light flashed across her and she turned to see the communication crystal glowing rhythmically. She immediately laid her hand upon one of the curvy planes of the statue. Flynn, as a woman, appeared within the crystal but didn't venture into the room. "Hey, Flynn, how are the girls?"

Flynn screwed up its mouth. "They are well. I have the name of the…woman for you."

Lily sat up straighter. "Who is it? Do I know her?"

"Her name is Cleo, Cleo Nilsson." It waited expectantly for Lily's reaction.

"I don't know any Cleo Nil—" Her heart lurched in her chest. A flashback flooded her mind. She was once again in the metal box, sweating in the heat of a desert day. A man in uniform was sneering at her, surrounded by the shorter pale forms of the alien Greys.

"The major," Lily gasped. She stared at Flynn, who nodded in response. "Has he been put to death?"

"No," Flynn said. "He has been sentenced to death for… treason…but it has not happened yet."

"So why is she here? Why is she doing this?" She pulled on her bottom lip, thoughtfully. "I need to talk to her."

Silence fell as Lily pondered her next move.

"You cannot," Flynn said finally. "She cannot know of our existence."

"So, she doesn't know what her husband did, helping the Greys kidnap me and hold me prisoner."

"No, she does not know the…exact nature of the treason, just…crimes against the nation."

"I guess she blames me for her husband's sentence. How did she find out I was involved, I wonder? She shouldn't have access to the statements I turned in."

"He told her," Flynn said.

Lily studied Flynn's visage through the crystal. "So, are you sure she doesn't know about the Greys? About you?"

Flynn's image flickered and Lily knew the IDB was being called away. "No, just you," Flynn said as it faded. "She is… dangerous. We will protect."

Lily was not happy. She stared at the now quiet crystal statue for some time, mulling the reasons for Cleo's attacks on Good Neighbor. The idea struck her as ludicrous. Major Leon Nilsson had been a middle-aged career military man drawn to the dark side by the promise of prestige and power. That meant his wife was probably middle-aged as well. Lily just could not imagine a woman of that age doing the things she'd been doing. She wished suddenly that she'd had more time to ask Flynn how they had ascertained that it was truly her. Suppose it was someone else using her car? There was so much to think about. She grasped her head in her hands, frustrated.

As it was so late, especially on the East Coast, she texted this new information to Uncally, adding that she was off to bed but he could call her in the morning.

She rose and turned off the light, then headed down the hall to their bedroom. Hunter was already abed and slumbering on. Lily envied her the peace of mind that allowed that slumber.

Flynn's comment that Cleo was dangerous kept circling in Lily's mind like some *Jaws*-sized shark. She found it hard to believe, but if the woman had indeed been working so hard trying to destroy the Good Neighbor cattle, who knew what else she might do?

Sighing deeply, Lily carefully crawled into bed next to Hunter and spooned her warm, slumbering form close, seeking comfort. Her thoughts wandered as always to how her precious Birdie was holding up. She tried not to think about it, instead begging for sleep.

The next morning Lily woke with new purpose. She told Hunter who the saboteur was without going into too much detail. Then, after breakfast and seeing Hunter off to work, Lily grabbed her cane and went to the bunkhouse, seeking Lanny. The long, low building seemed deserted, so she paused at Margie's office door and peeked inside.

"Hey, Margie, have you seen Lanny this morning?"

Margie was sipping her morning smoothie through a straw and choked on it when Lily spoke. Lily hurried to pat her on the back and take the smoothie from her hand before it spilled.

"Omigosh! Are you okay? I didn't mean to scare you."

Margie regained her composure and cleared her throat, her wide, brown face flushed. "Yeah, yeah, I'm good. I shoulda heard you come in, but I was tryin' to figure out this email. Is it for me?"

"Email? Who's it from?" She moved around to see Margie's computer screen.

The email was from lifestole32@hotmail.com, and the message was clear. *You'll pay, bitch.*

Lily stumbled backward, rocked by the venom of the message.

"Lily? What's—"

"It's not for you," Lily muttered. "Do you know where Lanny is?"

"Sure. Him and Lunan went to check on the herd in westside pasture. Is everything okay?"

"It will be," Lily said through gritted teeth. She briefly greeted Simmy, who was coming for her morning visit with Margie, and hurried outside where she mounted the remaining four-wheeler. She gunned the engine and raced westward.

# CHAPTER THIRTY-ONE

## *A Shot Rang Out*

The west pasture at Good Neighbor Ranch was one of the biggest. As such, it required a lot of maintenance so the road leading to it was well trodden and Lily could relax and let her thoughts wander as she traversed it. She needed to tell Lanny who Cleo was. He, of course, knew very little about the kidnapping, but she would say that it had something to do with her government job and that should satisfy him. She was truly blessed having Sage and Lanny as her immediate family. Whether from their Native American way of thinking or their own personalities, they were always accepting and understanding. Either way, Cleo might just be the significant threat that Flynn had implied she was, and Lanny needed to know that.

She came to a trio of vehicles parked by the main entry gate. Lunan, loading an orange cooler of ice water onto the back of his four-wheeler, spied Lily and his mustachioed face broke into a wide smile, lighting up his leathery, tanned face.

"Miss Lily, you come to see us," he said raising one arm in a welcoming wave.

Lily couldn't help but return the enthusiastic greeting. She swung off the four-wheeler and limped toward the worker. "Hey, Lu, do you know where Lanny is? Maybe you could give me a—"

A shot rang out and Lily felt the force of the bullet as it grazed her shoulder. Spinning from the impact, she saw Lunan turn his horrified face toward the mountain range just behind Lily's huge observation boulder. He reached a protective arm toward Lily. Stunned, she stepped toward him. Another shot fractured the quiet and she watched the projectile slam into his extended forearm. Heart pumping a staccato beat, Lily grabbed Lunan and pulled him to the ground. She rolled to her side so she could peer in the direction of the mountain range. It was too far away to see anything clearly.

Lunan was writhing in pain. After hurriedly studying him, Lily reached up and grabbed the collar of his worn T-shirt right in the middle. With a mighty jerk, she pulled, ripping the cotton material off in a long strip. Gaze roving across the landscape, hoping to stay hidden, she used the material to bind the through-and-through hole in Lunan's forearm. Blood coated her fingers as she pulled the bandage tight.

"St…stay down," she rasped. She looked toward the closest four-wheeler and wondered if they could make it. Even if they did, they'd be sitting targets for the shooter. She looked back at Lunan's ashen face. His lips were trembling from the shock. She had to get him some help.

To her immense relief, she spotted Lanny crouching behind a large juniper bush, just outside the now partly open gate. Looking toward where the shots had come from, he dropped to his belly and began a speedy military crawl toward them.

He was out of breath by the time he reached their side. Gasping for air, he laid a comforting hand on Lunan as he peered toward the rocky range. "There!" he said suddenly, pointing.

Lily followed the direction he was indicating and saw a far-off shadow figure, arm elongated by a rifle barrel, clambering down off the rocks.

Lily reached into her pocket for her cell and hurriedly rang Hunter's direct line. She answered almost immediately, but Lily could hear voices conversing in the busy hospital background.

"Lil, what's wrong?" she asked urgently.

"Ambulance, right now. Lunan's been shot. We're in the west pasture." She hung up, trusting that Hunter would respond immediately. Eyeing the range, she scooted herself toward Lunan and laid her upper body across his chest in an effort to keep him warm until help got there.

"Miss Lil, you're bleeding all over him," Lanny said loudly. "You shot?" He grasped at her shirt, trying to see if there was a chest wound. Finally spying the slice on her upper arm, he rolled up the long sleeve of her button-down shirt to put some pressure on it. He held it in place as he scanned the expansive lands around them.

"Who's doing this, Lily?" He studied her face, his gaze harsh and unyielding.

Lily's arm was really stinging so she pressed one hand atop his as she answered, "It's from the job, Lanny. Someone has a vendetta against us. Against me. Her husband got in some serious trouble with the government and she's not happy about it. Blames me."

"Shit," Lanny said, shaking his head. "This world's full of crazy people."

Lily nodded in agreement and rested her forehead on her forearm, willing her heart to slow down just a bit. She took in a deep breath filled with the scent of greenery and dirt. And blood.

"It's all right, Lu," Lanny was saying, his strong hand patting Lunan's unwounded arm. "Help's coming."

Lily lifted her eyes, propping her chin on her forearm. She noted that some color had returned to Lunan's face. He was watching her with his dark, expressive eyes. "You okay, Miss Lily?" he whispered. "You wasn't hit again, was you?"

Lily shook her head in the negative, even as tears rose in her eyes. "I'm all right, Lu, I'm all right."

"Help's comin', Lu," Lanny said again. "Help's comin'."

Lunan nodded and closed his eyes.

Hunter was, of course, with the ambulance when it arrived. She rushed to her wife and quickly treated her flesh wound. "What the hell, Lily?" she scolded as she cleaned the wound with peroxide and then iodine. "I can't leave you alone ever again. You either get bit by a snake or…" A huge sob shook her, and she looked away for a brief moment. "Or get shot at!"

Lily studied Hunter's dear, sweet face as it frowned in concentration and sought control. "I love you, Hunter," she whispered.

"You all right, ma'am?" a paramedic asked as he came close. "We're taking your friend to the hospital. Maybe you should ride along? Get checked out?"

"She's going to need stitches, Jimmy. The bullet grazed her upper arm." Hunter and Jimmy helped Lily get to her feet and onto the second stretcher in the back of the ambulance. Lunan had already been loaded and, ever ready, they already had an oxygen feed on him. He smiled at Lily and gestured a thumbs-up with his uninjured arm.

Lily nodded at Lunan but grabbed the lapel of Hunter's shirt. "Watch out for everyone, for Simmy. Cleo shot us and she might hurt some of the others."

Hunter told Jimmy to wait a bit and then hopped out the back of the ambulance. Lily saw her talking with Lanny as their gazes scanned the landscape. Moments later, she climbed back into the ambulance, laid Lily's forgotten cane on the bed beside her and closed the door. Jimmy eyed them with concern, but Hunter nodded at him, then took Lily's hand and patted it. "I told Lanny. He's going to shut everything down and make everyone stay inside, okay?"

Lily relaxed back against the small, hard pillow. "Okay."

Hunter looked up at the paramedic. "Good to go, Jimmy." The ambulance moved out, rocking on the rough road like a ship at sea. It reminded Lily of the glass-bottom boats she used to go out on when living in Florida.

# CHAPTER THIRTY-TWO

*Protection*

Hunter's shift wasn't finished, but she waited by Lily's side until the doctor had stitched Lily up and given her the all-clear to return home. Lunan was going to be kept overnight for observation. Luckily, the clean shot to his forearm hadn't severed any important bits, narrowly missing an artery, so no surgery was required. Still, it was a serious wound and they wanted to make sure he had full use of his arm muscles before they released him. Lily insisted that one of the ER nurses take her to him when Hunter went to fetch the car. His sister Helen had arrived, and the three talked briefly before Lily would agree to leave the hospital.

"He'll be okay," Lily said as she got into Hunter's SUV, as though affirming the thought in her own mind.

Hunter laid a hand on Lily's knee as she navigated the crowded parking lot. "Yes, he'll be okay."

"So, this is the wife of the military guy who kidnapped you, right?" she asked after they drove onto Central Avenue. Luckily, as it was late afternoon before the mad rush of workers heading home, traffic was light.

Lily turned and studied Hunter's profile. "Well, he assisted. It was the damned little monsters who actually transported me."

"You remember that, then?"

"Not really. Just fleeting memories. I was in the truck, then I woke up in that metal box I told you about. I saw him later, with them."

"Why, Lily? Why would he help those bastards?"

Lily shifted and the stitches on her upper arm pulled. She sighed and closed her eyes. "The same reason all criminals do what they do. Money, power, prestige. They promised him power when they took over the world."

Hunter raised her shoulders and lowered her neck down into them, scowling at the road. "Could that happen, Lily? Could they conquer us?" She guided the car west onto the highway, heading home.

Lily thought about it a long moment, realizing anew how important her government position was in the grand scheme of things. "Sure. Sure they could, hon, but that's why our government is working with Flynn's people. They're kind of a security system, letting us know when things get dangerous."

"Like now," Hunter stated, glancing at Lily. "Is that why the girls were taken? To protect the planet? How worried should I be?"

Lily took in a deep breath. "I'm not really sure. I've been getting sketchy information. I have faith in Flynn's people, though. In the Collective. And I certainly trust the girls."

"They're so young," Hunter said sadly. "Just babies."

"I know," Lily replied, taking Hunter's hand. "I know."

Hunter's fingers caressed the nub that was all that remained of Lily's left pinkie finger. "I have my doubts, Lil," she said, her lips tightening. "Look what has happened to you because of that damned Collective. I gotta say that you are the only thing that matters to me, you and Birdie. That's it. And if the Collective gets in the way of that…if they fuck with harming either of you, well…" Her voice trailed off and Lily squeezed her hand.

She changed the subject. "Did I tell you how heroic Lu was? He reached out to protect me without a bit of fear. So brave."

She continued on, relating again all the details of the shooting and how Lanny had come to them.

It had to be serendipitous timing. As soon as they pulled the SUV into the parking area in front of the Good Neighbor ranch house, a black military helicopter settled into the cleared grassy area next to Hunter's car. Hunter was helping Lily from the vehicle and they had to duck down behind it to avoid the wash of air and dust from the small prop blades. Raising up, they spied eight soldiers scrambling from the body of the helicopter, each carrying a large pack. They stood in a small group as another man in a blue camouflage battle uniform stepped from the copter, phone to his ear. He spied Lily and Hunter and waved, his devastatingly handsome smile a beacon in the lingering desert dust.

"Uncally!" Lily returned the wave and she and Hunter raced forward to greet him.

After a quick hug, Colonel Collins pulled back and studied his goddaughter, head to toe. "The air report says you were shot. Are you okay?" His gaze found her bloody sleeve and fastened on it. The T-shirt under it was bloody too, but he had no idea that it was mostly Lunan's blood.

"It's just a bullet graze, on my arm," Lily told him reassuringly. "One of the hands was shot through the arm, though."

"It was Lunan Dix. He's going to be okay, but they're keeping him at the hospital for a day or so," Hunter added, gently herding the two of them toward the house. "Let's go in so she can sit down. I'm sure she'll want to tell you all about it."

"Sure thing, let me just give these soldiers some direction and I'll be right in," the colonel said.

"Yeah," Lily said, looking back at the troops. "What's with the soldiers, Uncally?"

"Just some protection. They're gonna keep an eye out for this Cleo before she does any more harm."

"Here? They're staying here?" Hunter seemed amazed.

"They'll be bivouacked all around the ranch. You probably won't even notice them," he replied reassuringly. He stepped away toward the group of soldiers, and Lily saw him pull a map from his pocket and spread it out on the hood of Hunter's car.

"I sure hope I get to see the bitch before the soldiers take her away. I want to give her a good talking to," Lily muttered as they stepped into the coolness of the ranch house. Sage and Simmy were waiting just inside the door, and Sage immediately engulfed Lily in a huge bear hug. She reared back to check Lily's face, their gazes mingling.

"Are you all right, my girl?" she asked in a low voice.

Lily nodded, but her eyes filled with unshed tears. "Lunan was hit," she sobbed. "He was helping me and his arm...his arm—" She broke off, unable to continue, and Sage quickly ushered her into the front room. They sat knee to knee on the sofa, Sage holding Lily's hands. She didn't need to speak. Her loving, maternal presence was exactly what Lily needed.

"I'm gonna make a tray of tea," Hunter said from the wide, arched doorway. "I think we could all use a good strong cup." She pulled Simmy along and they disappeared down the hallway.

"Lu's gonna be okay," Lily said sternly, freeing one hand to brush away the tears dampening her cheeks. "He's going to be okay."

Sage just nodded and held Lily's hands tightly.

# CHAPTER THIRTY-THREE

## *Birdie Says Hello*

True to Uncally's statement, the soldiers seemed to disappear into the desert vista. The only evidence they were even there was the lone soldier patrolling the house grounds, and in his desert gray camouflage and pale tan boots, he seemed to blend in with the landscape.

After introductions, Colonel Collins stayed for tea, chatting with Simmy and Hunter while Lily washed up and changed. After visiting with everyone, he had a quick debrief in Lily's office before climbing into the helicopter and lifting off with a sad wave through the bubble-like window.

Once he was gone, Lily took a seat in the front room, sprawling on the large, overstuffed sofa. In Sage's, and no doubt Simmy's, efficient way, the coffee table had been cleared of all the tea fixings. It made Lily sad to see that no goodies remained. She turned her body so she could look out the large picture window, losing herself in thought. She had to admit, having the soldiers there on the ranch did provide some relief to the stress that had been plaguing her. Now that that worry had abated somewhat, her fears about where Birdie was and what she was enduring grew exponentially. She tried to push away thoughts of her being tortured by the Greys. Had they imprisoned her in a hot metal box as they had done to her? Were they even still on Earth? Or had they taken the girls to whatever planet they hailed from?

She found it hard to believe that the Greys had been created by the same IDBs that had created the greatest civilizations here on Earth. What key ingredient had gone sideways that allowed the evil little monsters to exist?

She sighed and wondered if she would ever be privy to the actual workings of the Collective. She had hoped that Birdie would help to give her some understanding, even an inkling, of what the Collective knew. And why they did what they did. Realistically, she understood that their power and knowledge could only be completely foreign to a human. When it came to this, humans were like infants trying to understand Einstein's Theory of Relativity. It had taken Birdie several years and rapid aging to understand most of her own people's capacity, and she was half IDB.

She envisioned Birdie's beautiful face in her mind and a keen ache filled her. She so missed her daughter. There was a large hole where that child had lived, and Lily seriously wondered if her darling girl would ever come back to her. And if not, if life would be worth living without her.

"A penny for your thoughts," Hunter said, entering the front room.

Lily grunted and sat up. "Just missing Birdie. The ranch isn't the same without her here."

Hunter sat next to her on the sofa. "I know. Too quiet. I've gotten used to her noise."

They sat in silence a long beat.

"How's your arm feeling?" Hunter asked finally, eyeing Lily with concern.

Lily looked at the bandage under the sleeve of the clean T-shirt she'd changed into. "Okay. It stings a bit."

Hunter stood. "Let me get you another pill."

Suddenly, without preamble, the television sparked into life. Both women turned as one. The station switched, as they watched, to a station of nothing but static. Lily's heart lurched in her chest, first from fear and then alarm. Was Flynn going to appear in front of Hunter finally?

Then, catching them both off-guard, they heard the dearest voice they could have imagined.

"Mummy? Are you okay, Mummy?"

"Birdie?" Lily whispered. "Birdie?"

"Mummy? Does your arm hurt? I'm sorry I wasn't there…"

Lily ran to the TV stand and laid the palms of her hands on the big, snow-filled screen. "Oh, Birdie!" she exclaimed. "We miss you so much. Are you okay? Where are you, honey?"

"We're still here…on the ship. We should…back soon though. How badly…you hurt?" Her dear voice was breaking up and frustration filled Lily. She needed to touch Birdie physically so very badly.

"I'm fine, Aili, just stitches. When will you be home? Are they treating you well?"

Hunter moved close and laid her palms on the screen next to Lily's. "Birdie, it's Hunny. We miss you so much. Please come home." A sob shook her voice.

"Sorry TV not best…I miss you both, love you both. Soon," Birdie said, her voice fading.

The television went dark and Lily felt shell-shocked. She looked at Hunter, who was fighting back tears.

"At least we know she's okay," Lily told her. "She sounds okay."

"But my Rosie?" Simmy had come into the room and must have heard some of the exchange. "Did she say about my Rosie?"

Lily rushed to Simmy and took her cold, trembling hands in hers. "Yes," she hastened to reassure her. "She said they were both still on the ship. They're together."

Simmy shook off Lily's hands and sank into a nearby chair. "A ship? Then it's truth? They're real? Aliens have my girl? I thought…"

Hunter knelt on one knee next to Simmy's chair. "What did you think, Simmy? About where the girls were?"

Simmy shrugged as tears leaked from her dark eyes and formed new rivers along her weathered cheeks. "I just figured that Collective needed them back for a spell. The Collective don't have no ship, though, do they?"

Hunter sighed. "No, I don't think so. But the girls are doing a job for them."

"They're doing good work, Simmy. It's part of the reason they grew bigger, to help the Collective with a mission," Lily added in explanation. She stood in the center of the room, her arms hugging her waist as though for comfort.

"She said soon." Simmy eyed Lily with a hopeful, trembling gaze. "Does that mean it almost done? That they might come back to us?"

Lily nodded. "I think so. That's what it sounded like." She crossed to the sofa and sat down. "We'll believe that, okay?"

She turned to look out the window again. This time her thoughts were lighter than before. She'd heard from her precious Birdie and that would just have to sustain her for the next little while. It was really all she had.

# CHAPTER THIRTY-FOUR

## *Simmy's Grief, Lily's Joy*

Hunter and Lily lay side by side that evening, fingers entwined as they silently basked in the joy of knowing their daughter was okay. Her being away from them was still an issue, but at least they knew she and Rosemary were still alive and on track with their mission. And that they might be headed home soon.

Simmy had grown quiet after the TV encounter, as if overwhelmed by the enormity of the girls' abductions and the nature of the work that had been thrust upon them. Lily and Hunter had more history with the Greys and the IDBs, but remembering their own shock and acceptance certainly helped them understand her plight.

"Do you think Simmy will be okay?" Hunter asked finally, her soft voice wafting on the companionable silence they'd built. "She's really missing Rosemary. And worried about her."

"I think she's homesick, too," Lily whispered. "I saw her face when she was telling Uncally about the bayou. She's not really happy here, in the desert."

"Yet she's torn, not wanting to leave the place where Rosemary might come to," Hunter added.

"Exactly."

"Maybe if we could find something for her to do…" Hunter rolled to her side to face her wife.

Lily nodded. "To take her mind off things."

"Yes. Any ideas?"

Lily thought a moment, studying Hunter's sweet, sleepy face. "I might have one, but you need to go to sleep now. You have work tomorrow."

They pulled the sheets and blankets across themselves and soon Hunter, curled on her side, was slumbering deeply, her breathing slow and even. Lily lay awake a long time, unable to make her mind slow down enough for rest. She sighed quietly and slid from the bed.

The house was cold and Lily was grateful for her warm slippers and the flannel shirt she'd put on over her pajamas. She limped along the hallway, running a hand on the wall to support her weaker leg. Her cane would have been too noisy, and she didn't want to disturb Hunter or Simmy.

Once settled in her office with the door closed, she turned on the space heater under her desk and briskly rubbed her hands together. Sitting back in her wheeled office chair, she eyed the short stack of record books she'd left on the desk as a reminder for her to update them. Margie was crackerjack at the accounting, but Lily liked to keep a daily journal and a daily expense report, just for her own records. If she went back through the personal ones, she knew she'd see so many entries detailing Birdie's accomplishments, the cute things she'd done on a daily basis, the extremes of her knowledge. The expenses listed would be for Birdie's book addiction and, if she went back only a few more years, she'd see expenses for diapers. For educational baby toys.

Tears welled in her eyes. She'd been hard-pressed to enter anything since returning from Bayou Lisse. She pushed the record books aside once again. At loose ends, Lily stared at the crystal statue. She thought about seeking out Flynn, but actually, she was afraid that her anger and her frustration would spill forth, falling like a mallet onto the head of the IDB. Not good Liaison behavior for sure.

Looking around the room, she noticed that there was a sizeable stack of paper on the output tray of the printer. She hadn't printed anything, and everyone, even Hunter and Birdie, was discouraged from using her office—and especially her computer—unless she was with them. Was this something that Simmy had done? She didn't know the house rules, of course, so she could have unwittingly used the printer. She frowned. Simmy had not brought a laptop with her, and the office computer was password-protected, the files encrypted.

Lily rose and moved across the room to the wireless device. She flipped the paper, and as she read, her heart raced with excitement.

## *Aili's Journal*

### *The Ship*

We knew what to expect. Or thought we did. Obviously, the Collective had never felt a need to penetrate the depths of the Greys' spaceship technology. We didn't expect the ship to be partly organic, crafted on the interior from an excreted material, similar to the flesh of the Greys themselves. The Collective, learning this information from us, decided that the Greys no doubt had crafted this ship lining much the same way as they manufactured almost everything, pulling it from their own bodies. We found this to be true later, witnessing several times when a crew of what could only be called janitorial workers cleaned the ship's surfaces and patched them with their own extruded flesh. It was sort of gross.

The Greys, and their more evolved ruling class, the Elite, are surprisingly kind to us. We have been sequestered in a comfortable room, somewhat alien to what we are used to on Earth but passably comfortable. The food and drink are tasteless but certainly energizing, imparting an almost immediate boost after eating. Though I can't help wondering exactly what we are consuming, the energy boost is welcome. Hammering out a treaty is exhausting work.

It would be so good to be home again, even if only for a few days. We so miss our families. Living in an alien environment with our human bodies is difficult—the ships are made for smaller, squarish bodies. The required communication is difficult, as well. Worker Grey thoughts are conveyed much differently than human thought, consisting primarily of random, quickly appearing and disappearing images that deliver complex information. I must admit, we have a hard time keeping up. Thankfully, the Collective has jumped in to help us translate most of what they say to us a little more easily.

Rosie and I feel brave, feel we are fulfilling the destiny of who we have become. There's some nervousness, but we operate with the reassuring knowledge that the omniscient Collective can and will pull us away immediately if we are threatened in any way. Yes, we are their eyes and their ears while we are here, but only to provide extra impressions. They may have created the Grey beings in the beginning, but free will has many offshoots and many have been overlooked as unimportant. This mission is as much discovery as peace-seeking, and all of the Collective's energy is now focused on this once-minor irritation that has become a viable threat. We need to understand the Greys' full motivation.

## Aili's Journal

### The Complaint

We knew it was coming. The showdown of sorts. We had been waiting. Still, the sight of the little gray worker aliens lined up ominously in our bedroom had been alarming. We still quake even now that it's all over and we're in the midst of them. They are truly horrible creatures, their huge blank eyes somehow menacing, their thin lips often twisting in disdain for us. Their picture thoughts seem to disparage us, especially due to our youth. Actually, humans, and maybe even IDBs, don't seem to be their favorite beings.

Luckily, the tabletop treaty discussions have been with the more ethereal creatures, the more highly evolved ruling class of these female aliens. Ones who actually speak our own language politely into our senses as we communicate.

We now know exactly why we are here. The planet they inhabit is a planet of workers and the Elite. That's it. Very little flora, no fauna. The workers, all of whom are also female, mine the huge, beautifully veined stones used in the construction of the grand palaces where the Elite live. The workers also mine all the ore for the metal implements and tools they use. The most precious of these, an ore with a name that is unpronounceable to us, is refined only to power their ships. It has had a negative effect on the miners but especially the space exploration crews. These Greys can no longer procreate. Daily exposure to the ore has made impossible their usual parthenogenesis, the kind of asexual reproduction that planaria and plants use on Earth. The bud membranes are too thin to allow the fetus, of sorts, to come to term. The Greys never developed full reproductive organs, so they are essentially dying out as the clone-like beings they produce from their bodies continue to fail. Their numbers, especially for the worker population, were falling. The only reason they'd lasted as long as they had was their innate ability to inhibit apoptosis, or cell destruction, giving them more time.

The Elite, most of them, who'd been little exposed to the ore, could still reproduce but poorly. Their floating, ethereal forms are more suited to atmosphere than flesh. And their fragile buds produced Elite, not workers. But this inability to reproduce well oddly doesn't concern them as much as their ever-growing need for workers. Their comfortable lifestyles depended on their huge labor force.

When the problem first appeared, their best scientists had explored how mammals reproduced, experimenting on Earth's animals and humans. With their relatively easy space flight, they sent out legions to explore other Collective-created planets in this solar system, seeking workers who could mine for them. Few had feasible options or creatures who could withstand their planet's pressure and atmosphere. Even humans would have had a hard time surviving on their world.

Backed into a corner, a bright light shone on them finally. The hybrid children of the Collective! Surely the type of energy reproduction that generated them could work for them as well. It was so mutable and could be adjusted to produce exactly what they needed. Just imagine it, workers who were half IDBs– perfect!

Their creators, two minds of the Collective, had explained to the Grey Elite that this type of reproduction would never work for them, as it required an excitable ovum, an egg capable of reacting to the environment, and a womb to nourish it as it developed. Still, the Greys demanded this god skill.

And therein lay the debate. And the reason for the persistent declarations of war from this dying culture. The planet that they had destroyed, Ist, had been a favored one, with primitive Earth-like humanoids, cherished by the Collective and its Collective creator. Destroying Earth would be the Greys' next strike, they threatened, if the Collective did not provide them with the god skill.

As Collective, we wondered why they would seek out war, something that would shrink further their dwindling populace. It made no sense to my community. Obviously, it arose from pure desperation. The very thought that they could win was ludicrous to the Collective. We are their creators. Their god. Their planet could be destroyed in an instant. But we had to hear them out, even after they destroyed Ist. This was a serious offense, already punishable by their destruction. But yet, they persevered in their demands. Foolishly stretching the boundaries of our compassion.

# CHAPTER THIRTY-FIVE

## *But First Coffee*

Lily clutched the small sheaf of paper in her hand, excitement thrilling her soul. She wondered about the transport medium. How had Birdie kept this journal? How had she transmitted it to her printer? Regardless of the answers to those questions, this was completely classified material. She needed to scan it and encrypt it into her computer before destroying the originals.

She placed the papers carefully on her desk and moved to the coffee machine located under the office window. She placed a pod of her favorite coffee in it and mindlessly waited for it to drip through. Adding sugar and powdered creamer, she sighed shakily and carried the full, warm mug to her desktop.

The fact that Birdie had managed to get the journal entries to her somehow was reassuring. But trepidation loomed as well. Was this an indication that she'd been hurt or killed? Would her story end badly? Had this been her final communique before she was destroyed? A shudder shook Lily. Resuming her seat, she read on.

## Aili's Journal

*My Light to Guide Me*

Rosemary is as wise as she is beautiful. I respect her as well as cherish her. She does well with the Elite, better than I. My certainty about the ultimate futility of their demands and threats tends to interfere. Rosemary actually has empathy for them, saying her heart hurts when she thinks about their people gasping their last as they die childless deaths. She wants to help but as yet we have found no practical solution.

DNA, deoxyribonucleic acid, is a fundamental building block created from the remnants of our old universe. We brought it with us, refined it, adding various chemical bases to create life similar to what we once were, many trillion eternities in the past. Unfortunately, the DNA of the Greys veered and developed into a heavy kind of satellite RNA chemical base, something caused by the environment in which they developed or by a natural mutation. In structure, they resemble some type of dry land oyster rather than a human. Our methods of procreation simply would not work with this type of gamete.

So, our discussions have been difficult. The Elite Greys believe that if enough of our energy is directed their way, children would develop. Their procreation, their genesis, is based on something other than energy, but they insist we are holding out intentionally in order to let them die out.

And the discussions continue, Rosemary even physically touching the wispy tendrils of the Elite leader, trying to make it understand the true issue. Their scientists have gathered now to brainstorm solutions.

## Aili's Journal

*Rosemary's Idea*

The Greys have given us two small platform beds, which make it hard for us to be as close all the time as we would like. They are made of the same metal and body material coating as the interior of the ship and immoveable, fixed in place. So, we sometimes simply extend our arms and hold hands as we discuss silently what to do and what to say to the Elite. We are exhausted from the most recent roundtable discussions with the Elite, arguments and ideas that lasted many hours. And with no suitable resolution. They are adamant that only the god force of the Collective would suffice.

I persist doggedly, mentioning again the wearing of protective gear, of suits, when mining the ore, but Rosie reminds me once again that it's too late for that. There have been no new, uncontaminated offshoots in quite some time. And it's too big an undertaking due to the huge number of workers to be protected. The Collective concurs.

I ask again about parthenogenesis, trying to become clear on how it works with the Greys. I know that reptiles, some sea creatures, and also bees and wasps procreate this way. That is perfectly apt as the lower Greys are very much like worker bees. But many of the Earth creatures rely on fertile eggs and male proximity, something not available to these all-female workers.

We fall silent, our exhausted minds whirling with useless possibilities.

"Queen bee," Rosemary finally said aloud, her voice excited.

"No, they require drone sperm for the workers. Only the males are asexually created," I explain. Again, the Collective concurs.

Rosemary released my hand, and I felt bereft at the disconnection. She sat up, swinging her long legs over the side of the bed. She studied me with her beautiful crystal blue eyes, her newly unbound curls a thick dark corona framing her head.

"The Cape honeybee," she explained. *"Apis mellifera capensis."*

And then I saw it. I saw what she meant. "Binary fission?"

I knew then that we'd possibly come upon an answer to the dilemma. The Collective buzzed with the possibility of her solution as they saw it as well.

"But the bud," the Collective asked. "The buds?"

"We can't, like, jump-start them. Making every bud viable would be ridiculous, impossible. We've discussed that. There have to be some less-affected workers, somewhere. If not, we'd have to find something, some substitute from Earth that would work." Rosie rubbed her brow. "Lizard, or frog, or Komodo Dragons. Yes, Komodos would work."

"We're going to make the Greys half-lizard? Gross," I said thoughtfully.

"No, no, I hope not. If we can find just one viable worker, one not exposed, and…" Her thoughts flew to me and formed in my mind.

"Let me get this straight," I said out loud, haltingly. "We designate one worker as the so-called queen, keep her as far away from the ore as possible. Sealed away. Have her make her own buds. Or provide and implant Earth eggs, from a parthenogenetic species, so they can safely multiply within her."

I sent a quick query to the Collective, who responded favorably, though thoughtfully.

"Thelytokous parthenogenesis, the production of diploid daughters from unfertilized eggs, like the nineties capensis calamity. It was a disaster for Earth," I said quietly. I could feel the nods of the Collective.

"But how could it hurt the Greys?" Rosie asked. "The more production, the better."

"They have already populated most of their world," said the Collective.

"Do they even have true gametes? There's no womb." I was immensely frustrated, my thoughts whirling chaotically. I gave the idea some serious thought. "I think we need to consider that the queen probably could not harbor a lot of budding. There's no biology for it. How long would that be viable?"

Rosie leaned forward and her thoughts bombarded me. Then I understood.

The queen would produce buds, hundreds of them, that would be taken from her, cultivated in vitro or in fake wombs probably. The identical workers would grow there until sustainable, then be born into their self-made toxic world. To work in the mines and spaceships with impunity. More would simply be born as the older ones failed.

"But to imprison her—" I began. "That doesn't seem right."

Rosie nodded sadly. "Maybe it wouldn't be forever. It could be like a rotational duty roster. Each viable worker would serve a time there."

## *Aili's Journal*

### *A Solution?*

We drew up a plan, a schematic that we entered into the ship's rudimentary computer. The bewildering machine was designed for flight through space, not drafting or art, so we had a hard time finding software that would allow us the freedom of creativity.

I never knew Rosie could draw so well until I saw the building she crafted on the screen. It was situated on the surface of the Greys' planet and the outside was lined with thick walls of the safely mined stone slabs the Elite used for construction. The Collective researched it and said that one meter of stone wall would protect those inside from the fumes of the necessary but destructive mineral that powered their spaceships. A queen would be installed there, with her buds. Rosie worried about the aspects of sacrifice. Yet it had to be this way if they would survive as a people.

Further drawings showed a honeycomb of growing pods, where the encased clones could grow to size. These pod walls were also within the stone walls, protected against the fumes so the buds and the clone children would remain viable as they grew to adulthood.

Now the question came to how we were going to generate enough buds. The Greys could produce three pairs of buds a year, if they chose, and for more than a century the leather-like shell, or outer membrane of those buds, had been growing too thin from the particle onslaught of the ore exposure to be viable.

We talked about a way, whether chemical or energy-derived, to stimulate new production among the workers. Rosie suggested first testing the budding capsules that were still inside many of the workers. They might have some early buds that could be culled by their scientists, especially from the workers who labored farther from the mines. Maybe even those working as wait staff in the homes of the Elite. After many more discussions, we narrowed our focus to those who had worked for many eons in the elite homes.

## Aili's Journal

### Space

Knowing about space from the perspective of the Collective is very different from actually being *in* space on the Greys' ship. When Rosie and I looked out through those curved viewscreens, the full extent of the cosmos lay before us. It was revelatory, and I learned something that I did not expect. Space is frigid. It is vast. It is terrifying.

Great minds on Earth believe that there are at least one hundred billion stars in the Milky Way alone. We humans, with the naked eye, see about forty-five hundred of these stars. Each of those stars could have aggregated planets and moons, spawned during the star's creation as well. Lots of stuff, it would seem. But then you have to think about the black vacuum between these celestial bodies. You have to think about it containing the framework of dark matter and microwave light only, both unable to be readily seen by human eyes. To our eyes there is only black hollowness in these voids.

The Collective sees space as a warm, nurturing nest, full of wondrous possibilities. Many parts of the Collective entities break off and circle the many trillions of colorful, far-off galaxies in this expanding cosmos, debating whether or not to lose themselves into them and separate from this Milky Way cluster.

Collective curiosity seekers even now joyfully traverse the dark matter of space seeking new seeding possibilities on rogue planets found on the outskirts of those huge galaxies. They also document the constant changes of the cosmos and then report back to the many trillions of beings of the Collective that stay and seed this particular galaxy. There's no fear in them, of course, partly because they have travelled the endless spaces of their previous expansive environment, on the other side of the black hole, that big bang, for as long as their collective consciousnesses could remember.

For Rosie and me, well, our human halves, we found it too intimidating. Too horrific. There's a keen knowledge of our fragility, our vulnerability. We need an atmosphere, air to breathe, if we wish our flesh-and-blood selves to survive. The Van Allen belts that discourage humans from traveling in space, made up of the Collective force, are there for a reason. The Collective wants to protect the fragile humanoids they have come to cherish.

If I take a moment to think about it, I understand why the energy Collective often craves to manifest flesh and to be in that flesh. It's so different from their current immortal selves crafted of star energy. I get that. I wonder if they feel as vulnerable when they manifest as human as Rosemary and I feel when we stand at the window, staring into that endless, unknown speckled void.

I've discovered that there are several places on planet Earth called POIs or Poles of Inaccessibility. They are places far inland, the farthest point from any coastline. For example, there's a place in Antarctica that used to be a Soviet research station. It is the point on the Antarctic continent most distant from any coastline, and it is actually even closer to the International Space Station than to anywhere else on Earth.

Space is like this. If you stand in a central location, you will see cold, airless emptiness as far as the eye can see. There are some beautiful colors, glowing novas, galaxies, but the rest is simply the profound dark hole of space.

The silence at the POIs is said to be extreme, and though I've been told by my interdimensional family that the stars do sing as they shift fire, I feel as though I will never hear it for myself. The distances for me, and for Rosie, as hybrids, are impossible. Space is for stardust.

# CHAPTER THIRTY-SIX

## *Last Rites*

This was the final entry, and disappointment surged through Lily, followed by terror. Her daughter and Simmy's granddaughter were in space. Airless space where they could be in danger. Suppose the Greys became unhappy with the solutions they were being presented with? What would stop them from tossing the girls out of the window, or hatch or airlock, or whatever, to get back at the Collective. She remembered then what Birdie had written about their failsafe, that the IDBs would rescue them if the meetings soured. But would they? Flynn said Birdie was its baby, too. Lily would just have to remember that and hope for the best. It was agonizing.

# CHAPTER THIRTY-SEVEN

## *The Pain of Loss*

Lily electronically scanned and then shredded Birdie's correspondence. Sadly. But she knew it was necessary. She was just glad that Birdie had shared more information about the mission and what was entailed in it. She felt more informed at least. She didn't feel ready to share this information with Uncally yet, however. And there was some guilt about that. She wanted to keep something back for herself. Even though she knew it could be important, especially if the solution the girls had worked up fell on deaf ears with the Greys. She *would* contact him. She would. Just not right now.

One day fell into the next.

The patrolling soldiers seemed to be keeping the threat of Cleo at bay. Lily felt more relaxed as each uneventful day passed. Plus, she was still riding the joy she felt at having heard from Birdie and knowing that the girls were all right. At least for now.

Lily turned her worry toward Simmy. Seeing the grandmother sitting alone and forlorn each day, posted on the front room sofa, glancing hopefully now and again at a silent, blank television was more than Lily could bear. Her heart hurt.

One day, after meeting briefly with Margie at the bunkhouse, she made her way back to the main house. She peeked her head around the wide arched doorway and found Simmy sitting as she'd done since Birdie had spoken to them.

"Hey, Miss Simmy. Are you busy?"

Simmy turned to face Lily. "Naw, naw, I'm all right. You need help with somethin'?"

Lily came into the room and perched on the arm of the easy chair closest to Simmy. She sighed. "Well, it's like this. When we had our taxes done this past year, it was a bit of a mess. Connor Doe, our tax man, gave us hell because our files were so messed up. Somehow, some of the newer files were mixed in with the older folders, and we had to take time to search them out for him. We promised to get our act together and Margie has been trying to work on it but…"

She paused and straightened her shoulders. "Well, we've been culling the herd and with the ads she's been making up and placing around locally and online…There's just not enough hours in the day."

Simmy scratched her head. "That's a pure dee shame. Can I help out? You might not know it, but I been doin' the books for de bait and tackle fo' nigh on five years now. I can get m'self all over some paper, if you need me to."

Lily smiled and leaned to hold Simmy's hands. "Oh my gosh, Miss Simmy. If you could clean out those old files from the filing cabinet, sort them, and pack them into some banker's boxes, you'd win our undying gratitude."

Simmy released Lily's hands, stood, and smoothed her shirt. "You just point me to dem ol' filing cabinets and I'll fix them right up for you. No need to worry yo'self anymore."

Lily stood and frowned at Simmy. "That would be so sweet of you. I know you're sort of on vacation right now so if you wanted to say no, my feelings would not be hurt, I promise. We would get to it."

Simmy shook her head from side to side. "Naw, I'm good. Truth tell, might be good to have somethin' to do. Feelin' kinda useless jus' waitin' around fo' my Rosie to talk to me."

Lily nodded. "So, when would you like to start?"

"I just helped Sage with clearin' lunch so I'm free. How's about now?"

Lily was stoked by Simmy's enthusiasm for the project. "Well, sure. Let's go see Margie and see if we can get you started."

Lily and Simmy made their way slowly across the grounds, chatting about farm expenses and how high they were, even as their eyes searched the surroundings, looking for danger. They entered the safer, cooler dimness of the bunkhouse and strode along the plank floor until they reached Margie's office.

"Hey, Margie, guess who's coming to help you out with those file cabinets?"

Margie rose and gave Simmy a quick but heartfelt hug. "Oh, thank you, Lord! I was beginning to think we wouldn't get those files pulled before next tax season."

"Happy to help, happy to help," Simmy said, already eyeing the four metal filing cabinets and the pile of ready-to-assemble banker boxes tucked in between two of the tall cabinets.

"Listen, you two," Lily said. "Dad has, well, we have a vault at the bank in Morris and this is where we'll store everything you cull out. Just label the boxes with everything you put in there, and I'll get Felix and Ed to help me get them inside the vault. I guess we should keep only about one year's worth of past files here in the office."

Margie was pulling one of the flat boxes free from the pile, and she handed it to Simmy, who immediately started unfolding it, making it into a sturdy storage structure. "Sure thing, boss."

Feeling somewhat useless there, Lily made her goodbyes and left the office in the women's capable hands. She headed out, planning to check in with Flynn to see if the Collective had seen any sign of Cleo. As she stepped carefully out into the hot midafternoon sunlight, she felt a comforting sense of accomplishment. Keeping Simmy's mind and body occupied might help her get through the time until Rosemary and Birdie returned.

If they did. As the days passed Lily found her faith in the girls' return fading. Receiving the journal pages had been a boost, but that had been three days ago and she'd heard nothing since.

Coming around to the front of the house, she was surprised to see Sage sitting in a rocker on the front porch. That was very unusual for this time of day. She didn't seem aware of Lily's approach, staring off into the distance.

"Hey, SaySay, you doing okay?" Lily mounted the porch and took a seat in the rocker next to Sage's. She placed her cane quietly on the floorboards and hung her hat on the upright of her rocker.

A companionable silence fell, but Lily could tell that Sage was chewing on something. She waited patiently, following Sage's gaze across the rusty-colored desert landscape. A jackrabbit startled itself and ran just outside and along the picket fence almost to the driveway.

"It's too long," Sage said finally, speaking in her characteristically soft tone.

Lily lowered her gaze and stared at her denim-clad thighs. "I know, SaySay, but I can't seem to get them back here," she whispered.

"What do we need to do?" Sage twisted her hands together, then studied her fingernails. "No child is gone from her mother for that long. It's not right. You just tell us what to do."

"There's nothing to be done. I wish…I so wish we could do something. I get…messages from the people she's staying with. They say the girls are okay, just doing some chores, some projects that need doing."

Sage made a grunting noise and lifted her eyes back to the ranch lands. "And what about our need? We *need* to see those children. To make sure they're all right. Simmy is beside herself with worry. Lanny can't sleep. I…He's getting angrier every day. We trust you, Miss Lil, but things here just aren't right. We got shootings, mystery, things left unsaid. Now, Lanny and I try to trust you, like I said, but this just ain't the right way to live. You didn't *do* anything to those sweet girls, did you? You didn't harm them somehow? Is that what this is about?"

Lily felt horror creep up her spine and settle like bitter, stinging gall in her mouth. "Like...like what, SaySay? I would never...never...!"

Lily, overcome, rose and lurched through the screen door and into her bedroom. She locked the bedroom door, her heart beating like an Irish bodhran in too youthful, unrhythmic hands. She couldn't catch her breath and felt a full-on panic attack approaching. She pushed against her chest, willing it to expand and pull in much-needed air. Tears completely obliterated her sight, and she did not care. Her misery was too intense, and the hot tears scalded her eyes and cheeks as they escaped her body.

The losses were too great and too many. They'd finally broken her. She'd lost her father. Then her mother. She'd almost lost Lu. He could have so easily been shot through the heart. Her hand crept to the scar on her arm where the stitches had once been, and she pressed it hard.

She'd lost so much in Alabama. Her peace of mind, her close relationship with Flynn, then Birdie and Rosemary, lost to the evil Grey aliens. But Lanny and Sage had been there. Had always been there. Now...now it seemed she had lost Lanny and Sage as well. She was completely broken, and she could not be fixed.

# CHAPTER THIRTY-EIGHT

## *Broken Beyond Repair*

Hunter banging on the bedroom door woke her from an exhausted slumber some hours later.

"Go the fuck away," she shouted.

"Lily. Supper's ready. Come eat with us?" Her voice was low but held a pleading, puzzled tone.

"Not hungry. Go away!" Lily shouted again. She pulled the pillow over her head so no further sounds would penetrate. She hated the scents it held from her tear-ravaged face and breath but eventually drifted off again.

When she awoke several hours later, she could tell by the quiet of the house that everyone had gone to bed. Part of her felt bad denying Hunter the bedroom, but another part was filled with such anger and self-hatred that her thoughts would not coalesce into any sort of empathy or compassion. She stumbled to the bathroom, used the toilet, and then splashed cold water on her face. Looking at herself, she saw no joy in her eyes. They were cold and lifeless, much as Birdie had described outer space.

Birdie. Lily put down the toilet cover and sat thinking about her sweet, beloved Birdie. She suddenly brimmed with anger toward her daughter. How dare she leave her family to go die in outer space! It was just wrong! She decided she would simply write Birdie out of her life. Make her memory disappear. She would never mention her to Flynn again, to Uncally, to Hunter.

She toyed next with the idea of moving away from Good Neighbor. Selling out. Without Lanny and Sage, there was nothing here for her. She would no longer serve as Liaison. Let some military lackey come in and do it. She did not need any of them or the Liaison job. She knew how to waitress and with no one else to take care of, she could survive just fine.

She pressed her lips together. Hunter would not understand. Lily would try to explain it to her, though. Would try to tell her that loving people was simply not an option for Lily Dawson. She would just have to understand. Maybe Hunter could get her apartment back, with her old roommate. Or even move back to the Acoma Pueblo. Probably not, as it would be too far from her oh-so-precious job. Hell, she could even reenlist in the Air Force. She wasn't too old. They'd take her back.

Or maybe Lily wouldn't tell her anything at all. She would just go. Put this whole stupid life she'd built right into the rearview mirror of her car.

Lily seethed with anger until her skin felt tight and raw. She was trembling, throbbing with rage. Or maybe it was anguish for losing everything in her life in one fell swoop.

She needed to plan. She swiped at her eyes and stood. Her suitcase and her backpacks were in the hall closet, unfortunately. She wondered if she could get anything out of the closet without Hunter hearing her. Maybe the large backpack on the floor just inside the closet door. She idly wondered where Hunter was sleeping. Maybe the couch or maybe in the bedroom where that unremembered person used to stay when she was a child.

She sat on the bed and sighed. Tomorrow morning would bring too many questions, too much concern. She knew she would not be able to handle it. She had to leave tonight. Before she saw Hunter. Before she saw Sage and Lanny again. Sage and Lanny, who could believe…could actually *believe* that she would hurt that unremembered person or anyone else for that matter. No, it had to be tonight.

She opened her bureau drawers and pulled out pairs of underwear and socks, piling them neatly on the bed. She moved to the closet and only took out her most comfortable clothing, her jackets, and just three pairs of shoes, angrily ripping shirts and pants from their hangers and folding and piling them. Luckily, she was a simple dresser by nature so the stack on the bed didn't look too unmanageable. She paused and studied the room.

It had been her parents' room once, then her father's after she and Sandy had moved away. Now it was hers and Hunter's. But not for long.

There wasn't a lot in the room that was important to her. She grabbed her father's tablet from the nightstand and placed it atop the clothing. She would keep that as the journals had already been transferred to the Maryland compound. Limping quietly into the bathroom, she grabbed a few toiletries and put them in a cosmetic bag she pulled from the under the sink cabinet. Her watch was in the kitchen, though, by the sink where she left it after washing her hands earlier. She made a mental note to not forget it. The computer in her office had been given to her by Wendell. It was government issue so that had to stay. She did want her notebooks, though. They were personal and they were hers.

She glanced at the stack on the bed one more time, then quietly turned the lock and cracked the door. The hallway was dark, and someone, probably Sage, maybe Hunter, had left her cane leaning against the doorframe. She lifted it and tossed it onto the bed.

Making her way carefully along the hallway, she stepped into her office. She looked at the output tray on the printer first, finding it empty. She felt along the surface of her desk and switched on the small desk lamp. Her eyes fastened on the crystal statue nearby. Only the thought that it would make too much noise preventing her from yielding to the almost overwhelming urge to pick it up and smash it onto the floor. She turned her back on it and lifted her notebooks. Flipping through them, she took only the journals she'd kept. She knew she would want them and even if she never opened them again, she certainly didn't want anyone else reading them. She might very well burn them to help her forget everything.

Now for the watch, something she could get a good price for in a financial pinch. She crept back into the hallway but paused at the slightly open door to the room of that unremembered one. By the light of the small nightlight, she could see that Hunter was sleeping there, a Raggedy Ann doll clutched in her arms.

Lily sighed quietly but hardened her heart and moved on.

Oddly enough, there was light coming from behind the large swinging doors that led into the kitchen. She paused. What if Sage hadn't gone home yet? She was not ready to face the pseudo-mother who had betrayed her. She was turning to try the hall closet and then head back to her bedroom when a strange giggle piqued her curiosity. Who in the world was in her kitchen in the middle of the night? Simmy's bedroom door had been closed, so it wasn't her. Shock widened her eyes. Was Cleo back somehow and sabotaging something else? Lily wouldn't put it past her to burn the house down with all of them in it.

Anger strengthened Lily's resolve and she pushed the door wide and stepped through.

# CHAPTER THIRTY-NINE

## *The Sweetness of Ice Cream*

The scene that met her eyes was unbelievable to her. Stunning. They were there, both of them. Both of those beautiful children. They had their foreheads together across the round kitchen table and were giggling at one another, their mouths full of ice cream. Lily clutched at her chest above her pounding heart, balling up her T-shirt, sure she was going to have a heart attack. Her legs gave away, and she sprawled onto the cold, hard kitchen floor. Sobs wracked her body even as her head thudded against the kitchen tile.

Then they were there, both young women touching her, making sure she was okay. She could only stare in wonder at first one face, then the other. "You're here, you're real," she whispered through her tears.

"Oh, Mummy, you are so, so sad," Birdie said soothingly. "It's coming off you in waves. Oh, Mummy, no."

Rosemary stacked Lily's dropped journals onto the table, then fetched a paper towel from the counter and handed it to Lily. Lily pressed it into her face as she let Birdie and Rosemary help her to her feet. They helped her into one of the chairs, then they took their seats, just studying her as a couple of minutes passed.

"When...when did you...?" Lily had dried her face, but she could barely see them through eyes that were mostly swollen and raw.

"Just a few minutes ago," Rosemary offered. "We were trying not to wake you guys until morning."

"We just had to have some ice cream, though," Birdie added. "The food there was so awful. They had nothing we really liked." Birdie reached out and laid one hand on her mother's forearm. "Mummy? What's happened?" Her voice was low and heavy with concern, her eyes sad. "SaySay did something? I can't see it."

Lily took in a deep breath and smiled at Birdie, covering her hand with hers and holding it firmly. "It doesn't matter now, sweetheart. You two are home and that's all that matters."

Birdie eyed her doubtfully. "So, did you read the journal pages I sent? Isn't it great what Rosie came up with?"

Lily studied Rosemary, who was serenely enjoying every mouthful of the nondairy ice cream she was consuming. "You mean the beehive thing? I think it was a great idea. Did you find one of the Greys who had workable eggs?" She turned the question toward Birdie.

"We did. One of the workers who looked after an elderly Elite. She had served in the household for more than two hundred years and she had no family that worked in the mines. We were immediately able to find two ready buds in her, and we stayed on and made sure they had viable shells and life growing inside in the growth chamber before we left. Well, before they would let us leave." Birdie wrinkled her nose but leaned to savor another bite of chocolate ice cream.

"And the hive structure? Has that been built?" Lily's stomach growled and she reached into a nearby drawer for a spoon. She pulled Birdie's pint of coconut milk ice cream closer and took a hefty spoonful.

Rosemary nodded and swallowed. "Yes, they had it up within two of their rotations. We couldn't get off the ship, of course, too much pressure, but we got to watch it being constructed through the window. Those Greys are really strong!"

"Yeah, it was pretty amazing." Birdie offered the ice cream to her mom for a second spoonful.

"How did those…Elites feel about the solution?" Lily took some and shoved the ice cream back so Birdie could get a bite.

"They actually thought it was brilliant after they thought about it a minute." Lily reached her spoon toward Rosie's ice cream and Rosie passed her the pint before continuing. "I mean, think about it, they will have more production than they did before the buds went all fragile. When we left, the Elite scientists were already testing the budding of household workers from all the Elite homes."

"Most have been exposed," Birdie said, picking up the sentence. "But there will be some. Plus, the new babies that hatch out will have good buds and some of them will be made queens, as well."

"It's a good deal all the way around," Rosemary added, reclaiming her pint of pistachio. "If we had waited too much longer, I believe the entire population of the planet would have been doomed, though."

"You guys are amazing. No other word for it," Lily said, setting her spoon on the table. "Was the Collective happy?"

"We all definitely were," Birdie said, replacing the round top on her empty ice cream container. "Those directly involved in seeding the Greys were really happy that their creation didn't have to be destroyed."

Rosemary offered Lily the last of her ice cream, but Lily held up a thumb saying she was good. "The others, too, I bet because they didn't have to destroy anything, right?"

"Right," Birdie said.

Rosemary capped her empty pint and the two younger women pushed them together into the center of the table.

"So, are you okay, Mummy?" Birdie was studying her with that bright blue gaze.

Lily smiled tremulously. "I...we've all been worried about you guys, so things have been pretty weird around here. Sad."

"Is my Meemaw okay? I know she's here..." Rosemary's eyes seemed doubtful somehow.

"Of course! We've looked out for her. She's part of the family now. You both are," Lily reassured her.

"We didn't expect it to be dark when we got home, with everyone in bed," Birdie muttered.

"How did you get home?" Lily asked, suddenly curious.

"They let us off right here in the kitchen. The minerals they use allow them to fold space, sort of," Birdie answered. "So we were here in no time."

"And they have developed a rad cloaking technology. They can go anywhere without being seen," Rosemary added. "That's why they can just appear out of nowhere. They also have these little pods for surface excursions."

"They're like tiny shuttlecraft from the main ship. They reek of the rock fumes, though. It's what they brought us to the surface in. One of the Elite scientists told me that even if a Grey with a pod gets left behind, the pod will get her home through space. It'll take forever, because they can't fold, but that's how well the pods are crafted," Birdie said.

Lily was getting whiplash from the conversation. She rubbed the back of her neck. "Sounds like these aliens are pretty smart."

Birdie shrugged. "Not really, not like our Collective. But the Elite scientists are the smartest of the bunch."

"The workers? Not as much. It's like talking to a box of rocks," Rosemary added, shaking her head. "I hate that they're being enslaved this way but it's what they did before. You know, before they went all sterile. Now they are doing it in a protected way. It's actually better all the way around."

Silence fell and a sense of peace wrapped them in a cocoon of warmth.

"It's so good to be home," Birdie said with a sigh.

"It is," Rosemary agreed. "I wonder if I should wake my *Sha* or see her in the morning."

"Let's wait," Lily said, retrieving her journals. "Let her get a good night's sleep. She worked a lot today, helping us out. You guys are probably exhausted anyway, all that jet-setting around space. You need to rest, too."

Birdie snickered. "Jet-setting. Right."

The three women rose, and Lily impulsively drew the younger women into a lengthy embrace. They returned the hug, all reconnecting and reuniting from their extensive time apart. Lily fought back renewed tears and took a few deep breaths. Then she remembered Hunter.

Birdie picked up on her thoughts. "Hunny?"

"Yes, she's in your room. Why don't the two of you take our room. No, wait, the bed is covered in crap." She thought a minute. "Let's just wake her up and get her to move."

"Mummy, why is she in my room?" Birdie queried as they prepared to leave the kitchen. She took her mom's hand and suddenly knew the answer. She looked at Lily with wide eyes. "Mum? You can't just do that. And you can't give up like that. What's the deal?"

Lily sighed, feeling exhaustion overtaking her. "Just a mistake, sweet girl. It's gone now, all finished. Sometimes adults can be foolish, that's all."

# CHAPTER FORTY

## *Explaining*

"Hunter? Hunter, sweetheart." Lily gently shook her partner awake. She made a shushing motion with her finger over her lips when Hunter's eyes focused on her. "Please be quiet, we don't want to wake Simmy."

"Lil," Hunter muttered. "What's going..." She broke off abruptly as her eyes focused behind Lily and settled on Birdie. "BirdBird?"

Birdie climbed onto the bed and flattened herself atop her mom, moving the doll to one side so she could reach her better and give her a big hug.

"Oh, my God, it really is you." Hunter lifted and examined Birdie's face, then swiveled her head and saw Rosemary. "Rosie! You guys really are back?"

Rosemary nodded then started to glow a little bit. She seemed happy to be back with the two moms.

Birdie climbed awkwardly off Hunter and then the two girls pulled her into a sitting position. "We need the bed, Hunny. We've traveled an awfully long way."

Rosemary snickered and shoulder bumped Birdie.

"Sure, sure. Uh, will you guys still be here in the morning?" She was obviously still half asleep and maybe concerned that she might be dreaming the whole thing.

Birdie smiled and laid one hand on Hunter's shoulder, and Lily could see Hunter's face relax as she smiled.

"Okay," she said, getting to her feet. "See you guys in the morning."

She let Lily lead her from the room. Lily winked at the girls as they passed through the door. She closed it quietly.

Opening the door to their bedroom, Lily suddenly remembered that she had been planning to leave Hunter and to leave Good Neighbor Ranch. The evidence was piled all across the bed. Hunter realized it as well, as soon as she stepped into the lamp-lit room. She turned to her wife, questioning eyes wide. "Lily?"

Lily laid her journals aside and hurried to shove the socks and undies back into the bureau drawers. "Sorry, hon, just made a mistake is all." She placed the stack of clothing she'd gotten from the closet on top of the bureau and gently dropped the shoes to the floor. She propped her cane against the wall and laid her father's tablet and the cosmetic bag on her nightstand.

Hunter moved to stand next to her. Too close.

"Were you really going to leave me? Why, Lil, why? I don't understand."

"I...well," Lily stammered. It all seemed so stupid and embarrassing now that the girls were home. Her anger and hurt had made her a fool.

Hunter sat on the edge of the bed and pulled Lily down beside her. "Go ahead. Tell me."

Lily hung her head as she began talking. "It all started when SaySay was on the porch and she said...she said, she asked me if I had hurt the children or done something with them to, like, get rid of them. I don't know. She said Lanny was wondering that, too, and that they were both upset. That Lanny wasn't sleeping because he was so worried about what I had done to Birdie."

"That makes no sense," Hunter said when Lily paused.

"I *know*," Lily wailed quietly. "That she and Lanny thought that I was capable of hurting our precious girl, our girls. Oh, Hunter. It hurt so badly. I wanted to die."

Hunter seemed perplexed. "Surely, she didn't mean anything..."

Lily angered anew. "I heard what I heard. It'll be hard facing her tomorrow, but I want to see what she was talking about. What she really thought. And Lanny...I don't know what to do about him." She sighed. "Having the girls here will help."

Hunter frowned at her. "I dunno. They're like full-grown, in their twenties now. That'll be weird for them."

Lily pressed both palms to her temples. "Ahh, geez, I hadn't even thought about that!"

Hunter touched her arm to get her attention. "Lily, why were you leaving *me*? I didn't do anything."

Lily took a deep breath and straightened her shoulders. "It wasn't you, hon. I just...well, I'd lost too much, you know? It's like that thing with SaySay made me think that I had lost them. Their love and trust. And then I went way back. To losing my father, then Mama. And I was sure the girls had been killed by the Greys since I hadn't heard from them for so long."

"So, you wanted to leave me?" Her dark eyes were sorrowful as they studied Lily, seeking answers.

"Not really. I was trying to escape it all. Everything. To go back to a time when all this wasn't happening. You know, go back to being a waitress, not being the Liaison, not dealing with all this alien stuff. If Birdie was gone, well, maybe you should be, too."

Her sad gaze fastened on Hunter. "I just decided I shouldn't love anyone. That it was too painful to care so intensely. Leaving in the middle of the night, without seeing anyone, seemed like the right answer. I'm...I'm not that good with confrontation, I guess."

Hunter shook her head. "I don't know about that, but I'm a little pissed that you thought you could leave without a word to me...or anyone. You just can't do that, Lil. It's...it's cowardly and just plain wrong."

Lily shrugged. "Yeah, that's what Birdie said. 'You just can't do that, Mum.' You're both right. It was stupid and selfish and, but I...I was so frickin' *angry*."

"Angry? At who?"

"Well, Sage for starters. And Lanny. And the Collective for taking the girls from us." Her voice lowered. "And even you, though I'm not one hundred percent sure why."

Hunter sighed deeply and rose to her feet. "I dunno, Lil. Sounds like the spirit was definitely beating your drum." She walked to the other side of the bed and lifted the coverlet. "Let's get some sleep. Maybe things will look better in the morning."

Lily felt her heart break. Just a little more. Hunter was hurt, and she had caused it. She lifted the coverlet on her side, then went into the bathroom to change into pajamas. She would not, could not shed more tears. She was all cried out.

Though they were both obviously exhausted, it was a long time before either of them fell asleep. The distance between them seemed as vast as the void of space that Birdie had described.

## *Aili's Journal*

### *The Agony of Home*

The pain and disharmony at home was alarming, putting a dent in our happy homecoming. I brushed it off as simple worry, maybe pointless. Then I saw Mummy in the kitchen, her eyes swollen, her hair limp and mussed, her clothes wrinkled. Afterward, when I realized where Hunny was sleeping and felt the disconnect between them, it was almost more than I could bear. I reached out to the Collective and the entity Mummy calls Flynn came to reassure me. It said it believes all will be well between Hunny and Mummy, probably, but there is danger lurking. It couldn't tell me much because of the free will variable. Only that I needed to watch my back.

Other than that worry and tension, it was so amazing to be back at Good Neighbor. Rosie had loved what she saw of the house, which was mostly just the kitchen, and I was looking forward to showing her the whole ranch in reality, not just in my thoughts. I couldn't wait to really introduce her to Lanny and SaySay and Margie. To Lu and Ed and Eddie, Felix and Alice. I wanted to show her the cows and introduce her to Mom's horse, Shakey. This place has been my human life and I wanted to share it with her, the way she had shared her bayou home with me.

It's weird to think that this plane of existence, this home we call Earth, was actually created by the Collective. By my cosmic half. They seeded this earth with their own life force and then let it run rampant. The human mind grew, evolved, into what it is today. Sure, the Collective stepped in from time to time, when things became too dangerous or veered off the path of right and good. Or they came to Earth and influenced someone to experiment and see where free will would take things when variables were tossed in. The search for knowledge and self-improvement had been one aspect of the human interaction with us and, among those higher evolved on the mental spectrum, it still existed. The thought of this made me…well…satisfied. The future looked promising.

# CHAPTER FORTY-ONE

### *Breaking the Fast*

Simmy's cries of joy roused Lily from the depths of slumber the next morning. She reached out one hand to the other side of the bed and discovered that Hunter had already risen. The scent of her shampoo was wafting from the bathroom on waves of humidity, and Lily knew she'd even showered.

Lily rose slowly, her head throbbing, probably from dehydration. She used the bathroom, drank three cups of water, and combed her hair but decided to wait on showering and dressing. She felt that she should be present to monitor whatever was happening with the discovery of the two girls. Two grown girls. She shrugged into a robe to cover her sleep shorts and T-shirt, trying to look at least a little pulled together. There was nothing she could do to remedy the state of her still swollen, bloodshot eyes.

Voices, happy ones, drifted to her when she stepped into the hallway. Leaning heavily on her cane, she moved toward the kitchen. Birdie was the first to greet her, with a big hug, when the door opened. Then she saw Sage, who'd been standing at the sink alongside Birdie.

Sage's big grin of happiness faltered when she spied Lily. The regret caused by her earlier words to Lily was immediately plastered across her deep brown eyes and the drawn planes of her face. Lily was filled with empathy and understanding. And love. How she loved this woman who had always, always been there for her. Sage had been grasping for understanding during what, to her, had to be a mystifying situation. Was it all that different from the panicked plans she had considered the night before? Lily saw it clearly now and she moved to pull Sage into a close embrace.

"I am so, so sorry," Sage whispered against her ear.

Lily pressed her moistening eyes closed. She could not speak, so she held Sage for a good long hug. Birdie joined them, hands still wet although she held a dish towel in one hand.

"SaySay made pancakes, Mum, and my favorite veggie bacon." Birdie pulled Lily away and guided her toward the dining room, where Rosie, Simmy, and Lanny were discussing the possibility of adding a flock of sheep to Good Neighbor Ranch.

"Sheep?" Lily said, joining in the conversation as she seated herself.

Lanny reached out a hand and pressed his warm, callused palm atop her fingers. She returned the caress, piling her other hand on top of his, letting him know too that everything was all right between them. "Sheep are cool. Can we do it?"

"They are messy, but we can if you want them. Old Christian Young, across the river, passed last week, and his wife has offered the whole flock up for sale," he said.

"Can we graze them? Will the land support it?" Lily released his hand and leaned forward eagerly. Simmy took a seat next to her.

Lanny nodded. "My people keep sheep. The Navajo, too. I think they will do fine here. It's not as green as Young's river bottom land, but they will do okay."

Lily thought it over as Birdie wrapped arms around her from behind. "Let's do it. Price them and let me and Margie know."

"Can we have a few goats, Mum? Baby ones? They are so cute."

Lily turned and gazed into her daughter's bright eyes. Her heart thrilled because it implied Birdie planned to stay. "You bet, but you'll have to look after them. Check around and see who has some."

Simmy, settled finally, was staring across the table at Rosie as though being in the spaceship had left some kind of stain on the girl. Birdie moved to sit next to Rosie as Sage placed a tall stack of hot pancakes in the center of the table.

"Simmy? Are you doing okay this morning? We didn't work you too hard yesterday, did we?"

Simmy pulled her eyes from her granddaughter. "Oh, pshaw, I kin do dat kinda work in my sleep. Today a new day, a good day. Can't remember de last time I's dis happy."

"We so appreciate your help. I can't even…"

Birdie placed a short stack of pancakes and two slices of the bacon on Lily's plate. Lily's stomach growled loudly. Lanny even noticed.

"You'd best tuck in," Rosemary told her.

"I think I will," she replied, staring at the hot goodness on her plate.

*She went to the gym early.* Rosemary's thought gently eased into Lily's mind. When Lily lifted her eyes, she saw Rosie watching her, a smile on her curved lips. *She's okay. She just needed time to process.*

Lily took a bite of pancake and nodded her head slowly, letting Rosie know her message was received.

*She loves you more than life itself,* Birdie added into her mind. *She is trying to understand, and she will.*

Lily had no idea how to think back at them, to converse in this manner, so she just nodded again, her gaze meeting Birdie's. She had been worried about Hunter's absence and the girls had obviously picked up on that.

"Mmm, SaySay, I don't know what you put in this batter, but these pancakes are amazing," she said, taking another, bigger bite.

Sage had taken a seat next to Lily and she grinned widely at the praise as she took two pancakes onto her plate. "Just lots of love and care," she replied.

"Plus, a good griddle and many days of practice," Lanny added.

Sage nodded in agreement. "I've been making these for you since you were just a little thing. You were so scrawny when you moved here. Too much city life, I'm thinking."

"Probably," Lily agreed around a new mouthful of deliciousness. "Chunked up quick, thanks to you and Margie."

Birdie chuckled. "She *is* the chocolate queen," she added. "I swear I think she pipes the smell out the door just to draw me in."

Rosie laughed and poked a thumb toward Simmy. "I think my Meemaw was the one who invented that process. She got me hooked on chocolate when I was just a baby."

"Prolly helped make you sweet as you is," Simmy offered as she bit into a slice of bacon. "Word. You say this bacon don' come from no pig?" She eyed Sage incredulously.

Sage nodded. "Yes. Chocolate is okay around here, but no pig meat."

Lanny laughed and took another bite of pancake.

"Don' that beat all," Simmy muttered, eyeing the vegetarian bacon suspiciously.

## *Aili's Journal*

### *Rosie in My World*

We spent the day roaming the ranch. The soldiers stopped us at what had to be a checkpoint and after they contacted Mum's godfather, Colonel Collins, each subsequent soldier let us pass, though the next unit we encountered watched us curiously as we cheerfully waved and drove by in the four-wheeler.

Margie just loved Rosie and they developed an instant comradeship. They had much in common as my girl has an affinity for the organization of numbers. Numerology was even a hobby for her, following the Pythagorean number systems— she counted everything—so accounting was a cakewalk for her. The structural aspect of keeping books also appealed to her and they conversed a long time on the topic.

My physical appearance, looking another decade or more older, only caused a momentary blip of disbelief with each worker we saw as we traversed the ranch. Margie took it in stride, praising the way I looked and just honestly glad I was back at Good Neighbor. I quietly quelled any fear that cropped up with the others, giving each a hug or handshake, though Alice Garcia, Felix's wife, was strangely resistant, continuing to watch me, us, distrustfully.

We examined Lunan's wound, and he regaled us with a much-dramatized version of events surrounding the shooting. We played into it, although at this point, we had both Mummy's and Lanny's points of view. We even had Hunny's after-the-fact memories of the ambulance ride and the hospital. It was strange to see how large this event was in Lunan's mind, big enough to reshape his psyche from that point forward.

He took us to some of the cows, a grouping gathered together in the shade of a large juniper tree, trying to escape the midday heat. We walked to them, dodging cow piles, and they allowed us to scratch their rough-haired noses and softer ears. One even licked Rosie with a huge hot flat tongue. Through her, I could feel the silkiness of it, as well as her delight at the affection shown.

When Rosie met Shakey, Collette, and Stoney, the three ranch horses we owned, I thought her head was going to explode. Who knew that she would love horses so much? The images I got from her were idyllic, filled with manes flying high in the wind, horses trotting powerfully across expansive green plains, even strongly muscled flanks expanding and contracting under a covering of rusty roan velvet. I was frankly amazed until I received messages from her featuring the soil of Earth, messages of grounding, of heavy flesh. Then I understood and I viewed these majestic animals with new eyes.

I took her to Mummy's rock at the base of the mesa and we sat together, sides touching, as we surveyed the expansive Good Neighbor lands. She especially liked the guardian mirrors, shooting sunlight from their sentry posts far out in the desert lands. It was all so beautiful, as was the radiance constantly passing back and forth between us. It felt like home.

# CHAPTER FORTY-TWO

*Placation*

"What the hell is going on, Lily?"

His green eyes were angry, lending credence to the fury in his voice.

"What?" Lily questioned, somewhat alarmed. "What's happened?"

Upon receiving the text from Uncally requesting a call, she had quickly finished dressing and hurried to her office to teleconference with him.

"Why didn't you tell me the girls were back? Don't you think that's something I might have...oh...needed to *know*?" His voice raised on the final word, and Lily felt well and truly yelled at.

"I was just trying to find the time," Lily protested. "Besides, they showed up in the middle of the night last night. My head is still spinning."

She remembered, with keen discomfort, the fact that she had been a hair's width from walking away from him and the entire ranch. She opted not to bring that up.

Uncally grew thoughtful. "I guess their solution worked… that's why they brought them home."

Lily nodded and breathed a sigh of relief. He'd obviously received the encrypted text message she'd finally sent about the journal entries Birdie had sent. Oddly enough, he hadn't acknowledged it by his usual email or text message, so she had been wondering if he'd received it.

"I'm not sure how I feel about this…collusion between them. I mean suppose the IDBs decide to, I don't know, help the Greys against the humans? What's stopping them?"

Lily was perplexed and could feel a bit of that old anger resurfacing. "How can you say that? There's been a firm treaty with the IDBs and modern humans for almost two hundred years. And, by what they tell me, they have been helping humans for the past five hundred thousand years and in eons of prehistory before that. They are the reason we are who we are! They have protected us hundreds of times, at least."

Uncally sighed. "I understand that. They're just so blasted powerful. It…it scares me a little. How do you trust someone, something, that powerful? I mean one of them could blink and humanity would cease to exist. Earth would look like the planet Mars."

"Uncally, trust is faith. We have faith, based on their word, that they have our best interests at heart. Their extreme intelligence makes me want to believe them. Their past history with us makes me want to believe them. Their proof of kindness makes me want to believe them. Are they perfect beings? No. But the fact that they even bother working with the governing bodies of Earth, making treaties and keeping their presence secret, that says a lot."

He didn't acknowledge her words and changed the subject. "So how are the girls? Are they okay?"

Lily smiled and sighed deeply. "They seem to be. They are glad to be home, I know that. The food and lodging on the spaceship weren't much to their liking, they said."

"What do you think of the beehive thing?" He was watching her with avid interest and a moment of worry blipped across her mind. He seemed to have some hidden agenda she hadn't been read in on. Did this new intense interest have something to do with the girls dealing with the Greys or did it have something to do with the brief information about Birdie's journal pages? Or worse yet, were they planning on taking Birdie away for examination? Her heart sped up at the thought.

"I...I think it was a stroke of genius. I can't believe they came up with it. Well, Rosemary did. She's a brilliant girl, as is Birdie. The Collective gives them so much knowledge. It's something humans can't even fathom."

He grew quiet for several seconds. He leaned forward across his desk. "Maybe you understand my fear now?"

Lily grunted, refusing to pander to him. "The soldiers say they've not seen hide nor hair of Cleo. Do you think she's given up? Should we send the soldiers home?"

Uncally lifted a sharp pencil and waggled it back and forth with his forefinger and thumb. "Good question. I did some background on her. She grew up dirt poor in Kansas City. Her dad was an abusive farmer, mean as a snake to his kids and to his animals. He was cited like a dozen times, but no one actually *did* anything about it. So, Cleo, who was interested in government and law, probably even wanting to get in with the rich and powerful, applied to be a page while in high school through her job counselor. Her class took a senior trip to DC and, as she had all her credits, she just never went back to Kansas. Got a roommate, got a job slinging burgers, and eventually got on as a page."

"Wow, that's quite a story." Lily rubbed her tired eyes. "So, I guess she met the major in DC while she was working there?"

"Yep, they got married like eight years ago. No kids yet, thank goodness."

"I bet she's pissed about that," Lily mused aloud. "I mean, now they probably never will, so her dreams of escaping her early life for a cushy life with a major in the military has gone away."

"And no conjugal visits for federal traitors on death row. No kids from him." Uncally pulled at his bottom lip, eyes thoughtful and disengaged.

"She should just move on. She'll find someone else to settle with, have a family with," Lily offered.

"Instead of taking her anger out on you, you mean? I agree. Let's give it a little longer. She might be laying low just to fool us."

"Okay." Lily paused a moment. "You're not really mad at me, are you?"

"Of course not. Wendell just came down on me yesterday about no news on the girls and I took it out on you when the soldiers told me they were there on the ranch. I apologize," he said, grinning at her. "Forgive me?"

Lily snorted. "Of course. No harm, no foul. It's just so weird to have them back after them being in fricking outer space for almost a month. Freaky."

"I bet Hunter is happy Birdie is home."

"You know it, but the sweetest thing is Simmy. She is beside herself with joy. I think she was beginning to believe, as I guess we all were, that the Greys had killed them. And that we'd never know for sure."

"Flynn would have told you. Are you still in contact with the IDB?" He was wearing his blue fatigues and they made his inquisitive gaze into sharp emerald as he awaited her answer.

"Not as often as I did before the girls went away. We normally spoke about once a week, for sure, but it seemed to be busy with this crisis. I guess we'll go back to it sometime soon."

"What I want to know is, how are you going to separate those girls? Rosemary will probably return to Alabama and Birdie will stay on with you and Hunter. How are you going to deal with that issue?" He watched her curiously.

Lily felt alarm bells ring through her at his words. She'd been so caught up in other things that she hadn't given that issue much thought. She groaned and buried her face in her hands.

"Hmm," Uncally concurred. "I thought so."

## *Aili's Journal*

### *Mum's Dilemma*

Rosie and I will always be together. We know this. No matter where we are.

I do wish that the colonel wasn't in such a bad mood. There's a lot of pressure on him and he is doing his best to be on our side, but he is making Mum even more anxious than usual. I don't appreciate it, but the Collective sends me soothing images. It seems the humans are at it again, fostering discontent just because they can.

Greed. Arrogance. One-upmanship.

We have very little patience for these. In small doses, they can move the humans forward, but as a sole focus, they take four steps back for every one step forward. Rosie views them with more tolerance than I do. I simply want to do away with that part of human society. Not that I ever would, of course. We're not allowed to harm humans, but the tingly thought persists. Must be the human half of me.

# CHAPTER FORTY-THREE

## *A New Worry*

When she hung up from her call with Colonel Collins, Lily pondered this new dilemma. With her being the Liaison to the energy collective, she would have thought things—decisions, plans—would have been easier. She sighed and sat back in her chair. How would she instigate a separation of the two young women? She knew their love, their connection, could not be broken, and she feared she might lose her daughter to Bayou Lisse. Living three thousand miles from her daughter just felt unacceptable. It was closer than outer space, true, but too far for her. This past month's separation had been brutal, and she did not relish experiencing anything like it again.

She reached out her right hand and rested it on the crystal statue. After a few seconds, pearlescent colors swirled within its depths and Flynn appeared as the silver woman. It didn't come into the room but rather spoke to Lily from within the statue's bright center. Its first words were alarming.

"We absolutely will not allow Earth to mine the Greys' planet."

Lily's eyes widened. Of course! They would want that, wouldn't they? An ore that folds space. "Oh, no," she said, letting out a heavy breath.

"You must tell them, folding space will not...work for pure humanoids. Many of the ones taken before...perished early after returning home. Then the Greys...discovered they could transport them in...pressure-stable carriers."

Lily grew pensive. Of course, the government would want to learn the secret of folding space. Forget the Trekkies' warp drive, they'd want the whole enchilada.

"How will I approach it? I...I don't have..." she began cautiously.

"The colonel is aware. We changed...perception to draw attention. Articles, news...posts that he read."

"Wait. I didn't mention folding space to him. Just that the ore weakened the bud capsules." Lily was perplexed.

"The major...knew and he told them to get his case... reheard," Flynn said sadly.

"Son of a bitch," Lily muttered.

"We are letting the colonel...know how dangerous. He will...fight it."

"He'd better. How do we know that the ore, or things made from it, won't keep us from procreating? Won't damage our eggs?"

"This is an...issue," Flynn said calmly.

Lilly sighed, so fatigued she felt like her brain might snap in two. "So, what do I need to do?"

"Ignore this for now. It is just a...caution. But know...we allow free will. We will not allow this. It will be...destruction."

"You overlooked it in the Greys, didn't you?" Lily said accusingly. "In their evolution."

"We failed," Flynn answered in the affirmative. "The creators of their world grew...complacent, even remarking on their ingenuity using the ore for powering the ships and... changing dark matter. We all became complacent and...now Ist has been destroyed."

"And we are essentially under attack again, this time by our own governing body." Lily shook her head from side to side in disbelief. "Why didn't you realize that the major was going to tell or had told the military?"

Flynn bowed its head and its face was lost in the cascade of silvery hair. "He was already…jailed. We looked away. We are not constantly…omnipresent. He was…bargaining."

Lily sighed again. "I get it. Once that door is open though…I don't know if we'll ever be able to close it."

Flynn raised steely chrome eyes and stared at Lily. "We will not allow this to happen, Lily. You need to…hear this. Understand this."

Lily nodded thoughtfully, fear raging through her. It seemed as though there was even more drama coming her way sometime in the future. She only hoped she was ready for it.

"Mum? Can you come out now?" There was a gentle tapping at the door, and the crystal statue immediately fell fallow. Lily checked her office to make sure all was in order before getting to her feet. She gave Birdie a big smile as she opened the door.

"Lanny pulled the grill out of the barn and he's cleaning it now so we can have a cookout," Birdie said, gently trying to pull her mother into the hallway.

"Oh, that sounds wonderful," Lily said. "Where's Rosie?"

"She's with Simmy, picking tomatoes from the garden. I texted Hunny and she's bringing veggie burgers and dogs, lots of buns and a couple different salads from the store. Lanny says the hands and the soldiers have to have real meat, so Sage and Margie got some burgers and regular hot dogs from the deep freeze."

"Wow, it'll be a feast for all of us," Lily said, finally stepping into the hallway and pulling her office door closed. She wrapped an arm about Birdie's waist, and they moved slowly toward the front door. "Let's go see what we need to help with."

As they moved along the hallway, Lily realized that she'd never gotten around to asking Flynn about separating the two girls. She frowned. She was really, really tired all of a sudden.

# *Aili's Journal*

### *Saving the Humans*

The Collective could easily destroy the entire planet the Greys call home. Easily. We made it, we can destroy it. We have no treaty with the Greys, not even the Elite, so we have no real moral restraints to doing them harm.

But we have compassion.

This compassion has allowed us to work out our differences. To allay the threats of harmful conflict. We have been patient and fostering with them.

Greed. Arrogance. One-upmanship.

These attributes have developed among them as well as among the humans.

We often ponder how such a thing could exist among our creations, on Earth, among the Greys' two levels of society, among the handful of other planets that are evolving, even those not particularly humanoid. What is it about the flesh that seeks what others have? It's a survival response surely, but we, as a collective of energy, no longer have such attributes. We are the utopia of good emotion, experiencing any destructive ones purely vicariously through the flesh we allow to evolve. And this always comes. The taking from others to raise status. How very foolish. We will continue to explore this further.

# CHAPTER FORTY-FOUR

## *The Gathering of Friends*

The pungent smells of charcoal and pinon wood wafting throughout the front yard comingled, conjuring up pleasant memories from Lily's younger days. She inhaled deeply as she carried a huge, shrink-wrapped platter of sliced onions, tomatoes, and shredded lettuce to the large food table the men had set up earlier. Two of Colonel Collins's soldiers were bringing long folding tables and chairs from the storage room in the bunkhouse and a third was wiping them down with window cleaner and the clean work towels kept on hand for the ranch workers.

Lily paused and watched the strange ballet of movement, marveling at how efficient these military recruits were. Even the Good Neighbor crew seemed in awe as they worked alongside them. She remembered friends in Florida who had railed against the military. Among themselves, anyway, just as a point of conflict. Lily had always scoffed at them, some lingering loyalty to her own father's career choice keeping her neutral. Now, seeing the efficiency displayed by these well-trained soldiers, she realized that their military training, indeed the discipline of the entire military complex, might have lasting value, especially for young people needing structure.

"Behind you," Sage said as she passed Lily. The scent of sliced cucumber and other vegetables supplanted the pinon scent for a brief moment, and Lily's stomach growled. She sighed and stepped away from the table as Hunter drove up and parked along the fence bordering the driveway. Lily strolled slowly to the car. Hunter paused at the open driver's door and watched her approach. Lily lifted her hand in a slight wave, worried about her reception after the painful revelations of the night before. To her relief, Hunter shot her a big grin that made it all the way up to her shining brown eyes.

"You're home. I'm so glad. I missed you this morning."

Hunter rounded the car to open the back hatch. When Lily approached to help, Hunter pulled her into an embrace. "I missed you, too. Just wanted to get some gym time before work."

Lily pressed the side of her face to Hunter's and closed her eyes. She could not imagine a life without her Hunter.

After one more quick squeeze, Hunter pulled back and handed Lily one of the large cloth grocery bags, then hoisted two herself. Lily pulled the hatch closed and they walked together toward the food table.

"How did it go with everyone this morning? Were the girls accepted okay? Birdie texted about stopping for food and she sounded all right."

"It was like nothing had changed," Lily answered with a shrug. "Everyone was just so happy that they were back, they sort of ignored the age change."

Hunter was unpacking hot dog and hamburger buns, stacking them along one side of the table. "And Margie? The men?"

"I haven't checked in with them about that, but Uncally read me the riot act for not letting him know they'd come home. The soldiers blabbed."

Lily unpacked containers of potato salad, macaroni salad, coleslaw, and condiments. She arranged them in orderly fashion on the table.

"Damn, they just got here last night in the wee small hours. What the hell was he expecting?" Hunter folded the empty grocery bags with jerky, irritated movements.

"I'll get some spoons," Margie said, eyeing the goodies Hunter had brought. "Be right back."

"Let's not open the salads right away, we'll wait 'til the burgers and hot dogs are almost done," Lily said. "We'll need the big cooler."

Sage came close and eyed the offerings. "Looks good, Hunter. Thanks for stopping." She picked up three heads of iceberg lettuce and headed toward the house to make a tossed salad. She turned back. "Tess called and said she's on the way. She said you called her?"

Lily nodded and handed the folded bags to Hunter so she could return them to the car. "I did. Told her to get her butt over here and she's even bringing a tray of baked beans. Did you call Cibby?"

"She's picking up the kids from camp and they're having a pizza party there," Sage responded.

"Shame," Lily said. "Would have been nice to catch up."

"I'm getting these veggie burgers to Eddie," Hunter said as she lifted two packages. "He seems to be the grill master."

"Tell him to keep 'em to one side, away from the real meat. You know how Birdie is," Lily cautioned.

Thirty minutes later, the grill was fully fired up and full of cooking food, the salads nestled in one cooler, iced teas and sodas in another. Yet another cooler was around the side of the house, well stocked with bottled beer that Felix and Alice had picked up on a run into Morris. The soldiers had all seated themselves, and there was a welcome lull as everyone relaxed, visited with one another, and waited for the food to be ready.

Unable to get enough of the two young women, Lily, Hunter, and Simmy sat at a table with them, Lily sharing the history of Good Neighbor Ranch with Rosemary. They all turned toward the driveway when a horn sounded, and Lily and Hunter rose to greet Tess as she drove up in a shiny new white pickup truck.

"Wow! This is nice," Hunter said, smoothing one palm along the sleek curved lines of the side of the truck. "When did you get this?"

"Hey, no fingerprints," Tess protested as she stepped down from the cab. "I had Barley order it for me. Came in just last week."

"And you didn't bring it by to brag on it?" Lily said. "I thought you were my friend."

"Well…got busy." Tess reached out an arm, and a beautiful, freckled woman with a sweet, cherubic face stepped into that outstretched embrace. "Y'all, I'd like you to meet Jenny Ruth."

Lily's wide grin was almost painful as she moved forward to give Tess's new girlfriend a big hug. She pulled back and studied the sweet brown eyes, the cute dimples bookending plump, rosy lips, and the mane of gorgeous curly red hair that rivalled Tess's. "Lordy, Tess, where'd you find another redhead! You guys are getting hard to find these days."

Tess gently shoved Lily. "You move on back, now. You've got Hunter over there so just leave my girl alone."

Lily laughed at the teasing, and the four of them unloaded several trays that were stacked between the two front seats of the truck.

"Man, that smells good, Tess," Hunter said. "What did you bring?"

"It *should* be good. My kitchen boys are amazing. They pulled together some baked beans, some home fries, and a big ol' tray of fried chicken."

"Oh, man, are we gonna be feasting tonight."

"The burgers and hot dogs should be ready in a few minutes so let's get all this food set out buffet style on that big table," Lily said as they carried the trays across the front yard.

"No problem there," Tess said cheerfully. "Jenny does food service for the Taylor County schools. That's how we met, at a food service conference."

"Well, that sounds like a match made in heaven," Birdie said, taking Tess's arm.

Tess's eye grew wide as she realized who was talking to her.

"Birdie? Birdie, is it really you?"

Birdie drew Tess into a fierce embrace, rocking the two of them side to side.

"It is so good to see you, Auntie Tess. Come with me, you gotta meet my girlfriend, Rosie. You're gonna love her."

Tess looked at Lily in confusion as Birdie pulled her to their table. Rosemary rose and gave Tess and Jenny a quick hug and Lily smiled. She knew everything was gonna be okay.

# CHAPTER FORTY-FIVE

## *Unexpected Heroes*

As the line moved through, serving their plates, she noticed one of the soldiers had a perplexed look on his face.

"Whatcha need, Todd? Are we missing something?" Lily asked, moving to his side.

He blushed and stammered a response. "I'm sorry, ma'am. I'm just wondering about ketchup."

Lily's eyes scanned the grouping of condiments. "Holy cow. We can't have hot dogs without ketchup. I'll be right back."

She limped quickly into the house, her cane tapping loudly on the porch floorboards.

Opening the refrigerator, she grabbed the bottle of ketchup. A sudden sense of dread washed over her. She let the refrigerator door close, uncomfortable with the sudden dimness that descended on the room. She could sense someone behind her. A real person, not imaginary fleeting ghosts from her past. She took in a deep breath and turned, expecting to see huge menacing black eyes above a stumpy beige body.

Instead, she encountered a woman. A woman she'd never met. But one that she knew, with sudden insight, was Cleo Nilsson, wife of traitor Major Leon Nilsson. Her heart began to race.

Cleo studied Lily with eyes that were an intriguing gray color—and dismissive. Lily studied her right back, taking in her shoulder-length graying hair, black jeans and T-shirt, and, most importantly, the pistol clutched in the right hand held close to her thigh. The moment seemed surreal.

"I'm wondering what makes you so very special," Cleo said in a low, sneering voice. "That the military would believe all your lies. You don't look like much."

Lily placed the ketchup bottle on the kitchen table before responding, "It was all true, everything I told them."

"Bullshit," Cleo spat. "Leon told me what happened. How he went out of his way looking for you when you were taken. He told me how he rescued you from those aliens. They were going to kill you. Almost did. Would have for sure. And how do you repay him? Show your gratitude? By making up those lies about him." Her voice had risen, and her top lip curled in distaste, visible even through the dim lighting in the kitchen.

"He's lying, Cleo." Lily shifted, taking a small, imperceptible step toward the swinging kitchen doors. If she could get to her cane that was propped just inside, she might be able to use it as a weapon. "He was working with them, helped them take me. He was planning on turning our government, hell, our planet over to them."

Cleo stirred impatiently. "Why would he even do that? It's ridiculous. There's no reason for it. He loves the military and these United States. He's sworn an oath to defend this country."

Lily nodded slowly. "Exactly why his crime is so heinous! He betrayed his oath, his military, his country, his world. Ask him sometime about what he planned to get for his treachery. The Greys promised he would have power and money after they took over planet Earth. He told me that himself."

"I really hoped you would die in that hospital. I prayed for it every day. I told Leon that and he said you were simply too privileged to die. To be held accountable for your lies. He said your father's cronies would bend over backward to make sure you survived. Make sure you thrived." She frowned. "Now, look at you. You got the ranch, the cushy life, the kid, the staff here to look after you and your lesbian lover. I guess he was dead-on with his predictions."

Lily was shocked that Cleo saw her life that way. Of course, she didn't know that Lily was the Liaison between the IDBs and the federal government. And that was a good thing. Let her go on thinking that Lily's life was simply so charmed.

Lily glanced toward the dining room window. Surely someone would miss her soon, come to check on her. Her heart leapt into her throat when she thought it might be Birdie. She had to defuse this situation to protect her daughter.

"I saw you, you know, with that ball of light. You were talking to it late at night when no one else was around. What's that about? How does the military know you're not the one working with some aliens? That was some Twilight Zone shit going on," Cleo said musingly.

Lily realized suddenly that Leon hadn't told Cleo about the IDBs and his trying to take the ranch and act as the Liaison. His hatred seemed to be focused on revenge and getting back at Lily rather than revealing national secrets.

But Lily wasn't the traitor. Leon Nilsson had received what a traitor deserved. His lies might hoodwink his wife, but they held no truck with the federal prosecutors. Or the international governing board that was responsible for monitoring the relations of Earth and the Collective. They all knew what he had done.

Lily rested her hand on the table next to the ketchup bottle, bracing herself as she tried to control her rampaging fear.

"Cleo, listen. Threatening me is not going to get your husband released. He is still going to be put to death eventually. For what *he* did! You had no part in it. You're still young enough to get on with your life. Divorce the major and move on. Don't do this."

Cleo tapped the pistol against her denim-clad thigh. "Easy for you to say. Suppose it was your half-breed lover who was where my Leon is? Would you just 'move on'?"

Lily answered immediately. "Yes. If she was indeed a traitor and it was proven to me that she'd tried to give our Earth to an alien race. Hell, yes, I would."

Cleo moved closer to the table where Lily stood. A ray of dusky sunlight showed her mouth twisted into a grimace.

"You know, I think I will move on, as you say. I've been giving it a lot of thought and I've come to realize that nothing I can do will get him released. But there is one thing I promised Leon I would do for him."

She lifted the large pistol and caressed the thick barrel with her left hand. "I may get caught or I may go on to live a life on the run. I know they're already looking for me. I don't much care at this point. Seeing this farm you have and seeing it in operation, I realize how insignificant I am. You are the golden child for sure and all I can do is kill you. Life for a life. Seems fair, doesn't it?"

Lily felt fear make her legs weak. She wasn't ready to die, to leave her family, her friends.

"You're not thinking straight, Cleo. This ranch is crawling with soldiers. There's no way you'll get away with this. They'll be all over you once they hear the shot."

Without saying a word, Cleo pulled a metal rod from her back pocket. Watching Lily, a victorious glint in her eye, she slowly screwed it onto the barrel of the gun. "Maybe. Maybe not," she said finally. She took aim at Lily and time stood still. Cleo lifted her other hand and held the weapon steady with both hands. "I won't miss this time."

Lily actually saw her life flash before her eyes and felt oddly comforted. She had no real regrets. Her life had been a good one. She wondered if the pain from the loss of Hunter and Birdie and the rest of her extended family would exist in the afterworld. She hoped that the feelings of loss would pass from her there. If there was a heaven. Her only other concern was about who would replace her as Liaison with Flynn. She hoped the transition would be a smooth one. She lifted her chin high and told herself she was not afraid.

"Cleo, this is a huge mistake. Once you take a life, nothing is ever the same again. You need to think about that before you do this."

Cleo laughed and the gun jumped alarmingly. "Do you really think I care at this point? You have ruined my life. You've ruined my husband's life. You deserve to die. That's pretty much it."

"Your husband ruined both your lives. That's pretty much it," Lily countered. She moved toward the door. Let Cleo shoot her in the back. Anger washed across her and she would not stand passively by and wait to be killed.

Abruptly, she was grabbed and bodily thrust to one side, and she was on the floor. A noise sounded, a pop followed by a hiss. Through wide eyes, she watched in horror as Rosemary took the bullet that had been intended for her. She screamed.

## Aili's Journal

*Humanness*

We sensed it, even surrounded by dozens of people conversing as they served their plates. We knew she was in trouble. We entered the house quietly and quickly determined who it was and what she was doing. I crept back out to alert the soldiers as my Rosie listened at the door. I returned to the kitchen just as Cleo shot my love.

Ahh, Rosemary. If fully human, she would have died. As part of the Collective, she was able to disperse her molecules enough to not be harmed by the bullet. Instead of seeing her fall to the ground, I watched as she ran forward and slammed the gun from Cleo's hand. The soldiers and ranch crew poured into the kitchen seconds later, like a cataract of salvation. Cleo was vicious as she fought against the soldiers but, her arms pinned, she finally relented and allowed herself to be led from the house as radio noise squawked all around us. Two of the soldiers, Ray and Elaine, helped Mum to her feet and I grabbed her and held on. The thought that I might have lost her, someday would lose her, made my heart thump hard in my chest, and I realized the full scope of my humanness. I wasn't sure I liked being so vulnerable and resolved to ponder it later.

# CHAPTER FORTY-SIX

## *Sufficient Unto the Day*

Shaken to her core, Lily sat outside in one of the folding chairs and watched as they shuffled the handcuffed Cleo into the black, insect-like helicopter and clipped her to a bar just inside it. The pilot closed the door and stood guard outside.

Suddenly, Uncally was crouched before her. Unbidden tears broke from her when she saw the sympathy in his deep green eyes. She'd managed to hold it together until seeing that loving kindness. He took her hands in both of his, resting them on his bent knee.

"Well, seems like you've had quite a day," he said, trying for humor.

Lily laughed hollowly, in spite of the tears streaming along her face. Birdie, standing next to her, lovingly dabbed at her cheeks with a paper napkin.

"It's okay now, Mum. It's okay," she cooed.

Lily looked up at the circle of soldiers and loved ones surrounding her and knew she had to do better. Her eyes found and rested on her beloved Sage. But could she? Could she hold back the tears? She kept seeing Rosemary take that bullet. The bullet that might have ended her life.

Rosemary, on the other side of her, laid a comforting hand on her shoulder and Lily pressed her cheek to it. She was immediately filled with soothing comfort. Yes, she would be okay.

The colonel seemed to sense her dilemma and he pulled her to her feet. "Let's let Cleo stew for a while. I want some of that good food you've got going on here. Man, I love a good barbecue. And yes, before you negate it, they do have them up in Maryland. They're the smaller, backyard type, of course, but this spread is amazing."

He called to one of his men as he moved toward the grill. "Mark, is there another burger on there for me?"

Lily used her T-shirt to mop at her face and she smiled at her beloved girls as Hunter wrapped one arm around her waist and squeezed her close.

"I just don't know," Tess was saying to Jenny. "It was some kind of revenge thing, I heard."

The female soldier, Elaine, was helping serve a plate for Simmy. Luckily, the grandmother hadn't seen what had happened to Rosie, and Lily fervently hoped she would never know the full story.

Lily snaked one arm around Hunter's back and returned the squeeze. "Well, what a cookout," she said, her voice sounding more hollow than she would have liked. She watched as the soldiers, calm again, took their seats and returned to their plates of food. They welcomed Uncally as he took a seat at one of the tables, his plate laden with a burger and a goodly pile of the side dishes. His glance strayed often to the two now grown girls before he dug in in earnest.

Sage came close and patted Lily's arm before handing her a plate of food. Lily looked down at the veggie hot dog, coleslaw, potato salad, and baked beans, and her stomach rumbled, flipping in gustatory joy.

Hunter laughed. "I heard that," she said. "Let's go find a seat at the table."

Surrounded by happy, conversing friends and family, Lily realized that her life *was* charmed. No matter the emotional and physical onslaughts she had survived, watching Lanny laughing at something Click said to him, watching Margie deep in conversation with Tess and Jenny as they ate, seeing the ranch hands studying and commenting on the soldiers, Lily felt a love for her life that could never be surpassed.

Later, after Uncally had finished his leisurely meal, he hugged Lily hard and left in the shiny black helicopter. Lily caught a glimpse of Cleo's sad face as she stared at her from the bubble window as the helicopter gracefully maneuvered around and flew away.

"Goodbye, Cleo," she muttered before fetching another veggie hot dog from the grill.

The soldiers stayed on so they could pack their belongings. The helicopter would return for them the following day. They helped carry the food inside, then returned the tables and chairs to the storage room, making sure that no residue remained of the front yard cookout. They disappeared to their campsites, and suddenly the ranch was very quiet.

Late in the evening, Rosie and Birdie joined the two moms and Simmy on the wide, wooden verandah. Dusk was warring with a rusty, streaky sunset off in the distance. A lone coyote howled and then was joined with a chorus of his friends.

"All in all, I think everything went well," Hunter said, rocking gently to and fro in one of the well-worn rocking chairs. "We should do that again real soon."

Birdie laughed from the porch steps. "Yeah, maybe. Let's leave out the crazy woman shooting Rosemary, though, okay?"

Lily groaned. "Oh, please. Don't even mention that. I was so terrified."

"I gotta say, I'm just glad I didn' see none of it. My old ticker just wouldna stood all that, I'm affeared," Simmy said in a low, somber tone.

"I did think of you when I was laying on the ground being rescued by your granddaughter. I was wondering how I could explain what had happened," Lily muttered.

Rosemary reached back and laid a calming palm on Lily's knee. "It's okay, Lily. I knew I'd be okay."

Lily grunted and pressed her hand atop Rosie's. "I'm glad you did. I so thought you were dead."

Rosemary chuckled. "I'm not surprised. It was pretty scary."

"Well, I have to say I'm glad that threat has gone away. We don't have to be afraid anymore," Hunter said with a deep sigh.

Lily frowned, wondering if what Flynn had told her was coming down the pike. Would the powers that be actually try to steal the ore from the Greys? And kill them all in the process? If humans couldn't reproduce, what marvelous solution would be available for them? Lily didn't think even brilliant Rosie could come up with that answer.

Best to ponder that disaster another day, she decided. Lily just wanted to bask now in the fact that she and Rosie were both still alive.

Birdie had clearly heard Lily's jumbled thoughts. She glanced at Rosie and Lily watched both their eyes glow with a bluish emission. She didn't know if she'd ever get used to that, but she had to. She loved them unconditionally. She glanced at Hunter and Simmy. All of them. Unconditionally.

## *Aili's Journal*

### *Taking Simmy Home*

Rosie and I rode with Simmy on the forty-hour bus ride back to Bayou Lisse. She doesn't trust airplanes. We had a great time swapping scary urban legend stories as we watched the small Southern towns roll past. Simmy was in a great mood, happy that Rosie and I were going to stay with her and Theo for a week-long visit before returning to the ranch. We didn't tell her that we wouldn't need a bus to get back there.

We both found it odd that the Collective had waited until now to explain the fundamentals of transmigration to us. Shifting to a new place was as easy as seeing ourselves there. We could also now create new human forms for ourselves, though I couldn't see a real need for it. Becoming wildlife and plants seemed more fun. In a different human guise, we would still be ourselves, just merely appear different. What fun was that?

We had decided to live mostly at Good Neighbor, but we saw Bayou Lisse as our second home and knew we would stay there often. Mum asked us to check in with Sophie and Delora and tell them she and Hunny said hello and that they hoped to visit soon.

Rosie and I held many silent conversations as we watched other passengers sleep around us on the bus that night. We discussed the past. We discussed the future. But most of all we discussed love, not human love, per se, but the much more evolved star energy love. The love that links everything. We have decided that it is that particular love that is the matrix of the universe. The Dark Matter that is so much more.

The humans' Bible says that there is a peace that surpasses all understanding. We believe in that peace. We know it as the love binding strong the energy of the universe.

Bella Books, Inc.

*Women. Books. Even Better Together.*

P.O. Box 10543
Tallahassee, FL 32302

Phone: 800-729-4992
**www.bellabooks.com**

CPSIA information can be obtained
at www.ICGtesting.com
Printed in the USA
JSHW061114221222
35297JS00003B/4